A Dark Chapter Press Anthology

WWW.DARKCHAPTERPRESS.COM

Also Available from Dark Chapter Press

The Cabinet of Dr Blessing, by Jack Rollins

The Séance: A Gothic Tale of Horror and Misfortune, by Jack Rollins

Kill For A Copy, 13 fantastic tales of horror featuring an introduction by best-selling horror writer Shaun Hutson

The Other Boy, by Ian & Rosi Taylor

Flashes of Darkness Halloween Special 2015 (Amazon exclusive e-book)

Eight Deadly Kisses - eight strong female writers bring eight strong female protagonists to life in this charity anthology raising money for CAMFED

Coming soon

Flashes of Darkness, a collection of bite-sized short stories, ideal for the horror fan in a hurry

Don't miss the forthcoming Dark Chapter Press Unlimited Short Story E-books

Tread Gently Amidst The Barrows, by Jack Rollins

The Last Witness: A De Omori Short, by David Basnett

Dark Chapter Press: A-Z series - 26 tales from 26 horror writers

Kids

Print Edition ISBN: 978-0-9930620-6-3
Published by Dark Chapter Press
20 Royal Oak Gdns, Alnwick, Northumberland, NE66 2DA

First edition: March 2016

This is a work of fiction. Names, characters, places, and incidents either are the product of the author's imagination or are used fictitiously, and any resemblance to actual persons, living or dead, business establishments, events, or locales is entirely coincidental. The publisher does not have any control over and does not assume any responsibility for author or third party websites or their content.

"Foreword" by Ryan C. Thomas. ©2016 Ryan C. Thomas. Original to this volume.
"Bad Little Boys Go To Hell" by James Walley, ©2016 James Walley.
Original to this volume.
"The Bones of Baby Dolls" by Feind Gottes, ©2016 Brian Minikime
Original to this volume.
"The Boy in the Apartment" by Josh Pritchett, ©2016 Josh Pritchett Jr.
Original to this volume.
"Little Angel" by Sharon L. Higa, ©2016 Sharon L. Higa. Original to this volume.
"The Apothecary's Hiccup" by Douglas F. Dluzen, ©2016 Douglas F. Dluzen.
Original to this volume.
"Raw" by Erica Chin, ©2016 Chin Lee Kam. Original to this volume.
"Twins" by Andrew Lennon, ©2016 Andrew Lennon. Original to this volume.
"The Ladder" by Pete Clark, ©2016 Pete Clark. Original to this volume.
"Born Bad" by Mark Parker, ©2016 Mark Parker. Original to this volume.
"Milk" by Michael Bray, ©2016 Michael Bray. Original to this volume.
"Anna" by Matt Hickman, ©2016 Matt Hickman. Original to this volume.
"Dig" by Alice J. Black, ©2016 Joanne McEntee. Original to this volume.
"Omens" by Chantal Noordeloos, ©2016 Chantal Noordeloos. Original to this volume.
"The Box" by Gary Pearson, ©2016 Gary Pearson. Original to this volume.
"Social Sacrifices" by S.L. Dixon, ©2016 S.L. Dixon. Original to this volume.
"The Butcher's Apprentice" by David Basnett, ©2016 David Basnett.
Original to this volume.
"The Seventy-Five Percent" by Brian Barr, ©2016 Brian Barr. Original to this volume.
"Pregnant With Freedom" by Christopher Ropes, ©2016 Christopher Ropes.
Original to this volume.
"Detention" afterword by Stuart Keane, ©2016 Stuart Keane. Original to this volume.

No part of this publication may be reproduced, stored in a retrieval system, or transmitted, in any form or by any means without the prior written permission of the publisher, nor be otherwise circulated in any form of binding or cover other than that in which it is published and without a similar condition being imposed on the subsequent purchaser.

A CIP catalogue record for this title is available from the British Library.

Cover by Michael Bray © 2016 Michael Bray

A Dark Chapter Press Anthology

KIDS

Things And Stuff What Is In This Book

Foreword

By Ryan C. Thomas

I was sitting in my backyard when I received the email to write the forward for this creeptastic anthology. My 19-month-old son was running through the rain-soaked yard--the aftermath of a week of El Nino storms here in San Diego. I said, "hey bud, don't lay in the mud." My son looked at me, smiled, and proceeded to belly flop into a fresh puddle of black goo. I immediately texted my wife. "Our son is evil."

Her response: "I know. Forget the college fund, we're going to need a bail fund."

But that's the thing with kids...they do just do what they do and you have to accept it. At least that's my philosophy. Still, no matter how insane my son acts--throwing rocks at the dogs, pulling his diaper off to pee on the floor, climbing up the bookshelves to paw at my book collection--he doesn't hold a candle to the devilish youths in this collection.

They're not just insolent, they're creepy and bloodthirsty. To say they push the limits of true fear would be an understatement!

And I enjoyed the hell out of them.

While some of these stories will wring a laugh out of you, most will shock you, terrify you, even disturb you. But if you dig beneath their violent overtones, you will find serious themes at work--the lingering effects of bullying, the insatiable curiosity of undeveloped minds, the undying devotion of parents who can't help but provide for a child no matter how many bodies it leaves in their wake, the corruption of innocence at the hands of true evil.

Yes, that's right, I said it: Evil.

Like you, I have always been a sucker for a good "evil kid" tale, be it classic films like *The Omen* or novels like *The Lord of the Flies*. Because unlike most horror tales, the "evil kid" archetype raises the stakes of terror into a realm of bleakness that assaults our hearts as much as our minds. Children, after all, are nothing if not the embodiment of total innocence. There is no malice in a toddler's eyes. They haven't learned hatred and they haven't accrued a lifetime of unfairness and heartache to ponder vengeance. There is just wonder and surprise and the need to feel loved. So when we see a toddler wielding a knife or a gun, or worse yet actively plotting to kill, it means we have lost every last vestige of purity and goodness on our planet.

How does one fight *that*?

How does one turn back a world where even our cleanest slates are doused in blood? And what does it say for the strength of demons, devils, and evil spirits, that they will possess that which is the most polar opposite of misanthropy. That they will corrupt absolute innocence and turn it against us? How do we fight such calculating evil?

You'll have to read these stories to find out.

From revenge stories to parents protecting their evil little ones to remarkable tales of friends fighting for their lives against otherworldly demons, this collection digs in to the blackest pits of horror, and dares us to ever look at children in the same way again.

Now if you'll excuse me, my toddler is trying to get something off the counter. There's a sippy cup and a knife up there. I hope he's ...yes...he's going for the sippy cup.

Whew!

Ryan C. Thomas
San Diego
February 1, 2016

Bad Little Boys Go To Hell

By James Walley

Harper's Meadow was a warzone.

Surrounded by dense forest, and bisected by a winding river, it was possibly one of the most idyllic warzones in existence. Every kid within a ten-mile radius knew it as a battlefield, a naturally hewn colosseum where rival schools and gangs would meet and wage adolescent war on each other, almost every weekend. Nobody knew how this particular meadow had gained such notoriety over the years; it was just one of those focal points which seemed to draw youngsters from far and wide, the staging ground for many a rite of passage and the perfect spot for a good old fashioned rumble.

Although several stray trees sprouted here and there within the clearing itself, one stood taller than the rest. Central and ancient, it had been dubbed 'The Big Fella' by meadow battlers who had long since grown up. As with any enormous tree, it seemed to issue a 'climb me' challenge which was irresistible to any teenager not visiting the spot for melee purposes. Standing silently amidst the swaying grass of this warm August evening, its challenge had been accepted by four small figures, who were busily traversing its massive boughs.

Clattering and hammering sounds rang out around the meadow, for once not caused by duelling children, and Wilson gazed down upon the makers of the racket with a mixture of excitement and pride. High up in The Big Fella's branches, planks were being laid, ropes tethered, and splinters inflicted, causing profanities to be uttered and laughter to be provoked in turn. The watching boy turned his attention to a scrap of paper in his hands. The diagram upon it was crude and crayoned, but seemed to match the construction below. Things were coming together.

They had arrived much earlier that day with all manner of equipment and raw materials which had been begged, borrowed, but mostly stolen, in order to facilitate Wilson's master plan. He was the oldest of the four boys, by a clear three weeks, and given the wayward antics of the group was often referred to as 'the ringleader', usually by an irate teacher or finger wagging policeman. As with all boys his age, he was never addressed by his own name, and had been given the nickname 'Wilson' after once being hit in the face with a volleyball, hard enough to leave a face print. Thanks to a rather well known Hollywood movie, the name had stuck ever since. *It could have been worse*, Wilson mused. Nicknames were notoriously unpleasant, and often referred to toilet habits, body defects or sexual orientation amongst boys his age.

The ringleader label was well founded, since Wilson was indeed prone to the odd master plan or three, and this particular one had all the makings of his greatest scheme to date. Most kids his age were already accomplished fort builders, but few seemed to care about location. Hell, the majority seemed happy to settle for upturned sofas in their living rooms. Hardly a defensive stronghold, and yet, way up here atop The Big Fella, not only could they build a defensible structure but it would also oversee Harper's Meadow in its entirety. Any assault could be seen and dealt with easily. Any invaders or marauders sent wailing back to their mommies with an earful of burst water balloon.

Wilson hopped down onto the wooden platform which had been fixed onto The Big Fella's uppermost branches, just as the last nail was hammered in by a heavy-set youth with a wooden mallet.

"About time you got finished, Tonk," Wilson crowed cheekily. "I thought you were using the wrong end of that hammer."

Tonk grabbed a handful of words and threw them back. "I know how it works. I'll show you if you like." He hefted the mallet and made a fake lunge towards Wilson, smirking as his friend flinched. "How many is it for flinching? I forgot," he cackled, already winding up the obligatory two-punch punishment for said crime. Tonk's fists, and his willingness to use them, were the reason for his charming nickname. Within the first few weeks of school, he had established himself as the new kid with whom it was not wise to mess. A few had tried, and been unceremoniously *tonked* for their curiosity. Wilson couldn't help but admire this sort of attitude, and whilst it had been viewed by some as the actions of a bully, Tonk carried himself with the sort of measured ruthlessness more often seen amongst the ranks of masked vigilantes.

Wilson took a few steps down the wooden ramp behind him, dodging Tonk's admonishing blows and half sliding out of the Crow's Nest which formed the fort's upper level. From below, bickering voices sprang up from the much larger second floor.

"Look, stop tinkering, it's pretty much done anyway," a shrill protest scolded. "You're just adding bits for the sake of it now."

More hammering followed, punctuated by a calmer, if somewhat frustrated, reply. "It's done when I say it's done," came the retort, followed by the unmistakable sounds of juvenile scrapping. Trotting down the gantry to the source of the commotion, Wilson found Beanie and Gerbil locked in a heated discussion which appeared to have descended into some kind of wrestling match.

The older of the two brothers, Beanie had his squirming sibling in a headlock, drawing yelps of rage as both boys jostled for control of a hammer on the floor in front of them. Gerbil, although only Beanie's step brother – and a mere six months his junior – was as diminutive as his nickname suggested, and was putting up about as much of a fight as one might expect a small rodent to muster under the circumstances.

Nobody knew why Beanie was so called, but he was a born craftsman. The boys suspected that he had been a great architect in a past life. Or possibly a beaver. He had jumped at the opportunity to oversee the construction of such a mammoth stronghold, and had contended with Gerbil's protests on 'how to do it right' throughout the whole process. Here, on the expansive 'main deck', it would appear that his patience had finally run out.

Amidst Gerbil's warnings that he was going to 'tell mom!', and Beanie's polite suggestions that he was going to 'cornhole him with the hammer' before he could do so, a pair of size sevens hit the deck hard. The timber planks shuddered as Tonk arrived spectacularly from the Crow's Nest above, and called time on the one sided sibling rumble.

"Stow it, both of you!" he bellowed, proving that his voice carried as much gravitas as his fists. He glanced down at the wooden citadel they had created. A smaller floor was accessible via a makeshift ladder nailed to The Big Fella's mighty trunk. It, in turn, housed ropes which would provide access to the ground. The floor on which they stood skirted all the way around the gigantic tree, boasting rails and covered areas, and above them, the small, heavily armoured Crow's Nest. A vantage point, and sniping spot for anyone with an itchy throwing arm and the desire to use it. "We're going to be up here for weeks!" an over excited Beanie boasted, bringing a smile to Tonk's stern face. "It's finished. Wilson planned it out. Beanie, you built it."

"Hey! I helped a lot!" Gerbil interjected indignantly.

Tonk raised an eyebrow. "Gerbil, you... fetched stuff." Gerbil held up his hands, heavy with splinters and scuff marks, as trophies of his 'hard work'

"The point is..." Tonk began.

"... the point is!" Wilson interrupted, stepping forward from the Crow's Nest gangplank. "We've built ourselves a fortress here, and it looks pretty much done to me." He afforded an appreciative nod to his friends. "Let's see anyone try to take Harper's Meadow from us now. This is our place from now on!"

Momentarily, Beanie and Gerbil forgot their squabbling and raised a cheer in agreement. Tonk gazed out into the field below them, its grassy carpet a blaze of orange as the setting sun spilled through the bordering trees. It was almost blinding, and yet impossible to turn away from. Tonk's smile broadened, and he took a deep breath. "This is our place now," he whispered, almost to himself. "Bring 'em on. Who's got the stones to go up against us in our own damn castle?"

Somewhere, deep within the wooden heart of The Big Fella, something ancient heard Tonk's question, and replied.

Four pairs of eyes opened within the tree line surrounding Harper's Meadow. Balefully green and unblinking, they stared up as one as the August sun retreated behind them, towards The Big Fella, and the four tiny figures standing proudly in its wooden arms.

The forest which spanned the meadow was a mysterious place, even in daylight, with all but the most rambunctious of kids wary of its ominous air. Now, in the failing light, the glinting eyes which peered out would have given even the most courageous of youngsters cause to head for the hills. For the four boys, high up in the boughs of their lofty fort however, the shimmering portents of impending doom were silent and hidden as the friends cracked open bottles of soda, and toasted their mastery of this most coveted piece of juvenile real estate.

Placing his bottle down, Wilson surveyed the array of consumable goodies which they had brought to supply their stronghold. Any survival nut who had planned to dig in for the long haul would no doubt have a larder full of useful items to sustain them, should a prolonged siege be on the cards. Then again, most survival nuts are not thirteen-year-old kids. What sat before them in a proud pile therefore was not what you might count as nourishing essentials. Chocolate, soda, chips, cake, and more chocolate lay piled up in a cholesterol choking heap in the 'canteen', a small wooden chest, which Beanie had meticulously hewn into the covered area of the fort's second, main floor. The downing of tools signalled that it was time to rest upon laurels. Packages were torn into and bottles swigged from as the boys celebrated.

"Hey! Who brought fruit?" Tonk yelled, gingerly holding up an apple by its stalk, as though it was a live grenade about to go off. "If I'd wanted to eat healthy, I could have gone home."

Gerbil snatched the offending fruit from his hulking compadre's hand. "I like fruit," he protested. "It's good for you. I'm a growing boy, dontcha know?"

Beside him, and himself halfway through a mouthful of cake, Beanie chuckled. "Play to your strengths, Gerbil. You ain't doing any more growing."

Gerbil made a face, and pitched the apple at his brother. It bounced harmlessly away, rolling past the railings and over the side of the fort, to much guffawing and jeering at the pitiful throw.

"If anyone's brought broccoli, I am so outta here," Tonk chuckled, tucking into a family sized bag of candy bars which he had claimed for himself.

The autumn sun was bidding its final farewells to the day and Wilson skirted the perimeter railings, lighting lanterns and candles to support the final rays of the dim orb in the sky. He munched on a bag of chips and allowed himself a contented smile as he took in the splendour of his brainchild. In the intimate glow of the candlelight, his small group of friends didn't look like an army defending a castle, but it sure as hell felt like they were, and that was what he had wanted it to feel like. They had all forged their alibis for the night, claiming to all be spending innocent sleepovers at each other's houses, and so they were here for the night, in a bastion of their own making. For any kid in the fun end of their teens, it didn't get much better than that.

A faint rustling pulled his thoughts momentarily away from the fanciful and down into the gloomy depths of the meadow, and he craned over the side for a better view. The sun's hasty retreat was nearing completion, and there was merely darkness below them. Darkness, and more darkness. In fact, some of the darkness appeared to be moving independently, and with it, several green, glowing objects. They seemed to stare back up at him as the bright, full moon made its first appearance in the sky, casting a pool of moonlight into the meadow.

Wilson's eyes fought to cut through the gloom, and the dark shapes fell into some kind of clarity. The glowing objects set amongst them like eyes, gleaming and trained on him. They *were* eyes. Green, cold and emotionless. They belonged to shapes that seemed to be made of the surrounding darkness, although small, slight and almost undetectable.

"Guys." Wilson took a step back from the railing, still unsure of what he had seen. "There's something down there."

Beanie sniggered, halfway through an attempt to force-feed his cake to Gerbil. "Moon's been up two minutes, and already Wilson's got the heebies."

Wilson snapped off a serious glance at his scoffing pals. "I'm serious, there's someone down there." More chuckling. "Come take a look." His offer seemed to stem the laughter, as bravado took a sucker-punch to the face.

Tonk, who was never one to misplace his co-jones, strode towards the railing. He peered out into the encroaching darkness, his back to the others as he craned and squinted towards the ground. Several moments passed, with only the sound of junk food being consumed and crickets chirping, before Tonk turned to address his friends. The look on his face caused the munching to cease, and seemed to provoke the crickets into stunned silence as well.

"He's right. There's something down there. Something... weird."

Young boys, when faced with the prospect of 'something weird' rarely require further prompting, and in unison, Beanie and Gerbil raced to the railing to see what all the fuss was about.

Four sets of unwavering green eyes stared back at them. Their owners stood in a line. Small, black as pitch and statuesque. "Who are they?" Gerbil ventured, a hint of concern in his voice.

"Listen up!" Tonk's voice pierced the air like a cannon blast and the other boys flinched. "You ladies better get lost, this here's our place now!" The command carried a force which echoed out into the night air, but Wilson knew his friend, and there was a hint of uncertainty that he had never heard from him before.

Far below in the moonlit meadow, silence fell again. Not just the boys staring down, but all of Harper's Meadow seemed to hesitate, ponder and wait for a response from the dark figures below. No reply was forthcoming, no rebukes, insults or taunts sprang from the motionless newcomers, and Wilson shifted uneasily as he continued to squint at the floor beneath them. There was a sound, though. Faint at first, but amplified and carried on the breeze to where the quartet of tree defenders stood. The sound of child-like, cheerful giggling, which could only have come from the tiny forms stood at the foot of The Big Fella. As it grew louder, the chuckling fell almost into melody, and Wilson felt his guts tighten. A barrage of insults would have been preferable to this creepy chorus of mirth, and a quick glance at his pals suggested that they too were experiencing a sudden urge to go to the bathroom.

A large, industrial-looking flashlight sat beside the second level ladder and Wilson snatched it up, flicking its switch nervously. The meadow had been bathed in steely moonlight, but not enough to make out very much, and he wanted to see who these chortling jokers were. He flashed the beam over the side of the railings, tracing a circle of spotlight to where they stood. Abruptly, the giggling ceased, as the torch beam picked out four squat, diminutive shapes, all staring back up at the tree. Annoyingly, the light only served to emphasise the black formlessness of the figures below. Only green eyes shone from somewhere in their void faces and Wilson's eyes widened as he spied four paths of smouldering grass, snaking back from where they stood, to a point in the tree line.

He snapped his head back into the safety of the tree fort and fumbled at the torch switch. "What?" Beanie asked, unsure whether to be concerned at the panicked look on his friend's face, or point and laugh. "What did you see? Are they big kids? Is there a lot of them?"

"Do they have guns?" Gerbil chimed in from somewhere behind them. Tonk snorted and gave the smaller boy a shove. "Idiot. How many tiny giggling psychopaths do you know?"

Gerbil shrugged. "I don't know any psychopaths," he muttered. "Except you," he whispered under his breath, smirking at having gotten away with a stealthy jibe.

Tonk nodded sagely. "There you go then." He seemed proud of his logic, even though it only made sense to other thirteen-year-old boys.

"So what do we do then?" Beanie was still half addressing Wilson, who still had the look of the lobster who had just been pointed at in a seafood restaurant. "Maybe they're just here to gawp. The fort is pretty awesome. Right?" His tone seemed to seek assurance more than anything else, but Wilson was in no position to give it. He cleared his throat. "I don't know what's down there, but I don't want it up here." He straightened, and edged back over to the railings. "Trust me, you don't either."

The boys eyed each other cautiously. They were all proficient in practical jokery, and succumbing to 'the heebies' would inevitably bring mockery and shame.

Just as Tonk was about to deliver a 'quit fooling around' jibe to his apparently spooked friend, a noise drew their collective attention ground-wards. Four uneasy faces peered over the railings and into the moonlit night below, as four dark, twinkly eyed faces peered back. The interlopers were no longer standing in a line, however. One was perched on the shoulders of another, and as the boys watched, a third figured hopped onto the second's shoulders. The fourth followed on, until the mystery arrivals stood tall, like some dark, freakish totem pole. They teetered and swung as the uppermost creature snaked out a blackened hand, questing for one of the ropes which hung from the side of the fort's first level. As it grasped, its eyes widened, catching the four boys in its gaze and winking slyly.

As one, and with all pretence of bravado thrown to the wind (now so much stronger as four bowels gave their own protest), the boys fell back onto the platform, scattering as Tonk voiced their collective conclusion to events. "Ah hell no! Screw that!" he shrieked, bolting for the ladder which led down towards the first floor. Whether his actions were heroic, or simply borne out of self-preservation, Wilson was unsure, but he watched as the lumbering youth scampered down to the lower level and snatched up the ropes which dangled so invitingly towards their attackers. Beanie and Gerbil ricocheted across the main platform, both brothers jabbering frantically and accomplishing precious little. It could of course be argued by any youngster that charging around yelling '*Monsters*' is a very effective way of reacting to said menace, but in reality, it's just as likely to get you eaten.

Wilson sprang to his feet. He was in no mood to join his friends in a rendition of the 'Monsters' chorus, and instead ran over to a large, Beanie-made cabinet in the corner. On its roughhewn shelves lay a cornucopia of adolescent weaponry. Super soakers, water balloons, cherry bombs, slingshots, and even a .22 air rifle that Tonk had liberated that morning from his older brother.

Tonk's head poked up from the hatch, sweating and wide eyed. "We have gotta get out of here. I don't want to be eaten by rabid monkeys!" he barked. Wilson made a grab for something offensive from the stash of ordnance and headed for the ladder. "They're not monkeys," he muttered over the still wailing brothers. "Monkeys don't wink at you and set fire to stuff."

"They don't?" Tonk replied, his wistful preconceptions of primates in tatters. "Maybe someone trained them."

Wilson paused, one foot on the ladder from which Tonk was hanging. "Who'd teach monkeys to terrorise kids and commit arson?"

Tonk chewed his lip, momentarily removed from the situation. "I would," he ventured. "That sounds awesome."

It did sound awesome but Wilson had no time to consider it further, and was already halfway down the ladder, a clutch of water balloons in his hand. Had the creatures made it up into the fort? And if they had, would a liquid barrage do anything but make them want to eat him and his friends all the more? Wilson's options were laughable and his waning courage even more so, but mercifully, no grisly fate awaited him on the tiny first level. Leaning gingerly over to the edge, he ventured a peep downwards, almost crying out as a formless face leered up at him, way too close for comfort.

How could they be this high up? There was only four of them, on each other's' shoulders. It didn't matter, the need to remain off the monster menu was more pressing, and

Wilson let fly his water balloon payload, shutting his eyes and darting back into safety as he did so. Steam shot upwards, filling the air where his head had been moments earlier, and with it, a shrill whistling sound. Wilson imagined Satan's kettle, piping and filled with souls as it boiled away in Hell's kitchen. The one that's actually in Hell, of course. The vapour shot up into the air like a mini geyser, before silence once again took hold of Harper's Meadow.

Was that it? Wilson hauled himself once again to his feet. Had he just vanquished a band of tiny demons? It seemed implausible given that his weapon of choice would probably not have bothered your average Boy Scout troupe, but the eerie quiet which had descended seemed to indicate that he had.

The coward concerto above him was continuing. Wilson made for the ladder to calm his brave troops, who had singularly failed to do anything useful throughout the whole ordeal.

"Everybody can relax." Wilson donned his best action movie voice as he emerged from the hatch. "I've dealt with them." His proud declaration might have carried more weight had the giggling not immediately started again. It emanated from the base of The Big Fella like a mocking rebuke, yet still held the same unsettling cheeriness as it had moments ago.

"By 'dealt with', do you mean, 'just pissed them off'? Because that's how it sounds to me," Tonk offered, wishing that he was wrong.

Before Wilson could answer, the giggling in the air was replaced by flying objects. Looping up over the railings, they glowed like fat fireflies and tumbled in droves towards the startled boys. One of the projectiles rolled past Wilson as he leapt back up onto the second deck. It burned with a deep orange light and sputtered like a hot coal as it came to rest at his feet. An awful lot like a hot coal, in fact. The other boys screamed as more of the flaming missiles peppered the platform, the unearthly giggling following them up from the ground beneath. In an act totally belying his inherent cowardice, Gerbil kicked and flailed at the fiery bombs as they landed hither and thither, threatening to ignite their leafy fortress.

The others took a cue from their rodent-like friend and began swatting the coals from where they came to rest. As any young boy will tell, fire is our friend. Apart from being a hell of a lot of fun, and damned useful in a lot of destructive ways, it looks hypnotically pretty. All these thoughts were stowed as the group fought to prevent their erstwhile fiery ally from taking hold in the boughs of The Big Fella. Here and there, small fires were breaking out and once again, water balloons were called to the rescue, as though they weren't held in high enough regard already.

Mercifully, the barrage appeared to be subsiding. Beanie and Gerbil scrambled to dispatch the remaining fires, which were threatening in turn to incinerate their precious junk food supplies. Hell, at least the marshmallows would be nicely toasted.

Tonk had taken to poking the less frisky of the coals which sat glowing on the deck, maybe half expecting a demonic entity to spring forth from one of them. Wilson was more preoccupied with goings on below. Clearly he had not defeated their mysterious foes with his water balloon assault, and if this wasn't over, they needed a plan.

A plan may have been easier to concoct had a small ashen face not loomed up over the railings, mere feet from where Wilson stood. He toppled backwards involuntarily as the horrific visage silently ascended, before plummeting back the way it had come and out of view of the startled boys.

“Hey!” Beanie protested, although at whom was unclear. “They can’t fly, that’s not allowed.” He picked up a stick and brandished it, sword like over his head.

“Wait, are you suggesting that there are rules here?” Gerbil almost laughed at the idea. “For all you know, they could have a tank down there.” All eyes fell on Gerbil, eyes which screamed as one, ‘If they’ve got a tank down there, it’s your fault now.’

Again, the face hovered into view. Big green eyes regarded the huddled group, and tiny hands grabbed for purchase on the railing, before it gradually fell away again into the darkness.

Despite the threat of something impending and awful, four pairs of hands gripped the rail, and four pairs of eyes peered over the side of the platform. Below, the impish darklings had formed a small group, and were alley-ooping one of their number up into the branches of The Big Fella. Even as the boys watched, the ‘alleying’ imp was mid ‘oop’, and sailing up towards them. Again it was time to scream. Not wishing to be grabbed by the ascending creature, the boys fell back onto the deck, scrambling away from the edge as creepy little fingers came within inches of grasping the railing.

Wilson was almost to his feet when Beanie charged past him, holding a long wooden panel. He reached the edge of the platform and set the panel into an oblong slot in the floor, creating a makeshift battlement which reached almost to the third level above them. Momentarily, the sheer unexpected brilliance of this new line of defence forced a grin onto Wilson’s face, which immediately retreated as Beanie again flew past, bellowing for assistance. Propped up against the mighty trunk of The Big Fella, lay a dozen or so wooden battlements of similar dimension. Wilson was already on his feet, lugging one over to the edge of the platform as Beanie explained exactly why he would one day, no doubt, be in line for some kind of wooden fort Nobel Prize.

"We're solid up here, right. Nobody can reach us," he wheezed, hefting another section of barricade. "But that doesn't stop kids from throwing stuff." They reached the edge, slotting their respective ramparts into the floor next to each other. "Water balloons, rocks, poop. We need to be able to repel any incoming. So I added this little feature." Between gasps for breath, and the still lingering panicked expression on his face, Wilson thought he could detect a hint of pride in Beanie's voice, and why the hell not?

"This is awesome!" Tonk whooped, echoing the sentiment, as he carried two of the panels over to where his friends stood. He pressed his cupped hands against this new wooden shield, shouting into them as he did so. "Screw you, beasties! Whaddya think of that, eh?"

Although not much by way of an answer, the heavy *thud* which rattled the other side of the barricade sent the boys leaping nervously backwards. There was a skittering, scratching sound as whatever had hit the outer wall scrambled for purchase, before silence returned, punctuated only by the oblivious chirping of crickets.

The boys eyed their new barricade nervously. Silence should surely be a good thing, especially after the fire barrage and the clutching, shuddersome fingers, and yet it was a sense of unease which slinked across the night air, carried by this sudden onset of calm. The wall had held firm and formed a small arc, six panels wide across the recently assaulted portion of the fort. As Tonk and

Wilson edged closer, buoyed by their newly heightened defence, Gerbil spoke up from behind them.

"Umm, guys," he ventured, casting a concerned glance across the un-battlemented sections of the main floor. "Shouldn't we be doing something about the rest of the perimeter?"

All eyes turned to their woefully exposed flanks. Nobody had considered the fact that their mysterious assailants could quite easily shuffle a few feet around the base of The Big Fella, and might even now be doing exactly that. The silence below would certainly suggest that such a bowel squeezing, ominous manoeuvre may indeed be taking place.

Beanie was already frantic. Partially due to the situation, but perhaps also as this represented an affront to his master builder status. "The slots go all the way round!" he blustered. "I just didn't get the chance to make enough panels for the whole perimeter yet." He threw up his hands, apparently now oblivious to the threat of otherworldly doom beneath them. "Gerbil, I told you we needed more wood. Dammit! Now I look stupid."

Gerbil's reply came amidst whimpering huffs of protest, as impending peril took a back seat to the finger of accusation. He wanted to point out that Tonk had been responsible for wood collection, but had no desire to incur his burly friend's wrath, and so vague whining took its place. "Why've you always gotta blame me? Every time? It's always my fault!" he babbled.

"Oh yeah, it's always your fault," Beanie countered. "Every time we get set upon by demonic midgets, it's always your fault." He rolled his eyes as his brother's griping continued.

Wilson had moved towards the already moored panels, and was wrestling one from its slot in the floor. "Look, this is getting us nowhere," he shouted, calling all eyes back to him. "We can all bitch and moan at each other, or we can try and avoid getting horribly murdered. Personally, I'm not really up for getting murdered." The section of barricade popped free in his hands, and he hefted it to one side as the arguing sputtered to a muted stop. Only mumbled sibling cheap shots continued between Deanie and Gerbil as the others took to uprooting the barricades.

Wilson peered down into the darkness below, half wincing with the expectancy of something hideous and grabby rising up out of the depths towards him, but nothing stirred. Had they already skirted to the other side of The Big Fella? Had they already scaled it? Was he going to be entree, main or dessert?

Trails of smouldering grass still lingered on the ground, but they didn't track around the mighty tree, rather outwards, away from them and back towards the tree line. As he squinted into the muddy moonlight, Wilson spied the figures, perhaps twenty or thirty feet away, huddled in a small circle. "Guys, look. They're over there!" He pointed redundantly into the night, as the rest of the group arrived at his side. "Does someone have the flashlight? They're up to something."

Once again, the impressively weighty flashlight was passed to where Wilson stood. It was Tonk's, or at least his dad's. Probably several million candle power and hefty enough to swing at whatever it picked out of the darkness. Wilson clicked it on and played the beam over to where the figures stood in their grotesque group hug. They seemed to be all facing inwards, and as the torchlight hit them, one of their number straightened. Reaching up, it extended a blackened arm, holding up something that glimmered and shone in the light. A keening, mewing sound slithered up into the night sky, like steam escaping from a fissure, and the gleaming something was flung into the air. It glittered, almost sparkling as it drifted within the torchlight which followed its course. Finally, it dropped onto the ground a few feet from the hunched group of eerie wailers.

"What was that?" Beanie ventured. "Looked like a marble or something."

"Maybe it was an eyeball," Gerbil simpered. "Or a nad."

"Beats flaming rocks," Tonk shrugged.

"It wasn't much of a throw," Gerbil chipped in again. "Bit pathetic really." He mustered up as much bravado as his tiny frame could contain, and managed a stuttering yawp. "Is that all you've got?"

Presumably that wasn't all they'd got, as the cricket laden silence fell away to a deep rumbling and shaking from the ground below. All eyes fell on Gerbil, who had clasped his hands across his mouth, as though attempting to reel in the rebuke which had escaped him.

Beanie punched his brother's arm sharply. "Gerbil. D'you wanna try not pissing off the demonic, monster, imp things?"

"Yeah, we really don't want an encore from these guys." Tonk rasped.

The tremors grew and Wilson fought to keep his balance, the flashlight beam trained on the ground. Where the gleaming marble thing had landed, small dark shoots had appeared, snaking upwards and growing thicker as they emerged from the earth. The figures danced and leapt amongst the turmoil of black vegetation which had been called into being, and still the shoots flung themselves upwards. Only now, they seemed more like branches, but obsidian and leafless, like something long dead and twisted to some dire will.

Four sets of eyes widened, and four mouths gaped open as the demonic flora continued to grow and climb beneath them. Within seconds, it was no longer just beneath them as thick branches carved their way up alongside The Big Fella, until a tree that could reasonably have stood along the banks of the River Styx stood portentously before them, as black as the sky behind it

The boys stood equally rooted to the spot, their own wooden fortress now standing trunk to trunk with this new hellish creation.

"Well, that's..." Wilson managed, before Tonk cut in with his own interpretation of events.

"...that's a whole freaky butt load of *hell no*." Even he was backing away now, seeking some means of escape which Beanie would no doubt have installed, had the threat of this horticultural hell spawn been any kind of realistic possibility.

As if the towering behemoth wasn't bad enough, the familiar, shimmering green eyes that had once stared up at them now peered out, only meters from the boys' perch upon The Big Fella. The figures seemed to be made of the same hellish substance as their perch, and it was impossible to see where they ended and their own tree fort began. Only the eyes were visible, and they glittered like tiny, dread searchlights, seeking out their prey.

No mean feat, as said prey took to rapidly seeking out hiding places and whatever could be hastily fashioned into a weapon. Wilson had relieved The Big Fella of one of its boughs, and was hefting it as though facing down a ninth inning fastball. With their arsenal severely depleted, Beanie had snatched up a handful of cherry bombs, and already had one loaded into the slingshot in his other, visibly shaking fist. Beside him, Gerbil had apparently drawn a blank in the weapons department, instead clutching a box of Twinkies protectively to his chest. It was open and he held a spongey projectile in his free hand, seemingly torn between bite and throw.

Tonk was still searching for something to brandish menacingly when something ear splitting and bladder squeezing shrieked through the air towards them.

Four figures, now no longer shrouded in darkness, took shape again from the infinite blackness of the new tree's looming form. From somewhere high up in its sinister branches, dark tendrils hung down, equally black and dreadful. At the end of each one, a tiny figure hung, or more accurately, swung. Wilson's eyes widened as he realised that his merry band of tree fort defenders were being boarded.

"They're coming over!" he bellowed, as their demonic assaulters cut a lightless arc through the night sky.

Gerbil, who had opted for lunch over launch, swallowed a chunk of Twinkie. "What are we gonna do? We have to get out of here!"

"How?" his brother gibbered. "The only way is down into the field. Past that... tree, and I don't really fancy picking my way through Satan's cabbage patch, do you?"

There was only time to issue a single command, and that command needed to be one word or less, ideally. Wilson assessed their available options and signalled his intentions to his comrades. "*Up!*" He pointed towards the Crow's Nest, and was already ascending the ramp towards it as their attackers landed.

The retreat was about as ordered and calm as one might expect from a bunch of adolescents fleeing in mortal peril. Tonk followed his leader, clutching the .22 that he had been wanting to use all evening. Gerbil scuttled on behind, lighting the cherry bomb in his brother's slingshot as he went. Beanie let fly the tiny red firecracker and also took to his heels as the last of the charred fiends descended into The Big Fella's mighty frame.

Behind the hightailing group, the flamboyant explosive blasted out an impressive rear-guard barrage which momentarily lit up the meadow. A sharp *crack* ricocheted through the [illegible] boughs and spurred on the boys' scampering exodus.

At the top of the ramp, Wilson whirled back to face whatever might come cavorting up behind them, his tree branch bat held high and as threatening as he could manage. He was, of course, more terrified than he had ever been in his young life, but he was the leader. The sheer power of the adolescent male bravado would not allow him to relinquish this most lofty of positions. It would never allow him to cower in the corner of their final and only remaining refuge, or spectacularly soil himself. Such was the mantle of the general, even if that particular commander in chief secretly wanted his mommy at that particular moment.

Beanie loosed off another fizzing cherry bomb as he arrived in their towering perch, steeling Wilson's courage and drawing another resplendent boom from the terror-filled darkness below. This was their last stand, their Alamo, a metaphor that would have carried much more weight, had Wilson paid any attention at all in history class.

Yet another firecracker terminated its volatile existence with a bright flash, as Beanie wielded his slingshot like a soggy grenade launcher. Grenade launchers, even of the slingshot variety, eat up ammunition like crazy however, and with a fourth, resounding blast, Beanie's weapon of mass distraction was spent.

Smoke wisped up from the tumultuous blackness of the platform below and the boys collectively held their breath, hopeful that their impromptu fireworks display had kicked some wholesale demon ass. The silence which fell across the meadow was encouraging, and the gang allowed themselves a few cautious grins of triumph. Tonk, ever the bravest of the group, edged closer to the ramp's aperture, seeking hopeful confirmation of an unlikely victory.

Something hissed ominously below them, followed by a now all too familiar giggling. The sound was not unlike a psychotic child unwrapping a chainsaw on Christmas morning, and snaked up out of the silent, inky mists below.

The horribly familiar, green eyed face which loomed up out of the smoke seemed almost serene, silently gleeful and way too close for comfort. Gerbil let out a startled squeal and dropped his box of Twinkies, any possibility that they might become the improbable secret weapon in the final battle against demon kind now irreparably damaged.

Wilson took a swing with his leafy club, which was easily evaded by the advancing creature, its kindred filing up into view behind it. If the tried and trusted 'Time out' rule, so often employed in schoolyard scuffles, was to be called upon, it would have been at this moment. It was unlikely however, that denizens of the deeper levels of Hades would conform to such protocols, and so the skulking advance continued.

The impish creatures fanned out into a line. Their formless features were almost visible in the gloom, rakishly spanned by orange fiery fissures, as though they had been hewn from hot coals whose embers still flickered and glowed with otherworldly light. Their bodies glowed with the same soot flecked incandescence, and the stench of brimstone hung heavy in the night air.

There was nowhere to back up to. The Crow's Nest was snug, designed only to house one or two sentries, and certainly not four frantic kids and their equal number in pint sized hellion.

Several resounding cries echoed around Harper's Meadow as the monsters congregated at the top of the ramp. Between flung expletives, pleas to deities and calls for maternal intervention, a single, full bloodied battle roar rang out.

Tonk, braced against the trunk of The Big Fella, screamed a frantic war prayer as he levelled his .22 at the lead devil-munchkin.

"This may not be holy water, but it's gonna hurt like holy hell!"

Even a shot from a .22 sounds like cannon fire to a thirteen-year-old, and Tonk pulled the trigger again, screaming at the bucking oblivion in his hands as it kicked out, screeching retribution towards the demonic phalanx stood before him.

Tiny, frankly pathetic-sized lead peppered the air as Tonk's gun continued to preach, and Wilson looked on in a daze. Water balloons were one thing, but his friend was stood next to him, firing a real gun at real demons. This definitely ranked somewhere between awesome and terrifying.

Bullets intertwined with cursing insults as Tonk added a verbal barrage to the one screaming from the weapon in his hands. Wilson peered into the whirling vortex of metal and expletive, as the impish figures before them buckled and dropped out of sight. A few seconds passed before he realised that Tonk's gun had spat forth its full complement of ammunition. Dry clicks rang out with each pump of the big youth's finger, although his reserves of cursing rebukes continued unabated.

Silence eventually fell. Tonk ceased his trigger pulling and ran out of ways to insult their mystery attackers' mothers.

"That'd better have worked." It was Gerbil who punctured the calm with his own, presumably patented brand of whining negativity. "Apart from this last Twinkie, we've got nothing but Wilson's stick to fend off the forces of evil now."

Sometimes, no words are needed in the face of such annoying pointing out of the obvious. Having been privy to it his whole life, Beanie delivered his now go-to response in the form of a deft cuff to the back of his brother's head, ironically drawing more moaning.

The aforementioned forces of evil lurked somewhere in the rising mist and darkness that shrouded the ramp. Curiously, they were neither wreaking brimstony terror, nor in fact visiting any sort of riposte to the cowering boys in the Crow's Nest. An uneasy calm had settled amid the branches of The Big Fella, interrupted only by the faint chirping song of the crickets and Gerbil's continued griping.

Wilson took a hesitant step forward. Maybe they had done it. Maybe all you needed to kill demons was a thirteen-year-old with a gun and a penchant for swearing. He turned to his comrades, who seemed to be simultaneously cautious and encouraged by the silence.

Gerbil had stopped his incessant whining, and only the crickets remained. The crickets, and something else, which issued from the floor below them, ever so quietly and oddly out of place after the chaos that had gone before.

Someone was crying.

Several 'What the hell?' glances were exchanged as the sorrowful weeping rose in pitch. It was still gentle and unassuming, but totally unexpected, mostly because the boys had expected to hear whooping cries of bloodlust and the rending of things that really shouldn't be rended. Wilson took another step towards the gangplank, peering down into the darkness, towards the source of the mystifying wails. Curiosity, as always the better of them, gripped the others, who joined their leader in his search for the mystery whimperer.

In the receding mists of the main platform below, three small blackened figures stood hunched over a fourth, stricken form. The apparently wounded imp rocked back and forth, clutching at something that may have been a leg, but was impossible to see against the night. Three sets of concerned, green eyes moved from their injured brethren to the gawping boys at the top of the ramp, and one set of tearful green eyes shone miserably, blinking back big obsidian tears.

"We bagged one!" Tonk crowed, holding his gun aloft, before lumbering down the ramp towards the huddled group. Riding the coat tails of their friend's courage, Gerbil and Beanie raced down behind Tonk. Even if the remaining three fiends had some fight left in them, at least the bigger boy was between them and a bitey doom.

Wilson, still clutching his makeshift club, almost redundantly now, slowly made his way down to where his friends had circled their besiegers. Something was not right here.

He had looked directly into the wretched eyes of their stricken foe, and recognised what he saw there. Before he had befriended Tonk, he had looked into the mirror, staring back with those same eyes as countless wedgies, swirlies and beatings had been delivered to him by countless random bullies that roamed the school halls.

Gerbil was poking at the fallen imp, his courage suddenly amplified by this surprising turn of events, as Wilson reached the bottom of the ramp. "Take us on in our own tree will you?" Gerbil mocked, seemingly revelling in his moment. "Bet you wish you'd stayed in Hell, or Cleveland, or wherever it is you came from, eh?"

The injured demon's whimpering ceased, as did Gerbil's early onset bravado, and he shrank back behind his friends as the little creature struggled to its feet. It fixed Wilson with an imploring stare, as if it somehow knew that he was the boys' leader. Words issued forth as it implausibly addressed him. "Please, no more," it beseeched, in a voice more befitting of a young Victorian chimney sweep. "No fair... no more," it repeated, those huge glistening eyes now trained on Wilson.

"Wait, wait," Tonk chimed in. He had done his fair share of ass whupping in the past, and had heard this sort of plea before. "You came after us." He hefted the .22 onto his hip. "You can't go crying 'time out' on us just cos you got your tail whipped."

One of the huddled number stepped forward with eyes, which had once been glinting and gleeful, now as doleful as his kin. "You called us," it ventured, almost cowering in the collective gaze of the four boys. "We came at your behest. At your challenge."

Wilson's furrowed brow lifted. He *had* seen that look before, and heard these appeals. He had been the hell spawn which stood before them, albeit without the fiery, smouldering creepiness. Granted, he had only gotten his head shoved down the toilet a few dozen times, and not been shot with a .22, but the sudden realisation stirred another question. "Who are you?" Clearly this was the question all the boys wanted an answer to, and had been since the creatures' arrival in Harper's Meadow, but as Wilson stared into the teary eyes of the injured demon, he already half knew the answer.

"We are like you," one of the imps replied matter of factly. "Only we are from down there." It pointed down at the patch of ground from which their Hell Tree had sprung, as if any clarification was required. "We get so bored down there. There aren't many other children like you to play with," it continued, shambling over to the edge of the platform and staring off into the night. "We heard your challenge and we decided to come and play."

Silence descended again. The sort of silence in which revelations are reached and acted upon. Gerbil, never one to embrace subtlety, and even less likely to ever win a Nobel Prize for tact, spoke up first. Loudly.

"Wait, they're *kids?*" He enquired, "So you're not here to eat our faces?"

Four pairs of gleaming green eyes cringed in unison. "What? No!" One of them squeaked. "Humans taste like crap. We just came up to play." Its tone dropped, almost recoiling. "We didn't think you'd have guns. That's no fun at all."

Accusers and accusees exchanged glances, and that all too familiar silence returned to give the crickets something to sing about. Clearly things had gotten out of hand here. Wilson and his friends had never in their wildest dreams expected to be facing off against the tiny adolescent forces of Hell. Similarly, the four little infernal Kinder had probably not planned on being treated like monsters. This had, after all, been a game. Capture the flag, not capture the soul. Shots had been fired, literally, and now the collective longing within the weighty branches of The Big Fella was to chalk this one up and head home.

In unison, every voice, both human and demon, spoke up: "So, we can go then?"

With a stale mate reached (although Tonk would later never agree that it had been a draw, having popped several caps into a demonic ass), both groups backed carefully away from one another.

Wilson made his way cautiously towards the ladder leading to the first level of the tree fort, paving a way for his comrades to beat a measured retreat. They quietly alighted from their mighty bastion, shimmying down to the cool grass of Harper's Meadow and heading for the tree line. All the while, their eyes were fixed upon the boughs of The Big Fella, which held silent, watching figures, who would also shortly retreat back to their own home, in the dark recesses of the world.

As they raced across the field to the safety of their houses, their parents and their beds, Gerbil offered up his own version of events, which he would almost certainly embellish to the open mouthed audience he would command when school was back in.

"Did you see me?" he shrieked, "I sure told that demon. I bet they'll think twice before..."

Even in full flight, Beanie's customary, back handed response to his brother's incessant jabbering was quickly forthcoming.

From its lofty branches, The Big Fella fixed the boys with a knowing smile, in that inimitable way that trees don't.

More kids would come to claim the fort.

To sit defiant in its branches.

Their boastful challenges calling forth any who might want to test their mettle in the field of battle. This age old meadow, which had seen countless skirmishes waged, would not stand idle for long. It was only a matter of time before someone found the fort and claimed it for their own, declaring themselves king of the castle, and master of Harper's Meadow.

And there were plenty more bad little boys in Hell.

The Bones of Baby Dolls

By Feind Gottes

Cassie sat cross-legged with her head down, as upset and distraught as a four-year-old girl can be. Any adult looking on would say little Cassie was pouting but that would be way off the mark. On the floor in front of her was the source of her massive disappointment. Four rubber limbs, a hard plastic, smiling head and cheap cotton stuffing strewn all about. Cassie had pulled the doll's innards out, disappointed to find that was all there was inside. When she had begun the doll dissection, she didn't know what she'd find or what she even wanted to find, but cotton stuffing didn't satisfy her in the slightest.

Cassie wasn't pouting; she was filled with rage.

Cassie lifted the butcher knife (the one she had taken from the kitchen when her mother wasn't looking) and plunged it as hard as she could into the doll's hollow plastic face. Her rage fueled her need to destroy the fake smile that seemed to be mocking her. The first strike was a bullseye right between the doll's baby blues, but it didn't satisfy Cassie in the slightest. She lifted the knife over and over until the plastic head was nothing more than plastic shards littering her pretty pink carpet. Cassie hated pink but her mother had seemed so happy with it, near glowing. Even at four, Cassie knew there would be an unappreciative, scornful look on her mother's face if she revealed what she really wanted was a black carpet. Something inside screamed out to her to just go along with it. She did love her mother after all, and didn't want to disappoint her.

Destroying the doll's face had quieted her rage to a certain extent, but Cassie still wasn't satisfied. She grabbed two more of her dolls and found the same disappointing result waiting for her on the inside of those as well. Nothing but rubber, plastic and cotton fibre. Cassie sat there for a time just stabbing at the assorted rubber limbs and hollow heads until she was just bored with doing it. She still didn't know what she wanted to find inside, but it definitely wasn't stupid cotton.

"Go away Lily! Shoo!" The family cat paid Cassie's words about as much mind as cats generally do anything.

The family feline stepped over Cassie's destruction because it felt like it, and nothing more. Cassie stroked the cat from head to tail, not really mad that it had come in, interrupting her moment. Lily the cat was about the only thing that ever brought a true smile to her little lips. Her visitor did remind her that she wasn't alone. She had a mess to clean up.

"Ok, Lily, I love ya, but I have to pick up this mess before mommy sees it." Cassie scooped up Lily, setting her out into the hallway with a quick look around to check no one was coming, closing the door behind her.

"Cassie? Baby, it's time for dinner."

"Okay, Mommy, I'm coming." Cassie was just setting the bag of doll parts inside her closet as her mother tapped on her door.

She gave a quick scan of the carpet to make sure she had gotten it all before heading to the dinner table. Her father was already seated at the head of the table in his usual spot, scanning the paper for whatever he would rant about over dinner. Always "can you believe this or that" about some "scumbag politician" or something similar. Cassie enjoyed hearing her father speak but cared little about anything he actually said. Her mother served her father first, as always, then set a plate in front of Cassie. Lastly she fixed her own plate, sitting next to her husband, across from Cassie.

"So, how is my little princess today?" Her father asked this same question every evening before launching into his own rant.

"Good, Daddy." Cassie was only four, but had her standard response down pat. It would most likely remain that way through her younger years.

Cassie's father then turned to her mother asking the other standard table question. "And how about my Queen?"

"Couldn't be better, my King." Cassie's mother replied with her own standard response which didn't yet have Cassie rolling her eyes with an embarrassed moan as it surely would in the years to come.

"Excellent! Did you see…?" With that, her father's rant of the evening began.

Cassie sat pushing food around her plate, occasionally taking a bite so as not to attract any undue attention to herself. She couldn't get her mind off her dolls. Why did they have nothing interesting inside? What *should* be inside? She couldn't help thinking about it while pushing peas around her plate as her father bellowed about his chosen topic. She thought she'd heard the familiar "scumbag politicians" line a few times, but had become completely lost in her own thoughts. Four was a little too young keep up a façade for very long as she'd completely forgotten to take a bite for a few minutes.

"What's wrong, Princess?" her father asked, though Cassie hadn't noticed he'd stopped ranting and was speaking to her.

Failing to answer, her mother chimed in. "Cassie, your father is speaking to you. Answer him."

It was her mother's voice that caught her attention finally. "Ummm, sorry…what?"

"What's wrong, Princess? What's got my baby girl so deep in thought? You're far too young to be pondering the meaning of life, Sweetie, so what's eating at you?" Her father's voice softened as though he was genuinely concerned.

Cassie considered for a moment whether to just apologize and take a bite so her father could go back to his concern of the day but she just couldn't. She knew she would get in trouble over the dolls, so she thought it best to just leave that part out. "What's inside me?" she finally asked.

"Well, you're a little princess so you, my dear, are filled with sugar, spice and everything nice. Now your baby brother isn't so lucky because little princes are filled with snakes and snails and puppy dog tails." Her mother scrunched up her face at this as if to say "ewww."

"*Noooo*, that isn't true, is it? What's really in there?" Cassie tried to hold back her anger, not wanting to be treated like an idiot no matter how well-meaning her mother may be. "Please, tell me the truth." Cassie had unconsciously changed the grip on her fork from an eating position to a stabbing one.

"Calm down, sweetie. Do you remember last week when you cut your finger?"

"Yes, Daddy."

"Ok, what happened?"

"It hurt."

"Yes, but what else happened?"

"It bled and Mommy put a Band-Aid on it."

"So you see? You've answered your own question. Inside of you, Mommy, Daddy, and little Jack – there's blood. Now, do you remember when we went to see the dinosaurs at the museum?"

"Of course, Daddy, that was cool!"

"Yes it was. So other than blood inside of us, there are also bones just like the dinosaurs at the museum, only smaller." Her father concluded, giving her a little wink.

"Is that all? Just blood and bones?" Cassie sounded – and was – a little disappointed.

"Well, there's a bit more princess, but blood and bones is most of it. You know some of the other things already though. Where does your food go when you eat? Like my little Princess should be doing right now."

"My tummy!"

"Right! And you know what's inside your chest, don't you?"

"Ummm… a heart!"

"Right, and that's where love comes from." Her mother joined in to end the conversation. "Now you know all you need to, so let's finish our dinner."

"Ahh, but I know there's *more*." Cassie gave her best grumpy face, but knew that was all she was probably going to get.

"Not much, Princess, now listen to your mother and finish your dinner."

Cassie finished her plate reluctantly, not really any more satisfied than she had been, but she would get no more out of her parents. The punctuation point was added as her baby brother, Jack, began wailing from his room. Her mother stopped clearing the table at the sound. She returned a moment later cradling the three month old in her arms, doing her best to soothe him.

"Cassie, wanna help Mommy? Will you feed your brother while I finish the dishes, please?"

"Sure, Mommy!" Cassie knew to sound more excited than she actually was.

Cassie took her place on the couch while her father turned on the news so he could find something else to complain about. Her mother brought over a burp cloth, a bottle and her baby brother. Cassie had done this a million times, but still her mother felt the need to give her instructions every time anyway, as though she couldn't remember by now. She knew to support his head and pat his back every ounce or so, yet her mother would remind her every time. Cassie's father had restarted his rantings over the news before her mother finished her repetitive instructions.

Cassie sat staring down at her little brother, lost in her own thoughts. She couldn't help wondering what his insides must look like. What were the other things that her father hadn't told her about? How much blood was inside? How big was little Jack's heart? A moment of panic washed over her at the thought of finding nothing more than the same cotton fiber she had plucked from the inside of her dolls. Some of her dolls were bigger than Jack, and yet all she found inside were hollow limbs, cotton and an empty head. *What was inside Jack's head?* She hadn't asked her father that question. Her curiosity had her mind racing with the possibilities. She had forgotten what she was doing.

Jack pushed the bottle away, turning his head toward her. Cassie, still lost in the fog of her own thoughts had almost forgotten she was feeding her little brother. He looked up at her with a big smile, which she returned, just as he spewed his formula into her face. She had been so lost in the thoughts of his insides that she had forgotten to burp little Jack. She was now coated in stinking formula spit up. Why did it always seem like more came out than went in? Jack immediately started wailing at a thundering volume, followed only a moment later by Cassie's own cries.

"Oh, Cassie, you didn't burp him did you?" Her mother's disappointed tone didn't help at all.

Cassie couldn't even speak through her own cries. She wanted to punch little Jack right in the face but dared not suffer the consequences of that action, which only fuelled the tears streaming down her face. Her father couldn't help finding the humour in the whole scene, breaking out in laughter as her mother tried to deal with two crying children. Cassie's mother was no more amused than Cassie was herself, as she did her best to wipe up the spewed out formula with the burp rag. After a few passes, it was useless. In frustration, she picked up the still wailing Jack, grabbing Cassie by the hand.

"Well, bath time it is then. Come on Cassie!" Her mother rarely got angry, but wasn't very good at keeping it in at this moment. Cassie was certain her father's laughter wasn't exactly helping matters, "There is nothing funny here, James, so help or hush!" A fresh burst from her husband helped even less.

Cassie's mother tugged her to the bathroom with renewed vigour and a loud huff directed at her husband. Once in the bathroom, she stopped pulling Cassie's arm out of its socket to draw the bath. She stood with a hand on her hip for a moment, trying to regain her composure while baby Jack still wailed away in her other arm. She took a couple of slow, deep breaths.

"I'm sorry, Mommy. I didn't mean to make Jack sick."

"I know, honey, it's okay. Mommy isn't mad at you. Hop out of those clothes and into the tub so we can get all that icky puke off of you." Her mother bent down and kissed the top of Cassie's head, stroking her hair lovingly for a moment to let her know everything was alright.

The rest of the night passed peacefully, other than Cassie's mother giving her father a little hell for being an ass. Bedtime came far too early for Cassie as it always seemed to do. She kissed her mother goodnight while her father, feeling a bit guilty, read her a story before tucking her in. She loved when her father would read to her. His voice was so deep and soothing to her, not like her mother's, which resembled nails on a chalkboard much of the time. Her father finished the short book she had picked out, giving her a kiss on the forehead before shutting off her light and saying goodnight.

The moonlight shone through Cassie's window, bathing her bed in its eerie glow. It wasn't the light that kept Cassie awake though; it was her racing thoughts. She couldn't help thinking about what insides would look like. Her little imagination was in overdrive with morbid curiosity and, try as she might, she found she couldn't stop. She tried thinking of other things but in no time her thoughts would turn back to the original. She *needed* to know. She had a fascination with seeing how much blood was inside. What did a heart really look like? What shape were the bones? What else was inside? She wanted to *see* it. Staring up at the ceiling brought no answers; just more questions to her four-year-old mind. She just had to *know*.

Cassie continued to ponder the intricacies of people's insides for days, turning to weeks. Her parents had grown tired of her questions about the subject. Her mother easily lost her patience at any mention of it and her father had even resorted to the finality of "no more of this talk, little lady," which was the end of the subject as far as he was concerned. Cassie's mind continued to race night after night until she was hardly sleeping at all. She rarely finished her dinner and dark circles were growing under her beautiful, little princess eyes. Her parents were at a loss as to the cause, and Cassie gave up asking her questions as all they drew were stern looks from both of her parents. She would lie awake, staring up at the ceiling, thinking about it all night.

She had begun creeping out of her room late at night, once she could hear her father 'sawing logs' as her mother called his snoring. She would creep down the hallway to baby Jack's room, staring at him as he slept in his crib. He laid in his crib sleeping quietly, making even less noise than her tip-toeing down the hallway. She would stand there staring down at him instead of up at the ceiling for hours on end. The moonlight didn't shine through little Jack's window at all. His room was as dark as it could get, but after a few minutes her eyes always adjusted allowing her to see him lying there still as the dead, other than the occasional sucking motion of his lips as though drinking from an invisible bottle.

Some nights she would stand there almost the entire night with Lily weaving in and out of her legs, while other nights she would sneak back to her own room, pulling apart another doll. She had a few left now. She had begun splitting the torsos open, methodically, like a coroner performing an autopsy. She would slip her knife in just below the plastic head, run a smooth straight slit down to the doll's ambiguous crotch, disappointed each and every time to find nothing other than cotton filling the interior. It was incredibly unsatisfying finding no blood, no bones, nothing but different types of cotton stuffing. Sometimes, Cassie would cry but mostly she only grew more and more angry, brewing with an unquenchable rage.

"There will be no more of this talk, young lady! Do you *hear me?* Little girls do not think of such things! *That is absolutely enough!*" Her mother was nearly screaming at her now.

"But…"

"*Enough!* But nothing! There will be no more talk of what's inside people. Not another word, Cassie!"

"Yes, Mom." Dejected, Cassie ran to her room crying, jumping on her bed to bury her face in her pillows.

Cassie couldn't understand what her mother's problem was. "Little girls don't think of such things?" Wasn't she exactly *that*, a little girl thinking of such things? Why did her mother hate her so much? The rage that had been building for weeks began to burst out of her eyes, in torrents of unstoppable tears. She wasn't sad, she was furious. She began punching her pillows out of sheer frustration, but found her anger not ebbing at all, instead only growing with each strike. Cassie sat up, trying to wipe away the flood pouring from her eyes. She knew what she had to do now. She found the realization stopped her tears from pouring down her cheeks. Her rage subsided as a smile grew across her lips. She had what an alcoholic would call a moment of clarity. She didn't know what to call it but she knew she felt better instantly. She wiped her tears away on her shirt sleeve, exiting her room to apologize to her mother.

Cassie was the happiest she had felt in weeks, gobbling down her dinner and even asking for seconds, which was unheard of. Her improved mood didn't escape the attention of her parents, with both feeling the need to comment upon it. Cassie had no answer for them, simply giving the standard child's answer of "I don't know." She did know, but knew it had to be her little secret lest she face the wrath of both her parents. She had no time for explanations as her little mind was busy on her plans for later. She couldn't help smiling the widest smile her face had ever seen, as though Christmas had just come early. Her parents were content that their daughter was finally happy after weeks of dragging through the house like their little zombie, rather than their little princess.

Cassie was filled with excitement, never had she wanted bedtime to come so quickly. She stared up at the ceiling, unable to stop smiling while she waited to hear her parents' door close. The wait was killing her. She waited and waited, finally hearing the door close, followed shortly after by her father's wall-shaking snore. She waited a while longer just to make sure both her parents were asleep. She slipped out from under her pink Cinderella comforter, squeezing her little toes into her pink carpet, trying hard not to sprint to the door. She knew it was nearly impossible to wake her parents, even if a train rolled straight through their house, but she didn't want to take any chances.

Cassie tip-toed her way to the door, opening it slowly, ensuring not to make a single noise. There was no interruption to her father's snoring and there was no light shining under her parents' door, which meant her mother wasn't still up reading. As she had done so many nights over the last few weeks, she tip-toed down the carpeted hallway to her baby brother's room.

She pushed his door silently open, creeping her way to her usual spot in front of his crib. Instead of standing and watching little Jack tonight, she carried the little pink chair her mother kept in the room over to the crib, setting it down with its back against the rail. She paused, listening for any sound other than her father's snoring, hearing nothing else. Confident her parents were sound asleep, Cassie stepped up onto the little pink chair and looked down at little sleeping Jack. With his eyes closed, he looked just like one of her dolls. She reached into the crib with her belly pressing into the rail to get her hands under her little brother's sleeping body, smiling as she lifted him up and over the rail. Little Cassie turned around on the chair's seat, careful not to slip, then sat down before standing up with sleeping Jack to creep back to her own room.

Cassie paused by her parents' door, listening intently for any sound of movement within, hearing nothing but her father's obnoxious noise. Confident she could proceed undisturbed, Cassie walked back into her room, setting baby Jack on the floor, bathing him in the bright moonlight coming through her window. Cassie had unknowingly picked a full moon night to satisfy her curiosity once and for all. Jack hadn't let out so much as a whimper on the journey so far, now lying there as peacefully on his big sister's moonlit carpet as he had in his crib. Cassie reached under her pillow for the butcher knife hidden there, turning back to her little brother with a grin granted a twist of the maniacal in the shadows cast by the moonlight. Cassie was aglow in silver light, ready to finally satisfy her curiosity. There would be no disappointing cotton this time, she was sure.

Cassie straddled her little brother's body, her knees pressed firmly at his hips, setting her blade down momentarily to unsnap his onesie, sliding it off his little arms and pulling it down to his waist. There was no hesitation in Cassie as she plunged the knife into her baby brother, like she had with every one of her baby dolls. Her baby dolls had never screamed and neither did baby

Jack. Cassie was giddy with excitement as she pulled the knife toward her enjoying the resistance it met along the way, until she reached the midsection, then there was hardly any resistance to her blade at all. Seeing all the blood pouring out made her happier than her little moment of clarity this afternoon. She began to unconsciously giggle as she set the blade down, diving her little hands into the incision, so happy to feel his wet squishy innards rather than boring cotton. She didn't think she could ever be happier than she was at that very moment. The thought of waking her parents was completely out of her head as she giggled and pulled out the mysteries of her little brother's insides.

Cassie couldn't believe how good it made her feel as she sent all the little pieces and parts to the side, diving her hands in again and again to pull out more. She didn't know what everything was, but pulling it all out was the most fun she could ever remember having. She held her bloody hands up in the moonlight, mesmerized by how the blood looked. It appeared so black, yet beautiful, shimmering with silver highlights. She loved how it felt on her skin and began rubbing it all over her face and chest. Her arms were coated, having reached inside Jack, elbow deep, and squeezing his insides between her fingers. She felt like a magician pulling out an endless handkerchief as she yanked out Jack's intestines while she laughed and laughed, finding it the most hysterical thing she had ever seen in her life.

Cassie dove into her work with great fervour, tearing out one little piece at a time, holding it up to glisten in the moonlight before setting it down. She had not yet heard that diamonds were a girl's best friend nor did she long to have one shoved on her finger; for her, the moonlight-kissed blood was perfection. Right now, the thrill of discovery and blood bathed in moonlight were her best friends and she couldn't possibly be happier. She used the knife where necessary until her brother's torso was nothing but an empty cavity, which was the only point of dissatisfaction. She wanted to see everything there was to see, using the knife to dive deeper, sometimes hitting bone. She couldn't stop herself from giggling the entire time, she was so happy until the moonlight began to fade at the approach of dawn.

She stood up finally as the first sunlight broke through her window, turning her carpet from a black glistening pool bathed in the silver that she loved, to a deep crimson she honestly didn't care for. Looking down on her night's work, she suddenly felt utterly exhausted. She slipped back under her warm Cinderella comforter, falling asleep the second her smiling little face hit her plush pink pillow. Sleeping Beauty had never looked so grim nor so serene.

There, Cassie slept, covered in blood with a smile still plastered across her face, better than she had slept in over a month.

She awoke to her mother screaming.

Cassie sprang up, rubbing her blood encrusted hands against her eyes. Even at being startled awake, she felt refreshed having slept so deeply, albeit briefly. A moment later, her mother burst through the door. There was a split second of relief seeing her daughter had not disappeared too, but in that same moment she also saw her little princess as she was, face and hair streaked in dried blood, covered almost head to toe in crimson. Her mother screamed again, frozen in place with one hand on the door handle, the other reaching up to stifle her scream of horror. Cassie's father entered a moment later, pushing past his wife who was still frozen in place.

"See, Daddy? Now I know what's inside."

Her father sat next to her, looking down to the floor where his little princess was pointing. His eyes grew huge in terror seeing his baby boy completely dissected on the floor. All of Jack's little organs were laid to the right side of his hollowed out torso, while on the left were all his bones and muscles neatly displayed like a museum layout. James Riggs looked to his daughter, eyes wide in terror, unable to speak a word, unable to comprehend how his little princess could have done something so absolutely horrible. His mouth stood agape searching for anything to say.

"What's inside you, Daddy?"

Cassie stabbed her butcher knife into her father's throat with a smile as her mother, still frozen at the door, screamed and screamed and screamed.

The Boy in the Apartment

By Josh Pritchett

Gareth Tennant stood on the balcony of his parents Parisian flat in the Ile St. Louis and tried not to sulk. Gareth's father had called to say he would be working late because he had come across an of interesting titbit for the book he was writing. Another broken promise, Gareth mused.

"Why did we have to come to Paris?" Gareth had asked his father a few nights before.

His father had smiled at him in that aggravating way a parent smiles at an angry child. "I have to do my research here, son.""But can't you do that on the internet?"

"It'll do you good to see more of the world."*Yeah, right,* Gareth thought. *Pull the other leg, Dad!*

Gareth had hated Paris since his first day at school. Gareth felt like a fish out of water, because he didn't know the language and all the school boys called him 'the English boy', and not 'Gareth'.

Gareth had been sitting by himself at lunch when the French boy named Jean approached him. "You are having trouble learning French, yes?"

"Yeah," he replied.

"Here, let me help you."

Jean then worked with him for the next few minutes to learn something in French. "This will impress the teacher," Jean said.

"What does it mean?""Oh, don't worry. Let's put it into action"

It impressed the teacher all right, so much so that she'd called his parents to the school. Mum rolled her eyes, but Dad at least thought it was a good laugh.

Gareth felt himself go pale when he found out what he'd said.

"I want to go back to England," he said that night when they got back to the flat.

"Oh, Gareth," Dad had said. "You'll get the hang of it all soon."

"I want to go home. They hate me here!"

"Gareth, honey," Mum said. "It just takes time to make friends."

"I want my old friends. I *hate* it here. I hate the people, the stupid buildings, and the stupid food. I hate all of it!"

"Easy on, son," Dad said, trying to put out a reassuring hand to Gareth.

Gareth brushed it away. "I hate you!" he shouted running to his room.

The next day Dad decided to work late, all the while forgetting he'd agreed to take Gareth to the park to play football with him. *Just another broken promise,* Gareth thought.

"Here now," Mum said. "I know it's been hard, but you have to bear up a bit."

Gareth just looked away. She then handed him some money. "Why don't you get yourself something at the sweet shop?"

Taking the money, Gareth left his room, took his football and exited the apartment. Rage was building up inside of Gareth as he walked down the hallway of the apartment building. All at once, he angrily dropped the ball onto the hallway floor and kicked it angrily down the corridor, hitting the wall next to the staircase and sending his ball rolling down the stairs.

Gareth ran after it as it bounced down the steps and rolled along the landing of the next floor down, coming to a stop as it hit one of the neighbours' apartment doors. Gareth was about to pick it up when the door opened suddenly, and a boy about his own age said, "Oi, what's all this?"

"Sorry, mate."

"You should be," the boy said. "The Landlord will have you out!"

"You're English?" Gareth asked surprised.

"Damn right I am," he replied with a grin. "And who might you be?"

"Gareth Tennant." Gareth held out a hand.

"Bergen Webb," the boy replied, shaking his hand. "Come on in."

The flat looked much like Gareth's except the paint was a little more faded and of course the furniture was different. Otherwise it mirrored the flat upstairs. "So why are you living in Paris?" Bergen asked.

"My Dad, he's a writer. He's working on a book here in France. So we had to come over here so he could write it."

"My mum met some bloke and dragged me all the way here to be with him, but it didn't work out," Bergen said.

"Sorry to hear that, mate.""Don't be," he said. "I think my Dad and Mum will get back together soon. Hey, let me show you something."

Bergen led Gareth back to his room, and what Gareth saw almost took his breath away. "Blimey."

Gareth found himself in awe of the huge train set that was arranged against a wall of Bergen's bedroom. It ran through a series of tunnels under and around what looked like an elaborate replica of Paris. Bergen reached under the table and flipped a switch. The two trains on the parallel tracks came to life and began their trek across the model of Paris.

Bending over, Gareth took a closer look at the moving trains. "There're people in the cars," he said. "Blimey! I think they're moving!"

"Mum says it's something called a Gestalt effect," Bergen said. "You only think they're moving because the train is messing with your eyes."

"Its way cool, though," Gareth said as he watched. He thought he could see the people inside doing things. One man looked like he was reading the paper and a woman seemed to be rocking a baby to sleep.

"Hey," Bergen said. "Want to play a game of Monopoly?"

Gareth actually wanted to keep watching the train. He had never seen anything like it. "Tell you what," Bergen said, as if reading his mind. "You can use the train piece while we play."

After an hour of intense spending and collecting, Gareth managed to capture most of the board and achieve a sound Monopoly. "Yes!" he announced; and then tossed up his paper winnings.

"Is everything going all right in here, Bergen?" a woman's asked from the door to Bergen's room.

Gareth looked up to see a tall blonde woman looking in at them. "Fine, Mum," Bergen said. "This bloke has just cleaned me out."

"Who's your friend?" Bergen's mum asked.

"Gareth Tennant, ma'am," Gareth said.

"Bloody swindler is what he is," Bergen said with a laugh.

"Will you be staying for dinner, Gareth?" she asked.

"I'd better not, my mum will be wondering where I am."

"Well, pop over again tomorrow, mate. You maybe a swindler, but you're better than those bloody frogs!"

"Bergen!" his mother said with irritation. "You know how I hate it when you use that word to describe the French."

"Sorry, Mum," he said. "But they are frogs!"

Bergen's mum rolled her eyes as Gareth laughed. "I'll see you at school, won't I?"

"No, I'm home schooled.""Lucky you," Gareth added. "I wish my mum would just home school me. That way I wouldn't have to put up with the frogs."

Bergen's mum sighed and walked off. "You're a bad influence, Bergen Webb."

"God, you're so lucky, mate," Gareth said. "If my mum caught me calling the French frogs, she'd have me out!"

Bergen laughed and walked him to the door.

Back upstairs, Gareth was all smiles as he walked in. "Mum, you're not going to believe it!"

"Shh," she said. "Your father's asleep. He's not feeling well."

"Oh, sorry. But I met a guy my age, just downstairs."

"That's good, Sweetie," she said. "What's his name?"

"Bergen. He's got this really cool train set that's got little moving people in it."

"Well, I'm glad you've made a friend, I really am. Now, I'll make us some dinner."

The next day after school, Gareth went back down to see Bergen again. Only this time Bergen had company. "This is my Aunt Betty and Uncle Ronald," Bergen said.

"Nice to meet you, Gareth," Aunt Betty said, holding out her hand.

Uncle Ronald didn't say a word; he just looked oddly at Gareth. Looking down, Gareth thought maybe his fly was undone. Then he looked up to see that Uncle Ronald was holding a napkin up in front of him. Slowly a biscuit levitated above the napkin, and Ronald bent his head to take a bite out of the levitating biscuit.

"Cut it out, Uncle Ronald," Bergen said with a smirk.

But Gareth was already laughing with delight. "Wow.""He's holding it up with a fork and his thumb and forefinger behind the napkin," Bergen said.

"Watch it," Ronald said. "Or I'll try the disappearing nephew trick on you."

Gareth laughed again.

"They're just here to see the new baby."Gareth looked over and saw a white cradle. Inside was a new born baby boy dressed in a light blue jumper. "Hello, little fellow," Gareth said.

The baby let out a cry. "Sorry," Gareth apologized.

"It's okay," Bergen's mother said coming out of the kitchen. "Why don't you boys go play in Bergen's room for a while?"

When they got to his room, Bergen reached into a desk drawer and pulled out a stack of comic books. "Wrap you mind around these," he said, handing the stack to Gareth.

Gareth sorted through the comics and thought his friend was showing him a secret treasure. He had old *Spider-man, Batman, Flash, Hulk, Ghost Rider,* and *X-Men* comics. There were even copies of *Tales from the Crypt, Swamp Thing*, and *House of Mystery*, all neatly cared for as if they were brand new. Then Gareth remembered the bag he was carrying.

"I brought you something too," Gareth said. "I stopped off at the little sweet shop on the Rue de Provence."

"Mere de Famille," Bergen exclaimed with delight.

Gareth opened the bag and produced two dark chocolate éclairs with cream filling. "I'll say this for the

French," Gareth began. "They may suck in every other way, but they make killer desserts."

"I agree. Be careful with the comic books!"

Gareth looked down and realized he was about to touch one of them with his chocolate covered fingers. "Sorry, mate."

"No worries," Bergen said and handed him a box of Kleenex. They spent the rest of the afternoon reading comics and watching the train.

When Gareth finally went back upstairs, his father was feeling worse and a doctor had been called.

"I'm glad you could come so quickly," he heard his mother say.

"I was in the neighbourhood," the doctor said with a very thick French accent. "We had a death here earlier today."

"Oh, yes… I heard about that poor baby that died. That poor mother, I can't imagine anything worse."

The doctor nodded.

"Is Dad all right?" Gareth asked as he stepped into the room.

"Oh, Gareth, I didn't see you there," his mother said as she stood up from the sofa.

"He's got a very serious stomach infection," the doctor confirmed.

"Is he going into hospital?"

"We'll see if it passes in a day," the doctor said to reassure him. "Sometimes these things clear up by themselves."

Dinner was just soup and toast, but Gareth didn't mind. In their family it was Dad who was the cook, not Mum. Dad was something of a Renaissance man, having majored in architecture and minored in cooking and literature in college.

"What did you do today?" Mum asked.

"I hung out with Bergen again," he said looking up from his bowl of canned chicken noodle soup.

She smiled. "Oh. So what did you lads get up to?" Gareth told her about sharing the éclairs, reading comics, and Bergen's new baby brother. "Oh, that's good news. What's the baby's name?"

"Uh," Gareth felt his face turn red when he realized he didn't know the baby's name. "I forgot to ask. Sorry, Mum."

Mum gave him a look. "Well, I'll write up a best wishes note for you to deliver tomorrow and let her know that I'll stop by for a proper visit when your father is up and about."

"He's got an uncle too. He does magic tricks," Gareth added.

"Does he?"

"Yeah, he did this trick where he makes a biscuit levitate…"

"Is this the one where he uses a fork and a napkin?"

Gareth looked down. "Why does everyone know this one but me?"

At first, Mum thought Gareth was making a joke, and she laughed until she saw her son's disappointed face. "Oh, love, it's just an old trick. Your great-granddad did it all the time."

Gareth let out a sigh. "I just thought you'd be impressed."

"I am very impressed. I was worried you'd be moping around your room all year. Now you've made a friend, and you're doing much better."

Gareth took another spoonful of soup and mulled over what his mum had said.

"It sounds like you had a good time today," she said. "Are you in the same class?"

"No, Bergen is home schooled."

"Hmm," Mum mused. "Well, maybe you could have Bergen up here for tea one day when your father is better."

That night, Gareth dreamed he was on a Metro station platform. Gareth had never seen that particular Metro station before, but he thought it could have been any old station in Paris. Looking around he saw a sign that read *Croix Rouge*. It stank of mold and dust. Gareth turned, looked down the tunnel and saw a light coming. The station rumbled with the sound of the oncoming train engine and Gareth realized he had no ticket. He wondered how he was going to board it without one. Suddenly, he wondered why the train's engine sounded more and more like a woman screaming in French.

The screaming got louder until he awoke, and he sat up in bed. He could feel his heart pounding as the dream faded.

Gareth got out of bed and rushed to the flat's door. He saw his mother sitting up on the sofa as he ran by. She had been sleeping there the last couple of nights because dad had been tossing and turning. "Gareth, don't open the door," she called in a groggy voice. But it was too late.

He only opened the door the length of the security chain, but it was more than enough for him to see out what was going outside in the hallway. Several people had gathered at the top of the stairs in their robes and pyjamas to listen as a woman screamed in French. Gareth still did not know enough French to understand her.

"Oh, God," hi mother muttered. "It's that poor woman whose baby died."

"What's she saying?"

Gareth's mum sat back on the sofa, her face darkened as she tried to listen. "Something about how she can hear her baby crying," she said.

When the police arrived, the crowd around the top of the steps broke up and went back to their flats. Gareth suddenly realized that his mum had put a hand on his shoulder as if fearing he would run out of the flat to see what was amiss.

Gareth didn't sleep very well for the rest of the night. When he did drift off to sleep, he thought he could hear a train's whistle in the distance.

Dad was not feeling much better the next day. It was Saturday and there was no school. The weather was fine and mum suggested that maybe Gareth and Bergen could go out and play at the Luxembourg Gardens.

Gareth raced down the steps with his football, the idea of kicking the ball back and forth on such a beautiful day sounded like heaven to Gareth. He was about to knock on Bergen's door when he heard a voice come up from behind him, asking him something in French. Gareth turned and saw a short woman with dark rumpled hair.

"I'm sorry, Ma'am. I don't know what…"

She grabbed his shirt and repeated what she said again. This time her voice rose in a desperate plea almost is if she were begging Gareth for help. Gareth could only stand there frozen with fear as this woman seemed to threaten him.

"Nikkei," a thin man with receding hair called out as he came out of one of the flats.

The man started to say something, but the woman raised her voice into a very loud and angry tone. He spoke even louder, almost shaking her, until she fell crying into his arms. Gareth could only stand there and watch, unsure if he should say something.

"I'm sorry," the man said at last, looking at Gareth. "We just lost our baby and my wife thinks he's in that apartment."

"Oh, I… I'm sorry, sir," was all Gareth could think to say.

"Thank you," the man said as he put his arms around his wife's shoulders and led her away. When they disappeared into their flat, Gareth let out his breath and knocked on the door. Bergen answered. "Hey, mate," Gareth said with a big smile as he held up the ball and tried not to think of what had just happened. "Fancy a game?"

"Can't."

There was a wailing sound of a baby crying. "Oh, bloody hell!" Bergen muttered. "You can come in."

Bergen turned and walked back into the flat; and Gareth followed, closing the door as he entered. Bergen walked over to his brother's cradle and lifted him up to hold him. "There, now, shhh."

Gareth watched his friend. Bergen seemed to be an old hand at taking care of babies. "You're babysitting?" Gareth asked, looking around.

Bergen nodded. "Mum had to go out. She said something about getting things ready for Dad when he comes."

"Oh, when's that?"

"A day or two, I think." Bergen turned to gaze out of the window.

"Hey, I forgot to ask," Gareth said. "What's your brother's name?"

"Alex," Bergen said, in a soft voice.

"Yeah," Gareth said. "My mum wants to pop by and see him, and meet your mum."

"Why?" Bergen said sharply, looking at Gareth.

Gareth thought he could feel the colour drain from his face. "Uh, you know," Gareth stammered, feeling an odd sense of fear about his friend. "It's a thing mums do. You know, come over see the new baby, gossip about all this and that."

Bergen seemed to ponder this, and then he gently put his brother back into his crib. "Sorry, mate, but it may not be a good idea just now."

"No worries," Gareth said.

"Hey, let me show you something," Bergen said as he led Gareth into the dining room.

The centre of the dining room was dominated by an oddly shaped table covered in white. Gareth thought the table a little high, almost waist high for grownups. With one swift motion, Bergen pulled away the white sheet and revealed a billiards table.

"Wow!" Gareth exclaimed. "You sure don't eat here!"

"Nope." Bergen reached down and pulled out two cues. "You ever play before?"

"A couple of times with my dad.""Look under there and hand me the triangle." Bergen pointed to the other end of the table taking out the balls.

Gareth pulled out the rubber triangle and began putting the balls into it. "Do you have any brothers or sisters?" Bergen asked.

"Nope, just me," Gareth said and then a glumness came over him. "Sometimes I think they just pack me in with the underpants."

"How do you mean?"

"Well," Gareth began as he dropped a ball marked '6' into the rack. "It's great sometimes that we've been able to travel; but sometimes I think it would be good to live in one place for a long time, at least a year or two."

"Yeah.""Yeah," Gareth repeated. "I mean when Dad's up and about he's a lot of fun, and we do stuff together like go camping and video games. But it would be nice to not have to go from country to country. I'd just like to keep the same set of friends, and never have to worry about people making fun of me because I don't speak the language."

"I could see where that would be a pain," Bergen said and then handed him a stick. "You can break first."

Gareth aimed the stick behind the white cue ball and struck it with his stick. The ball rolled fast down the table and scattered the other balls across the table.

Bergen took aim as the white ball slowed near a small cluster of balls. "What if we were brothers?" Bergen asked.

Gareth let out a chuckle. "Yeah, right!"

"I'm serious." Bergen used the cue ball to break up the cluster and sent the '10' ball rolling towards one of the pockets. "What if you could be my brother; and we could live here just playing all day long? Wouldn't that be great?"

Gareth looked at him for a second and realized Bergen was serious. But what would that be like? Living together, playing together, telling jokes, and getting into trouble together, even double dating together? Gareth was getting to that age when he was starting to become interested in girls. What would that be like for Bergen and Gareth, two English brothers with the run of Paris?

"It would be fun," Gareth admitted. Bergen smiled.

Gareth went back upstairs just in time to see the paramedics wheeling his father out of the flat with his mother and the doctor in tow. "Mum? What's happening to Dad?"

Without a word, she took him in her arms and

pulled him in close. For a second, the only sound he could hear was his Mum's tearful sniffles. "Oh, Gareth," she moaned. "It's bad. We need to take dad to the hospital."

"Mrs. Tennant," the doctor said in a low voice. "We have to go."

Gareth didn't really remember the ambulance ride to the hospital. He kept looking at his dad as he lay muttering something on the stretcher. At the hospital, Gareth and his mother sat in a waiting room with nothing but French magazines to read. Gareth thumbed through one of them as his mother wadded a Kleenex with her thumb and forefinger.

At last, Gareth spoke. "Bergen and I played billiards today."

"That's nice, dear," she said and then looked down the hall, waiting for what would come next. As Gareth watched her, anxiously staring down the hallway, he realized she looked like she was restlessly waiting or a train. After an hour or so, a nurse came to get them and led them back to a room in the ICU area. Gareth's dad looked pale, almost transparent.

The doctor came over to them. "Mrs. Tennant, may I speak to you outside?"

She nodded. "Gareth, stay with your father please, and call if he wakes up."

Gareth didn't reply as his mother followed the doctor out and into the hallway. He stood next to the bed and looked at his father as he heard the electronic beeps of the monitors. All Gareth could think was how much the weird breathing pump next to the bed sounded like Darth Vader's breathing.

Without thinking Gareth reached down and took his father's hand. It was so cold and dry that he almost didn't think he was holding his father's hand. It seemed like something alien. Suddenly his father's eyes opened, and his hand tightened around Gareth's own hand.

Letting out a startled gasp, Gareth looked down at his father's face and for the only time in his life, Gareth saw a terrified look on his father's face. "Don't get on the train, Gareth!" his Dad gasped in a hoarse and strained voice.

"Dad," Gareth stammered.

"Please, Gareth, do not get on the train," Dad said one last time before the electronic beeps became one loud dirge. His father's eyes rolled back before he let go of Gareth's hand, and slumped back onto the bed.

Gareth barely noticed the doctor push past him as he began the process of resuscitating his father. All Gareth remembered later was his mother pulling him in close, weeping as she prayed. "Please, God, no," she cried over and over.

He didn't know what to say, or if he should say anything. Gareth just stood there and held onto his mother. She held him so tightly that he could only hear, but not see what they were doing to his dad. After a few minutes, he heard them say something in French; and someone switched off the monitor. "I am so sorry, Mrs. Tennant," the doctor said, his face full of regret.

After they made some arrangements, Gareth and his mum went back to the flat. They didn't say much and it wasn't until one in the morning that he was able to fall asleep; and when he did Gareth had the dream again. Only this time, Bergen was standing next to the open door of a train that looked like the real version of one of his toys. He was dressed in an old-style conductor's uniform, like something from an old movie. Gareth could see Bergen's uncle, aunt, and mum as she held the crying baby. They were all sitting on the train, peering from the windows, and looking frightened.

Gareth saw his father, walking towards Bergen. He walked slowly, his head down, as if he was a condemned man. *"Dad!"* Gareth called out; and as he started to run towards him.

His father turned and looked back at him. His face was pale, unshaven, and his eyes were bloodshot. He held up a hand at Gareth in the way he used to when they played 'Stop and Go' when Gareth was four.

Out of habit, Gareth stopped and watched as his father turned and walked onto the train.

Bergen looked at Gareth and smiled. "You don't need a ticket, mate, just hop on board."

Gareth didn't like Bergen's smile. It reminded him of the barracudas he had seen when he and his family went to Sea World the year before. The fish all lined up in front of the glass watching the people go by, smiling and Gareth had wondered if those fish were imagining the taste of human flesh.

But this was Bergen, his friend, Gareth reasoned. He wouldn't hurt him, would he? "Just you and me, mate," Bergen said. "You and me playing games and having fun all day every day. Nothing but endless summer vacation and all you've got to do is hop on-board."

Gareth looked up when he heard something slam against the train's window. It was his dad looking out the window at him and yelling something, but Gareth couldn't hear him. Bergen looked up at Gareth's dad who suddenly backed away from the window, a look of fear crossing his face. Gareth just looked at Bergen and kept walking towards him.

"Just one more step, mate." Bergen's grin spread wider.

Then Bergen and the train seemed to ripple and fade away replaced by the Paris sky line. Gareth found himself standing on the outer edge of the flat's balcony, looking out at the city, his foot stepping out into empty space just as a hand was grabbing his shoulder. *"What are you doing?"*

The hand pulled him back over the balcony. He could hear the hysterical voice and see the face of his mother looking down at him. *"What are you doing?"* his mother repeated herself.

"I… I had a dream," he stammered. "About Dad."

She looked at him, tears welling up in her eyes. "So did I. He was told me you were in danger."

Gareth shuddered as he heard a train's whistle in the distance.

Over the next few days there were arrangements to make. It was decided that Gareth's father would be buried back in England. Gareth's maternal uncle Sean arrived to help, and Gareth found himself sitting around waiting for something to do. Nothing more was said about the dreams or Gareth's sleep walking episode although his mother had made him sleep in her room the previous two nights.

He was thinking about something when mum spoke. "I'm sorry, Mum. I didn't hear you."

"I was wondering if you wanted to go and play with Bergen for a while," she said. "You've been a grown up all day and I think you should be a boy again for a little while. You should spend some time with him before we go back to England."

"Oh," Gareth said with mixed feelings. A week before, Gareth would have given anything to be back in England. Now he felt like he was leaving his only friend.

Not just that, he thought he was leaving a part of his dad too.

But there was something different about Bergen when Gareth got to his flat

"What do you want?" Bergen snapped when he opened the door, and Gareth felt taken aback.

"My dad died, Bergen." His voice cracked. "Mum says we're moving..."

"Yeah, sorry to hear it," Bergen said; but his tone was saying something else. "Look my dad is here now, all right and proper; and I don't have time for you anymore."

"But, Bergen, I don't..." Gareth started to say as he felt like he had just been stabbed in the chest.

"Do I have to paint you a picture? Piss off!"

"But I thought," Gareth said, even as he was trying to find the words. "I thought you wanted us to be brothers."

"Oh, now you want that, do you?"

"Yeah. Yeah, I wish you were my brother."

Gareth watched as Bergen regarded him for a moment. "You could be, but you've got to do something."

"What?"

Bergen opened the apartment door all the way. "Come in and touch the train tracks," he said.

Gareth looked at him. "Touch the train tracks while I ramp up the current, then we can be brothers forever."

"Won't that... Won't that hurt?" Gareth asked, his mouth suddenly very dry.

"Only for a couple of seconds, but when it's over, it'll be endless summers for us, no more school or needing to grow up. Nothing but endless vacation and playing games, but first you've got to touch the rail."

Gareth thought about it or a moment. It sounded so good, too good really. Endless fun with his best friend, no more school or having to wander around lost in strange places. But what about Mum, he couldn't leave her, not now. "Can my mum come too?"

"We've already got one, and she's the best one yet."

The best one yet, Gareth thought. Something about the way he said that made Gareth nervous. He almost asked: "How many mums have you had, Bergen?"

Gareth suddenly felt like a spell had been broken and he could really see Bergen for the first time. He was something terrible and not his good friend

"Who is it, son?" a man's voice called.

"No one, dad," Bergen replied.

Gareth froze. He knew that voice, he had heard it every day since he was born. "No one is no one, Bergen," the man said stepping into full view behind Bergen.

Gareth felt his heart almost stop and his blood run cold when he saw who was speaking. It was not possible, but he was standing right there in front of Gareth, smiling at him. "Oh, hello, are you a friend of Bergen's? I've only just arrived."

Gareth tried to say something, anything to make sense of who was walking towards him, then he felt something powerful shove him out of the flat and onto his backside. He looked up, his heart pounding like a train engine going full throttle in his chest. For the first time Gareth thought he could see Bergen's real face now. It was an angry, red, and distorted face. *"You had your chance, boy,"* Bergen's voice yelled, sounding as if it came from some deep dark well. "Now, go away. You've missed the train!"

Bergen slammed the door hard enough to rattle Gareth's bones, but not before Gareth got one last look at his father's face and saw the fear in his eyes. Getting to his feet, Gareth dashed back up the stairs to his flat.

"Mum," he yelled as he burst through the door of his flat. *"Mum!"*

His mum came out of her bedroom wearing her dressing gown and a towel around her head as Uncle Sean sat up on the sofa, looking at his nephew. "Gareth, what is it, lad?"

"It's Dad," Gareth almost screamed. "He's downstairs!"

"What… What do you mean he's downstairs?" Uncle Sean asked.

"No, Uncle Sean," Gareth stammered. "He's downstairs in Bergen's flat."

"What are you saying?" his mother demanded.

"Bergen has him down there in his flat. I don't how, but he's got Dad brainwashed or something and…"

Gareth heard the slap before he felt it. His mother was standing there looking at him like a red faced stranger. "Sarah," Sean said. "Calm down!"

Then all at once, Gareth's mother crumpled and began to cry again. "I'm sorry, dear, I didn't… I'm so…"

"But he's alive," Gareth insisted. "Why won't you believe me?"

***

After a while, the doctor had to be called and both mother and son were given sedatives to calm them down and help them sleep. "It's very sad," the doctor said. "I am beginning to hate this building. I don't know if your sister-in-law has told you, but a baby fell out of its crib in another flat in this building a few days ago. It died."

"No, that's awful," Sean said.

"Yes, and a few weeks ago an old magician and his wife passed away just after moving into this building.

If I were more superstitious, I would say this building was cursed."

Gareth tried to speak up about what he had seen, but could only listen to his uncle speak. "His mum said he had been playing with a boy who lives downstairs, but I went downstairs to ask if Gareth was acting strangely, the door was open and the apartment was empty."

"Sir, I handle most of the emergency calls for this area your nephew is the only boy his age in this building," the doctor said.

"But how can that be?" Sean demanded. "Sarah said Gareth has been playing with him for most of the last few days."

"That apartment has is not occupied because no one stays there for very long. It has been that way for twenty years since a boy in that apartment died when he was electrocuted by a faulty toy train set in 1995."

***

In his dreams Gareth stood on the platform of an underground tube station and waited for a train that never came again.

Little Angel

By Sharon Higa

The child in the crisp green, gingham dress sat on the bus next to the lady, gazing through the half-open window at the passing scenery. The woman seated beside the little girl kept her head down, nervously fiddling with the strap on her black leather purse.

An elderly woman sitting across from the pair leaned forward and tapped the woman, whom she presumed was the little girl's mother, on the knee

The woman's head shot up with a start. She could have been anywhere from twenty-five to thirty-five-years old, hair prematurely grey; her dress slacks, blouse and low pump heels intimated upper-middle class. The dark circles and sunken eyes shocked the elderly woman, who drew back for a minute before remembering her manners. She leaned forward once more and nodded toward the little girl.

"Your daughter is so sweet and quiet. You really should be proud; such a polite little angel."

The woman shot a sideways glance at the child who had turned to observe the conversation between the elderly lady and her mother.

"Ye…ahem…yes...Martha is a well behaved little girl." The stammer and tremble in the woman's voice was not lost on the older lady. She cleared her throat and clasped the front of her blouse, hoping to break the ice as well as cover up the rudeness of her reaction. She smiled once more and leaned forward.

"Well, where are my manners? My name is Gloria Breene. And what," she turned her eyes toward the small child, "might your charming little girl's name be?"

The little girl turned her full attention to the woman who had just introduced herself. In a hauntingly sweet and too-mature-for- her- age tone, she replied, "My name is Martha Gordon and my mommy's name is Cynthia."

Strange, that the child should speak for her mother, Gloria mused, but she pushed the thought aside and addressed the woman sitting across from her.

"Well, Cynthia and Martha, it is a pleasure to meet the two of you. It appears we will probably be seat mates for a while. I've spent a delightful holiday with my grandchildren and am now headed back to my home. Where are you two bound for, if I may ask?"

Once again, Martha spoke up. "Mommy and I are coming home from my Grammy's funeral."

Cynthia flinched and turned to look down the aisle of the bus, as if she'd suddenly seen something of extreme interest elsewhere.

Gloria reached forward and placed a consoling hand on the obviously upset mothers' leg. "Oh my dear, I am so sorry for your loss; was she your mother?"

Martha answered the question while Cynthia looked down at the purse in her lap. "Yes, it was Grammy Wingate. It was unexpected, wasn't it, Mommy?"

Gloria saw the slight head nod from the mother before she turned back to the little girl; it was then that she really looked at the child.

Martha was on the petite side, the skin on her arms and cheeks flushed with a rosy glow of health, natural ash blond curls framing an oval face with a deep red cupids' bow mouth, and wide round hazel-gold eyes shining with an intelligence that seemed far too mature for a child of her age.

I wonder if she's wearing lipstick, Gloria thought. *Her lips are far too red to be natural.*

Her hands were tiny, the fingers seeming to be uncharacteristically long, as were her nails – filed to a sharp point, rather than rounded, as one would expect for a little one.

Something about Martha was both attractive and repulsive at the same time – Gloria just couldn't put a finger on what she felt was *off.*

Cynthia responded to what her daughter had said, only after Martha had given her a nudge. "Yes," she muttered so low Gloria had to lean forward to catch all the words, "my mother's death was unexpected."

Martha nodded happily, tucking her dress underneath her white stocking-clad legs and swinging her feet. Gloria noticed she was wearing black patent leather shoes. They reminded her of the shoes she used to wear as a child. *A bit old fashioned for a child in this day and age,* she mused.

The bus hit a pothole; the jounce brought Gloria back to the present and her two mutual travelers. She smiled once more at Cynthia, trying to invite and facilitate conversation with the woman. "Martha is certainly an eloquent speaker; how old is she?"

Martha spoke up before her mother could respond. "I turned five years old last March."

Startled, Gloria blinked – her gaze going from mother to daughter, then back to the mother. "My word, you must have found a very progressive school to send Martha to, and one that would take her at such a young age...?"

The question hung in the air between the two women, but it was Martha's young/old voice that cut through the expectant pause.

"Mommy and Daddy started home schooling me when I was two. They have always said I'm an exceptional child."

Gloria did not take her eyes off of the woman in front of her. She couldn't quite place what she was picking up from Cynthia, but she knew it was neither pride nor joy at her progeny's intellect. "Where is your husband now? Is he waiting for the two of you at home?"

Cynthia's eyes shot up to Gloria's, connecting for one brief instant before turning back to the purse in her lap. It was in that electrically charged second that Gloria was able to put a finger on the emotion coming from Cynthia: it was terror.

Martha leaned forward, placing a hand on her mother's shoulder. "Daddy died last year in an accident at our house; he fell off a ladder while cleaning the rain gutters."

Gloria flinched backward, slamming her elbow against her armrest. "Oh my dears – you truly have had your share of heartbreak, haven't you?" She covered her own uneasiness by focusing on rubbing her arm, avoiding any kind of eye contact with the girl. She was terrified the child would see the fear in her own face, which mirrored the mother's.

Martha stared at the older woman until Gloria once again looked up. Flashing a beautiful childlike smile, she patted her mother on the shoulder then leaned back in her own seat. "Mommy and I have been through a lot, but we have each other. Don't we, Mommy?"

Cynthia coughed into her fist for a minute, swallowing twice before she muttered, "Excuse me, I have to use the restroom," then abruptly rose from her seat. Martha watched her go, and Gloria watched Martha. "Don't be too long, Mommy; you know how I get nervous." The insinuation was not lost on Gloria.

Cynthia mumbled over her shoulder, "You know I'll be back; Gloria will watch you for now." Without waiting for a response from either the child or the older woman, Cynthia scurried down the aisle, clinging to the seats to maintain her balance.

Old woman and young child looked at each other. Gloria stared into Martha's eyes, which suddenly turned from hazel/gold to blood red, the pupils elongating until they were black, cat-like slits. Gloria gasped and grabbed her throat, cutting off the scream that tried to erupt from her while the little girl's features suddenly turned from angelic to demonic.

"Mommy's mine, you know," the sweet voice contrasted starkly with the evil leer, "so I would suggest you keep this to yourself; after all, *you* don't need to have an accident – do you, Gloria?"

Gloria's face lost all colour, her head shaking spasmodically back and forth.

Martha crossed her arms over her scant chest. "That's what happened to Grammy. I heard them talking on the phone; she tried to convince Mommy to 'do away' with me. Well, I couldn't have that - calling a priest and all – so Grammy had to have an accident. Mommy was so sad when she got the call from Uncle Johnny that Grammy had fallen down the stairs."

Gloria couldn't believe what she was hearing; her mind shrank from the words, logic trying to refute everything this child was saying, but the evidence was sitting right there in front of her. Just before Martha could say anything else, Cynthia returned from the restroom at the back of the bus.

When Gloria looked back at Martha, she was once again a sweet, angelic-looking child. For Cynthia's sake, Gloria mentally pulled herself together, terrified of causing the woman any more pain or tragedy. She forced a smile onto her face and glanced up as Martha's mommy took her seat.

"So, where are you two getting off?" Gloria made the question sound as casual as possible.

For once, Martha actually allowed her mother to answer the question, resuming her attention to the half open window and the scenery flowing by.

"We're getting off in the town of Braggton. The bus actually stops right in front of our home." Cynthia's voice had taken on a more [illegible] tone, her demeanour a bit more relaxed now that Martha's attention was drawn elsewhere.

The child continued to stare out the window which gave the two older women the chance to finally engage in small talk. They chatted about recipes, compared the weather, gardening – light topics that eased the fear, which had not dissipated but at least could be contained for the time being.

Soon, the voice of the bus driver came over the loudspeaker, announcing that Braggton was the next stop.

Cynthia's cheerfulness was suddenly and dramatically replaced by resignation. Gloria wept inwardly for her, but knew there was nothing she could do. Martha brought her attention back around to the two women and smiled brightly.

"It was a pleasure meeting you, Gloria Breene, wasn't it, Mommy?"

Cynthia simply nodded as she reached under the seat for a small backpack which she handed over to Martha, deliberately refusing to look at the child. Martha slipped the backpack over her shoulders and winked at Gloria. Mother and daughter remained seated until the bus had come to a full stop and the other passengers had cleared out.

Finally, Cynthia stood up and moved on down the aisle, bidding Gloria a quick goodbye. Martha allowed her mother to get a few feet ahead of her before she leaned down and whispered in Gloria's ear, "Give my regards to your granddaughters, Shannon and Carmen, the next time you talk to them."

Gloria's heart almost stopped; she was positive she had never mentioned her granddaughters by name.

She could only stare wide-eyed at the back of the retreating child, Cynthia waited at the bus doors for Martha to catch up. Together, they disembarked from the bus, which had stopped in front of two huge wrought-iron gates that led to a brownstone manor.

Gloria slid over to the seat that Martha had vacated. With tremulous anxiety, she peered through the window as mother and child stood on the sidewalk, waiting to collect their luggage from the cargo hold, along with five other passengers.

The driver eventually placed two bags down on the ground. Cynthia claimed them and subsequently handed him a folded up bill. Cynthia picked up one bag while Martha clasped the smaller of the two.

Gloria Breene watched as Martha reached for her mother. Cynthia flinched before she reluctantly clasped the proffered hand.

The bus pulled away, but not before Gloria heard the last comment the child made to the adult standing next to her; the comment which made the old woman frantically push the open window of the bus closed then shrink as far back into her seat as possible, no longer looking at the receding pair, wishing with all her might that she'd minded her own business.

Martha tugged at her mother's hand and, flashing a grin of pure evil at the shivering woman, said in her sweet child's voice, "That's a good mommy; now, let's go in and you can make me my dinner."

The Apothecary's Hiccup

By Douglas F. Dluzen

Paige took Henry's hand and pulled him towards another shop. All around, other families hustled to and fro. Frantic mothers pushed strollers down the dirt road and little girls in princess dresses danced about. Up above, the sun shone brightly down on the crowd and hinted at a beautiful and warm fall day.

"Let's go in this one," said Paige, reading the wooden sign. It read *The Apothecary's Hiccup* in bold red cursive, the words set above an ornate carving of a mortar and pestle, and underneath in black lettering – *Fine Herbs, Medicines, and Tonics to Soothe the Soul.*

"Whatever you want, honey," replied Henry. "I'm ready to get out of the sun for a few moments anyway." He squinted down the lane towards the beer stand. The line was long and it roped around the corner and out of sight. He frowned. "I didn't realize it was going to be so busy this weekend. When did the Renaissance Faire become so popular?"

"It's a beautiful day, who wouldn't want to be here?" said Paige and pointed at a young couple walking hand in hand with their small boy. The boy was dressed in a fluffy blue dragon costume, complete with a hoodie and cloth tail that hung down and swayed back and forth. "That's so cute," she said as she laughed and watched them walk by.

"Yeah, that is cute," agreed Henry. He placed a hand on Paige's belly. "We could pick one up for our boy too. He'll make a fine dragon." Paige giggled with happiness and held her own arms around her swollen belly. It was getting bigger every day now.

"Come on," she said, "let's go in."

They entered the shop and saw shelves upon shelves of sweet smelling spices and herbs. Lavender mixed with chamomile, which mixed with cinnamon and nutmeg to create a potpourri of aromatic pleasantness inside. Paige walked up to a large jar of cinnamon and picked it up. She opened the lid and took a long breath.

"*Oh!*" She quickly put her hand to her belly.

"What is it?" said Henry, over by another wall of goods.

"The baby kicked right after I smelled the cinnamon. I think he liked it." Paige walked over to another jar and sniffed again. The baby kicked again. "Ha! He likes cloves too." Henry walked over and put his hand on her stomach to feel. He felt the gentle bumps of activity.

"Wow, he really does," he said excitedly. "How strange, he's hardly moved the entire pregnancy."

"Well I wouldn't say that," said Paige. "I feel him all the time." She looked around the store. "But he sure likes it in here."

They continued smelling odds and ends near the front of the store. Occasionally, they would glance at the steady stream of people coming in and out of the front door. Henry noticed many of those leaving were holding a small paper cup.

"Paige," said Henry, "I think there are free samples somewhere. Let's find them." Paige put down another jar and followed. It didn't take much searching before they found a young boy sitting on a counter top and handing out small cups to those walking by. He smiled as they approached. He had cropped blonde hair and stone grey eyes and wore a simple white short-sleeve shirt with khaki shorts. Paige thought he looked a little under-fed, but he seemed happy and excited as he handed out the samples.

"Free sample?" he asked.

“Yes, thank you,” said Paige and grabbed a cup from him. She gave it a quick sniff. A pleasant aroma of mint and liquorice filled her senses. Her baby kicked against her stomach in response. “I think my baby likes it. Is this a tea?”

“I made it special,” said the boy, nodding. “I helped prepare it this morning.”

Paige smiled at him. “You prepared it, huh? How clever of you. What’s in it?”

“Star anise, lemon, even mint. It’s all natural,” he said, very matter of fact. “You have to be careful though, there are several varieties of star anise and you don’t want to mix them up or people can get sick.” He smiled at them. “But don’t worry, my parents made tea all their lives. I learned from the best!”

“Wow,” said Henry, impressed. Down further into the shop, Henry could see an older woman standing behind the cashier’s table. He guessed that was his mother. “You sure know a lot about spices,” he said, looking back at the boy. “I don’t think I’ve ever seen a kid so knowledgeable about tea. How old are you?” For a second, both Paige and Henry were caught off guard as it looked like the boy’s expression darkened. But it may have been a trick of the light as a second later he was smiling up at them.

“I’m old enough,” said the boy. “I’ve been making tea since I can remember.”

“Well thank you,” said Henry and he grabbed a cup for himself. He gave it a sip. The tea was piping hot but still pleasantly cool to the tongue. He noted the liquorice taste but it wasn’t overbearing. When he swallowed and opened his mouth it felt cool and crisp. “This is great, and quite refreshing.”

Paige tried hers. She too liked the taste. “It’s wonderful,” she agreed. She felt another kick inside as she put the cup into the trash can. *I've never felt the baby so active before,* she thought.

"Thank you for the tea," Paige said to the boy, who was already giving a sample to another gentleman. Paige turned to Henry. "Let's go."

"Wait!" said the boy, turning away from a customer and hopping down. He walked around the counter and picked up an opaque blue bottle sitting underneath and pulled the stopper off. Paige walked up to him as the boy poured another small cup from the bottle and handed it to her. "This one is for him." He pointed at her abdomen. "A special tea."

"Thank you," replied Paige. "What's in this one?"

"The same spices but in a slightly different combination. I think you'll like it. It will make him strong."

Paige held the cup in her hand and looked the boy over. He stood and watched her and she gave him a smile. *Cute kid.* "Good guess about having a boy," she said and took a sip. It did taste slightly different from the first tea but she found it just as refreshing.

"It wasn't a guess," said the boy, "I knew." He reached out and placed a hand on her belly. Paige felt her baby kick and she backed up in surprise.

"Your hands are so cold."

"Sorry, they are always like that."

"What's your name?"

"I'm Sam," he said. He winked at her and smiled. "I need to see to the other customers now." And before Paige could reply he turned and began walking towards the back of the store. Paige watched him go through a door and disappear out of sight. Shrugging, she finished the tea and threw the cup away and found Henry near the front of the shop.

"Come on," she said, "there's supposed to be a presentation at the glassblower's workshop. Let's check it out."

Henry nodded. "Sounds good. Let's stop along the way. I'd like a beer and sitting down for a while sounds nice."

They left the store and made their way across the faire. The sun had just reached its zenith in the cloudless sky and the day was heating up quickly. Henry and Paige watched as more costumed attendees filed into the faire and everyone in the moving crowds squashed closer together as they slowly navigated through the chaotic bustle towards the next store or food vendor.

Paige waited with Henry as he picked up a beer and together they found the glassblower's workshop. They sat down on a bench overlooking the demonstration area, complete with a large wood-burning oven and a nearby worktable supporting a collection of raw materials and dyes. The other benches quickly filled up and soon after a very tall man with long black hair and a goatee walked out from the workshop. He wore a leather smock similar to a cooking apron and he was already sweating from the heat of the day.

He introduced himself quickly and began demonstrating the basics of blowing glass. Paige watched with interest for a while, but eventually started looking at all the people around her. Henry seemed entranced by the process so she kept to herself and decided to do a little people watching. She looked about the crowd when she noticed Sam standing alone by a large oak tree a little way down the road, watching her through the moving crowd. She was slightly shocked to see that he was staring directly at her, his gaze fixated on her position with an almost hungry look in his eyes. She shifted uncomfortably on the bench and looked away. *Oh stop being so foolish, he's just a boy.* She looked back at the spot where he'd been standing but it was now empty. She shivered and looked back at her husband.

"Henry," she said, "I'm going to the bathroom. Wait here?" Henry took a sip of his beer and continued to watch the glassblowing.

"Okay," he said, "I think this will be going on for a bit."

"Okay, I'll be back."

She stood up and walked away from the workshop and made her way through the crowd towards the oak tree. She looked behind the trunk and around the area but she could see no sign of Sam. Extending onto her toes, she looked down the walkway in each direction, hoping for a flash of his hair or shirt amongst the sea of people moving to and fro. She saw nothing.

Well, that's weird. It must have been someone else. She felt her baby kick again and then a pressure built up in her abdomen. Down the road she saw signs pointing for the restrooms. She knew further beyond was The Apothecary's Hiccup. She decided to walk back quickly and check in before visiting the restroom. Perhaps he had gone missing. *I'll make sure he isn't missing and then come back.*

Moments later, she found herself outside The Apothecary's Hiccup. She walked up to the doorway and peered inside. All seemed quiet and well, Sam was sitting on the same countertop, handing out samples of his tea to passing customers and looking like he hadn't moved at all. She shrugged her shoulders and turned to leave the doorway, but just as she was turning her head Sam looked over and caught her eye. Paige didn't look away this time and instead raised her eyebrows questioningly. Sam gave her a slight smile and winked at her. Then he turned back to pouring more tea into cups.

Should I say something? What a strange kid, she thought. *He looks fine, though.* She lifted her leg to step into the shop but nearly lost her balance. She felt light-headed and put a hand on her stomach, leaned against the doorframe and collected her breath. *Whoa! Okay, bathroom first.*

She left the store and walked across the road to the nearest bathroom. Inside, she spent a few moments running water over her face and hands as she leaned into the sink. The cool liquid felt good against her skin and she felt her baby kick a few more times excitedly. *Must be the heat.* She turned off the faucet and stood up, but nearly fell over from the rush of blood to her head. Her vision darkened almost to the point of blacking out and she used her hands to steady herself against the sink. *I think it's time to go home.* Slightly worried, she waited inside for another moment and then walked outside. She stopped dead in her tracks.

There was no one outside. The road was bare, even of all the little bits of paper and trash that had accumulated throughout the morning. An eerie silence hung everywhere. The shops looked desolate and dusty and a slight wind blew dead leaves in small swirls along the ground. It was no longer sunny out. A heavy, grey mist hung above her and clouded the sky and the tree canopy, making the tree line and surrounding area look a patchwork quilt of ugly greys and off-whites, interlaced with glimpses of green. The air smelled musty and stale.

"Hello?" she called out. She listened but there was no reply.

She hesitantly walked forward and out onto the road. Down the length in each direction was more desolation. A crow called out in the distance and she pulled her arms into her sides and shivered. The air was cool and damp now. *Did I lose track of time in the bathroom? I swear it was only five minutes. Where is Henry?*

"Henry? *Henry!*" she called, but only silence greeted her.

A gust of wind cut through her light jacket and she rubbed her hands together again. *Maybe he's waiting for me at the workshop? He wouldn't leave.* There was another gust of wind and this time she heard a faint voice carried along with it. She stopped and listened. Sure enough, she heard it again. It sounded like someone laughing. She turned around and looked in the other direction, but saw no one. All she saw was dirt and the sign for The Apothecary's Hiccup. It swayed back and forth on the iron post it was attached too. *There it is again!* She listened. A delighted giggle escaped from somewhere nearby.

Paige walked back to the spice shop and the laughter grew louder. She carefully moved up to the front steps. The laughter was coming from inside. As she walked up the wooden staircase each board groaned quietly and when she reached the door, she peered inside. The apothecary's floor was covered in dust and broken bottles. Along the wall, jars and glassware were speckled with dry bits of cobwebs and there was a decidedly earthy smell to the air. Everything looked as if it had been frozen in time. She reluctantly stepped inside and walked around.

"Hello?"

"Hi," replied a young voice. She jumped backwards with a shriek. Sam was sitting on the same counter from earlier that morning. *How did I not notice him there? It's like he appeared out of nowhere.* Sam looked emaciated and sullen, his eyes sunken into his face. He hopped down from the table and, she noted, he made no noise when landing on the ground. Paige bit her lip as Sam walked up to her, feeling an urgency to stay away from him.

"Wh-where is everyone?" she said, backing up to a wall.

"They left," said Sam. He stopped in front of her and smiled.

"Where is your mother?"

Sam appeared to consider the question before replying. "My mother is long since dead," he said. Paige could see Sam's eyes were no longer grey but a sickly shade of mossy green. She flinched as he reached towards her belly. Paige knocked his hand away and noticed it was still ice cold.

"Please don't touch me." She moved away and eyed the door quickly, keeping her gaze on Sam as she inched her way closer to the door frame. "I need to go and find my husband."

Sam let out a high-pitched laugh, "I told you, everyone left. They won't join us until they are called."

"What do you mean?"

"Follow me if you want to see Henry," he said, and walked out of the shop.

Paige stood in the empty shop in disbelief. *What the hell is going on? Am I going crazy?* Torn on what to do, she breathed out to calm her nerves. *He's just a boy. Creepy… but a child nonetheless.* She walked out the door and down the steps and followed Sam down the dirt road.

Paige decided not to talk and, instead, kept an eye on the buildings as they walked and looked for anyone else. The closer they got to the glassblower's stand the faster Sam walked. He seemed eager to get there; twice he skipped in apparent amusement while kicking a small stone down the road. Watching him, Paige felt more and more like she was going to be disappointed when arriving. *Henry won't be there. I just know it.* She felt her son restlessly shift about.

"I don't understand," said Paige, daring to break the uncomfortable silence. "How did everyone leave so quickly?" She felt foolish for being so nervous around Sam, a child.

"They aren't far away. They are out there somewhere. Lost and wandering until they are called," he said as he waved a hand about in the air and motioned towards the mist that surrounded them.

"What do you mean?" asked Paige. *He sure doesn't sound like a child,* she thought.

But Sam didn't reply. Frustrated, Paige dropped her line of questioning and continued to watch the area around her. Finally, the mist revealed the benches. Her heart dropped to see they were all empty.

"*Henry!*" she called out. Sam sat down on a bench, folded his hands into his lap and watched her, his legs swinging in the air. Paige left him and walked quickly around the outside of the workshop and looked for Henry. When she completed her circle she found Sam in the same position, but now there was a smell of smoke and incense in the air. Near the front of the workshop she saw a fire illuminating the surrounding fog.

"Sam, did you start that fire?" He shook his head and pointed. Paige's eyes followed to see a vague outline of a man chopping wood in the distance. She ran towards him until he came into view. He had long black hair and wore a white tunic and had his back towards her.

"*Hey!*" Paige said after a swing of his axe. "Excuse me. Do you know where everyone went? I can't find my husband." The man didn't respond and continued chopping. After another swing, she ran forward and tapped him on the back. *He looks familiar.*

"Sir? Aren't you the one who was demonstrating how to blow glass?"

The man straightened and dropped his axe. He turned around and faced Paige, who gasped when she saw his face. The man was smiling. His teeth were yellow and rotten; layers of an oily black substance gummed and oozed between them, as if being squeezed out of his mouth when he pulled his lips back. The rest of his face was smooth and unblemished except for his empty eye sockets. Paige could see that his eyelids were torn away; leaving both holes in his head exposed and dirty.

Paige wheeled back and she felt her baby kick again, mirroring the panic she felt. The eyeless man stepped forward and silently grabbed her arm. Paige screamed and tried to pull away, but the man's grip was strong and all he did was smile wider. Black liquid oozed down his chin and fell on the ground.

***

Paige sat tied to a bench in front of the workshop, her throat raw from screaming. The smiling man had been surprisingly strong as he picked her up with ease and plopped her onto the bench. Sam had been underneath, and he had shut iron shackles around her ankles while the smiling man next bound her wrists. Then he began to feed more wood to the fire. She yelled for help.

"My ears grow tired of your incessant mewing," said Sam. He sat down next to her, kicking his legs back and forth in the air. "No one can hear you."

Tears poured down Paige's face as she struggled against her bonds. "What the hell is going on? Who are you?"

"It's a complicated answer. '*What* are you' is probably a better question."

"What are you then?"

"I am a Shilombish."

Paige gave him a confused look.

Sam sighed. "You know, there used to be a time when that word struck a primal fear into the hearts of men." He dropped off the bench. "In the more modern sense, you can think of me as a soul eater. My servant," he indicated, "is preparing a chamber for my new souls. We must collect them every few centuries if I am to survive." Paige watched the smiling man add more logs to the fire. It burned bright and hot.

"I don't understand," said Paige. Sam clicked his tongue against his teeth and walked back up to her.

"I may not look it," he said, "but I am an ancient creature. And before, I was human." He paused. "But that was a *very* long time ago. Now, I am different. I must dine on the willing souls of humans. I must reap another harvest for it has been too long and I grow hungry." Paige watched him lick his lips as he turned and stared at the fire.

"How… how do you collect the souls?"

Sam gave a snort. "Humans should pay more attention. Even a creature of another time, such as I, is still bound to give fair warning. So it has been since the beginning. A lasting custom, if you will. I told you and the others of the ingredients of my tea. But no one questioned which kind of each spice I used." He looked over at Paige. "Take the star anise for example," he held out his hands and, resting on his palm, Paige could see a single, brown and star-shaped pod of seeds from the star anise plant. “There are several varieties, many of which are indistinguishable from one another to the naked eye. Whereas one would be perfect for a mead or tea,” he smiled as a second star-shaped pot shimmered into view on his hand and identical to the first, “other natural versions can have side effects. In this case, the star anise causes the soul to disconnect with the host for a short time. I exploit those side effects to feed.”

“My God,” said Paige, looking away from him “Someone will figure it out. They'll stop you!”

“I doubt it,” said Sam. “Sure, there are signs when one loses one's soul. I daresay when everyone who drank my tea wakes they will feel dizzy and disoriented. Some will have even caught glimpses of what’s about to happen here. But, when things are investigated, all that will be was an honest mistake with the tea. It won’t be until years later when the effects are really felt.” He gave Paige his most innocent looking face and sad smile. “All anyone will see is a woman who mistakenly used the wrong ingredient. Anyone can confuse the star anise. It was just a little ’hiccup’ in the process.” He winked at Paige. “I’ll be fine.””Why are you telling me this?” Paige asked. She looked away from Sam in fear of the answer. *I’m going to die. He is going to eat my soul.*

“Because you need to know.”

She hadn’t expected that. “What?”

But Sam just smiled at her and turned to watch the fire. Paige could feel the heat on her face and she felt her baby kick again as her belly warmed. Thick, grey smoke billowed up into the air and mixed with the chalky-white mist that pervaded the entire grounds.

“Quickly now,” shouted Sam to the smiling man, “they are coming.”

The smiling man nodded silently. He tossed one last log onto the burning pile and then grabbed a long metal staff from inside the workshop. He walked up to the flames and pushed the tip of the staff into the fire's heart. Paige could see the flames changing from orange to red to yellow and back again, swirling around with accents of the mossy green that reminded her of Sam's eyes.

Sam, meanwhile, could hardly contain himself and bobbed up and down in excitement. The smiling man withdrew the iron staff and held it up high. On top was a molten glass sphere with a swirling black substance held within. It reminded Paige of the blackness she saw in the man's mouth.

The smiling man twirled the staff above his head and then plunged the end with the glass sphere into the ground beside the fire. At first, all Paige could hear was the glass sphere breaking apart. Sam jumped down from the bench and clapped his hands together. Immediately, there was a rumbling and the earth beneath the rod and fire opened up. Soil, ash, dust and wood all disappeared into a dark crevice that grew outwards until it was larger than a car. The fire was no more, having fallen into the hole. The smiling man now stood to the edge of it and stared down into the black depths.

Paige felt a sudden flare of pain on her shoulder. She looked up to see Sam standing next to her holding a small knife, the tip of which had just drawn some of her blood. He pulled the tip out of her shoulder and walked up the smiling man, who lowered the staff down towards Sam. Sam used his finger to wipe Paige's blood from his knife to the rod.

"What the hell is going on?" she said, shaking on the bench. Sam turned to her with a finger pressed to his lips.

"Just watch," he said.

The smiling man raised the staff with her blood up into the air and a flash of light erupted from the end, as if a beacon had been lit on the very top of a lighthouse. The bright light pushed the thick fog and mist away from the area. Paige began to see the outline of figures just beyond the cleared edges. As more mist burned off she could see hundreds of people milling about. But they weren't completely solid, more like gaseous vapours in the shape of humans. They were souls.

The souls turned to the bright lights and, to her horror, Paige could see that all of them were also missing their eyes. They slowly drifted towards the pit and, one by one, they willingly walked forward until they fell into it. As each disappeared, Sam laughed in delight. He no longer looked sullen and emaciated but full of vigour and strength as Paige watched him transform. She recognized the souls of the many people from the faire that morning. Dozens of children also stepped into the pit. *There are so many* she thought, disheartened. *So many of them drank that tea.*

"No!" shouted Paige. "Don't go down there!" But the souls didn't appear to hear her. Sam turned towards her. There was an animal look in his eyes.

"They can't hear you. The blood of someone in need is the perfect bait for a wandering soul, you know, it drives them. In a way you are helping me." Paige hopelessly struggled against the rope and shackles. Sam laughed. "Do you remember that second cup I gave you?" Paige shivered and nodded.

Sam continued. "That extract was a different form of the tea I gave to you and everyone else you see here. That tea was brewed especially for someone like you. For someone carrying a healthy baby."

Paige opened her mouth to reply but found she couldn't speak. She was too scared and confused. So she sat in misery as more and more souls disappeared into the ground and into Sam's possession. Eventually the stream trickled to a minimum and then there were none left.

"The gate will close soon," said Sam, "but we have time for one more." He turned and looked expectantly at Paige. She felt her body go cold and her baby kicked out yet again. She looked to her side for anything that might help and that's when she noticed that Henry was sitting right beside her. Startled, she tried to reach out for him. Her hands touched his leg but they went straight through. He was just as ephemeral as the others.

"Henry," she warned as he stood up and walked over towards the pit. At the precipice he turned and faced her and like the others, his eyes were gone. She cried out in silence, no sound escaping her throat as he turned his back to her and jumped. As soon as his head disappeared the crevice began to shrink and close. All that remained was a bare patch of earth.

Paige looked up to see Sam talking with the smiling man. Then he turned and walked up to her. "Delicious! A great haul this time." He put a hand on Paige's belly and she tried to squirm away from him. Her baby kicked.

"Don't you *touch me*," spat Paige. "Leave me alone. Leave my baby alone."

But Sam shook his head. "My tea lives in your son now too. The ceremony is complete and any baby who witnesses this magic is transformed like I was. He will grow to be like me one day." Paige just shook her head and sobbed as Sam continued talking. "In time, you will see even if you don't believe me now. He will eventually desire something more. He'll crave something you can't provide. When that happens, you'll know why and you will tell him about me. About all of this," he waved his arms around. "He is a Shilombish now. I will teach him the ways of our kind. He will be my apprentice."

"I'll never do it. I would never… he won't be like you," Paige struggled against the rope.

"I am not wrong in this," said Sam, and he placed his hands on her knees. "And you are his mother, his protector and guardian. You will do anything for your child including delivering him to me when it is time." Paige looked down at the ground and sobbed quietly. *What kind of nightmare did I stumble into?*

Sam let go of her knees and put his hand on her arm. "Now sleep," he said.

Against her will Paige felt her eyelids falling and she drifted off into nothingness.

***

"Paige!"

Paige opened her eyes to see Henry kneeling above her. He had a worried expression on his face but it seemed to lighten when he saw she was awake. Nearby were dozens of people on cots and blankets being helped by medical personnel. The sun was out and burning bright and there wasn't a cloud in the sky.

"H… Henry? What happened?" She tried sitting up and then nearly fell back to the ground.

"Easy, Paige. You had a little scare."

"What happened?"

"You fell down and got sick."

"What? No! I saw Sam. He was just here." But Henry gave her a bewildered look.

"Relax, Paige, it's okay. Just take it slowly okay? Who's Sam?"

Paige was confused. "The boy from the tea shop, remember?" Henry shook his head. "How long was I out?"

"Two hours or so." Henry put his hands behind her back and lifted her up. "Everyone's been getting sick. I was really dizzy at one point too and almost passed out. Dozens of people have gotten ill and the paramedics were called. You were the first to be sick, I think." He pointed at everyone being attended to. The crowds had dispersed as well and the faire looked empty. Paige shook her head, the memories of Sam and the smiling man still fresh in her mind.

"I don't remember a boy from the tea shop though," said Henry.

"What? You don't remember? It's the boy who gave us the free samples at the apothecary's. His name is Sam," said Paige.

Henry looked at her with concern. "You must have dreamed him, Paige. We picked up our samples from a countertop remember?" He shook his head. "Others reported visions as well. I think it must be a common reaction. Everyone who drank the tea has gotten ill. They've arrested the woman who owns the shop. I think the police think she was poisoning everyone or something. If that's true, she's a complete psychopath."

"What? No. It's the boy, Sam," she said. "He mixed the tea to make it look like a mistake." She leaned back onto the ground. *What is going on?*

"There's no Sam, honey," said Henry. "I'm sure it was a mistake though. Who would poison all of these people intentionally?" He picked her hands up in his. "Come on, I told the doctors I'd take you to the hospital to check on the baby." He pulled her up and together they walked back towards their car.

Just as they passed through the entrance, Paige spied Sam sitting along a fence and staring at her. Others walked by but took no notice of him. She looked at him and he winked at her and smiled. Her body grew cold and she felt her baby stirring inside of her.

Sam's words echoed in her mind. *'My apprentice' he had said,* she thought. She bit her lip as they moved through the mess of ambulances and cars in the parking lot. *What if it wasn't all a dream?* She put a hand on her belly as she considered Sam's words again. *He said I would do anything for my child… that I would protect him no matter what he is… that he would eventually become some kind of foul creature.* Paige didn't know what to believe. She hoped it was all a nightmare, but her mother's instinct told her Sam was right. Her baby had changed. She could feel it, even now as he grew inside of her. And monster or not, she loved her son and she knew deep down she would do anything for him.

Raw

By Erica Chin

Sarah fell ill before her first day at school.

Tim reluctantly made a call to the principal's office from the hospital. He was never good at explaining, never as good as Veronica had been.

"Good morning, Mr. Holliday," the headmistress answered the phone in her usual, pleasant tone of voice. "Is everything okay with Sarah? We were expecting her today."

Tim swallowed and warily tried to explain what happened that day. "Well...erm…Sa…" His voice quivered as he struggled to complete his sentence. "Sa…" Heat rose into his cheeks.

"Yes, Sarah," the headmistress completed the word for him, making him feel even more embarrassed. "How is Sarah?"

Tim bit his lip, forcing himself to focus better. It wasn't the time to stutter. Not now. He could do this without Veronica. Sarah needed him now. He took a deep breath.

"Sa…Sarah is…is sick," said Tim. He breathed a sigh of relief and took out a handkerchief from his pocket to wipe away the beads of sweat on his forehead.

"Ah, I see, so sorry to hear this bad news, Mr. Holliday," the principal said, sympathetically. "I will let her teacher know that she isn't able to come to school today. I hope she gets well soon! Please, take care, Mr. Holliday."

"Th…thank you," said Tim. The headmistress hung up. He snapped shut his cell phone and drew a deep breath. A small hand clutched his arm. "Papa?"

Tim turned to look at his six-year-old daughter. Sarah's face was as pale as a ghost. The colour had drained from her normally rosy cheeks. Her usually radiant green eyes were now swollen and watery. Tim's chest stung terribly.

He took her hand, which was as cold as a corpse. Liveliness was fading away from his only daughter, the apple of his eye, which tingled with the prick of tears. He squeezed her hand silently. If only Veronica were here with them. Veronica was always better at handling this than he was.

Look at what you've done with your daughter! He scolded himself inwardly. Sarah looked up at him and gave him a weak but reassuring smile. She seemed to have sensed his agony.

"Papa, it will be okay," said Sarah quietly, as she sat closer to her father. "We will be okay, right?"

Tim nodded frantically, not saying a word. Sarah glanced up at him once again and snuggled up to him with a smile on her face. Tim gently patted her back as they waited for their turn at the hospital.

As the clock ticked away, Tim grew more and more uneasy. Maybe he should give Veronica a call. She was Sarah's mother, after all. She had the right to know. He glanced at his phone.

Sarah coughed violently, nearly falling off the bench, and curled up beside her father. Tim pulled her closer to him as Sarah's eyebrows knitted in agony. Tim's uneasiness turned into anger as he gazed at her painful look.

Veronica hadn't cared about Sarah's feelings when she left. Why would Veronica care about Sarah now? That heartless woman had lost the right to their daughter the moment she abandoned her family for another 'more-capable' man.

His blood boiled when he thought about Veronica's new-found love. The bald, sneaky old man could have claimed to be Veronica's father and nobody would doubt it. Such men deserved no respect from him, nor anyone.

Sarah shifted uncomfortably. Tim glanced at the clock again. It had been an hour since their arrival. He should check with the nurses. He clenched his fists and was about to stand up when a nurse called them, "Holliday. Sarah Holliday."

Sarah opened her eyes. She seemed appallingly ill. Tim quickly held her up and followed the nurse to the doctor's walk-in office. Sarah broke into another fit of coughing.

"Good morning," said the doctor. He was a young man in his early thirties with wavy gold hair. "Please, have a seat."

Tim carefully placed Sarah down and sat nervously beside her. He was about to explain Sarah's condition when Sarah suddenly fell onto the floor and continued to cough more violently.

"Sarah!" Tim and the doctor helped the poor girl up. Tim froze when he saw a large spot of blood on the floor. He looked at the doctor helplessly.

"Blo…blo…blood!" He had wanted to scream out of utter anxiety, yet his voice came out wobbly.

The young doctor tried to calm Tim down. "It could be minor nose bleeding, nothing to be worried about, Mr. Holliday." Tim clenched his jaw tightly.

Sarah had stopped coughing. The doctor examined her body temperature, listened to her heartbeat, checked her pulse and blood pressure, did some other tests Tim did not comprehend, and finally wrote a prescription for Sarah.

"Doctor," Sarah said weakly as the doctor scribbled on the prescription note, "Will I be okay?" Tim squeezed Sarah's hand tightly.

The doctor looked up at Sarah and gave her a smile. "Of course you will. You have a fever, but you will be well soon after taking some medicine and getting enough rest."

He handed the prescription to Tim and said, "Don't worry, Mr. Holliday, it was only minor nose bleeding resulting from excessively high body temperature. Make sure she takes the meds, sleeps well, drinks enough water, and she'll be fine."

Tim took the prescription gratefully. The doctor seemed to have taken a liking to Sarah immediately. He gave her a red ink pen with a pink-coloured cap, which Sarah seemed to like.

"Thank you, doctor." Sarah waved goodbye as she and Tim left the doctor's office. Tim hurried to collect the medicine for Sarah and drove home.

Sarah fell asleep in the car as her father drove in the rainy afternoon. The city trapped them in congested street after congested street. Tim was frustrated, but each time the car had to stop, he glanced at the peaceful look on his daughter's stricken face and he was calm again.

She would be okay, *they* would be okay. He brightened up as the car in front finally moved forward.

Little did he know, then, that they were very far from okay.

***

"Good night, Papa." Sarah took her medicines and continued to sleep in her bedroom. The rain had not ceased when Tim tucked her in. Thunder rang as lightning flashed in the night sky. He shut the windows and pulled down the black-out blind.

Tim fired up his laptop on the dining table and continued working on his latest novel. The pitter-pattering of the rain drowned out all other noises. He took a sip from his mug of coffee and was soon in the zone to write.

It was almost midnight when he completed another chapter and shut down his laptop. He was supposed to finish the whole story by that day, but with Sarah falling sick, taking her to the hospital in the city centre and coming back, he'd run out of time.

After Veronica walked out on them, Tim and Sarah had moved further away from the city centre. They rented an apartment in the suburbs; they could no longer afford the rental to live close to the city.

Veronica never liked straying far from the city, she always loved the bustling lifestyle. The sights, the sounds, the senses. She enjoyed and thrived in the fast-paced régime. She was the life of the party and party was her life.

It was her vivacity and her vibrant take on life that had fascinated Tim. It was also the same exuberance that had pushed them further and further apart. Tim sighed. Luckily, Sarah wasn't anything like her mother.

Sarah was quiet and content. She seemed to enjoy the serenity in the suburbs. Tim was glad about the solitude as well, it appeared to generate more creative inspiration.

One drawback was that the air was always stuffy in the small apartment. Another drawback was that Tim didn't know how to cook, and was horrible at housekeeping, but he tried to keep organised whenever he remembered.

Tim was about to climb into his bed when he noticed his cell phone had recorded three missed calls and a text message from Veronica. He read the message. "How is Sarah? Please tell her that Mummy misses her every day." He deleted the message.

The next morning, Tim was woken up by a furious clap of thunder outside the window. He rubbed his eyes and looked at the sky through the rain-smeared glass. Dark clouds hung over the town.

Tim opened the door to his daughter's bedroom. Sarah was still asleep. He walked towards her. Her eyebrows were still knitted, her lips pressed tightly together.

Gently putting a hand on her forehead, Tim was shocked to find Sarah still had a temperature. The fever should have subsided by now. He had followed the doctor's instructions. He was, once again, thrown into helplessness.

"Papa," Sarah's eyes snapped open. Tim grabbed her tiny hand that was even colder than the day before. Sarah said in a croaky voice, "I'm hungry."

Tim's eyes opened wide. *Of course!* He had forgotten all about eating. The poor girl must be famished.

"W…wait a minute." Tim ran to the kitchen and rummaged through the refrigerator to find something edible that had not expired. He found a packet of sliced cheese and a loaf of white bread, and returned to his daughter.

But Sarah didn't appear as excited as Tim had thought about the cheese and bread. "Eat?" Tim put a slice of cheese between two slices of bread and handed it to Sarah. Sarah shook her head and wouldn't open her mouth.

Tim returned to the kitchen again and tried to find other food that Sarah might like. He heated up a few slices of canned ham. *Smells inviting enough*, he thought.

But Sarah continued to shake her head when presented with cooked ham, sausages, eggs, tomatoes, sweets, or chocolates. "But, Sarah, you… you have to… to eat!" Tim begged.

"Hungry..." Sarah said softly, "Papa, I'm hungry." Tim stared at his daughter, feeling even more frustrated, but she wouldn't eat anything he gave her.

Finally, Tim decided to drive out to buy more food. "W… what do you want?" Tim asked before heading out. Sarah closed her eyes and turned her back towards him. Tim didn't know what to do. He left and locked the apartment.

After driving aimlessly for ten minutes, he stopped at the nearest supermarket. He walked down the aisles, scanning for anything that Sarah might want to eat, and grabbed whatever seemed filling.

When he got back to his car, he had in his hands potatoes, bananas, crisps, fish fingers, chips, tinned spaghetti, lunchables, candies, and a tub of ice-cream. He didn't know how to cook, but he figured it wouldn't be hard.

Tim unlocked the door to his apartment and entered, feeling determined. He was confident he could cook something and Sarah would eat, finally.

He kicked the door shut behind him. "Sarah!" He already felt better that he had bought more food back, his tone became lighthearted. "I'm going to cook you something."

He froze as he caught movement in the kitchen from the corner of his eye. Someone was crouching in front of the open refrigerator. Sounds of chewing and chomping came to his ears, which made his hair stand on end.

Tim turned around. It was Sarah, her back now facing him. Cans and sweets were scattered on the floor around her. Her long black hair fell onto her shoulders and her back.

"Sarah?" Tim inched closer. He could hear his own heartbeat pumping louder and faster as he neared his daughter. Another thunderclap shook the Earth.

Sarah seemed to hear neither the thunder nor Tim calling her name. Her head continued to move as if grinding on something. Tim stopped beside her and his blood turned cold.

His young daughter looked up to him with that pair of mesmerising green eyes, her pale face smeared with fresh blood, a piece of raw meat dangling from the corner of her mouth. She continued to gobble on the raw chicken thigh she had obviously found in the refrigerator.

Tim was stunned. "No!" He snatched the raw chicken thigh from Sarah fiercely. The meat had already expired.

"Papa," Sarah pleaded. "I'm hungry." She blinked her eyes innocently at Tim.

"It's raw!" Tim yelled at her, feeling like he had plunged into ice-cold water.

Tim took a deep breath and tried to calm himself down. He gathered himself again and pointed to the stuff he had just bought from the supermarket. "Papa will… will cook."

Sarah stared at him expressionlessly. Tim closed the refrigerator and hurriedly prepared the stove. Sarah stayed squatting in front of the refrigerator, pink fluid from the meat glistened on her lips and chin.

Tim's cell phone rang when he was starting on the potatoes. He rubbed his hands on his apron and ran to the phone. It was the headmistress calling.

"Good morning, Mr. Holliday," said the headmistress, sounding concerned, "We haven't seen Sarah today. Is she still sick?"

Tim hastily answered. "Yes." The headmistress seemed taken aback. "Ah, okay. Please do not hesitate to let me know if you need any help," she said.

When the conversation ended, Sarah was no longer in the kitchen. Tim searched frantically for her in the small apartment, but she was gone. He fell into distress.

"Sarah!" He shouted again and again in the apartment, but no one was there to answer him. He rushed out of the front door and found the door of his neighbour's apartment ajar.

Without a second of hesitation, he pushed open the door. "Sarah?" His voice became stuck in his throat. He felt dizzy. His ears buzzed.

His missing daughter was right there, inside their neighbour's apartment, kneeling in front of an old lady's body, chewing and grinding on the lady's face, which was so damaged it was already unrecognizable. An acrid odour hung in the air. Blood oozed between Sarah's teeth.

It was all so surreal. Tim felt like he was in a nightmare. It was not real. It was not true. This wasn't happening. This wasn't Sarah.

Tim couldn't move or speak a word. He continued to stare at his daughter, chomping on the old lady's face. He didn't know how long it had been. Sarah bit off the lady's nose, chewed, and looked up at her father.

Sarah swallowed and said to him, "Papa, I'm hungry. So hungry." Terror had overtaken Tim. His knees turned to jelly. *Please, someone wake me up from this nightmare!* He knelt on the floor, his lips quivered. "Sarah..."

Another explosion in the sky brought Tim back to the reality of the situation. He finally took in the grisly scene he and Sarah were immersed in. He pulled a reluctant Sarah away from the unfortunate old lady, closed the door, and returned to his own apartment. He locked the door swiftly.

“No!!!” Sarah leapt onto him suddenly. Tim pushed her away, his whole body shaking with fear. Sarah pressed herself against the door and started banging he head back against it, hysterically.

“I'm hungry! Papa. I'm hungry! I want to eat!” She yelled and screamed in distress. Tim had to force his hand over her mouth to stop her from shouting. The last thing they needed now was attention.

An old lady had just died next-door and her face was dreadfully mutilated. How could he explain this? How could he tell anyone that it was his obedient daughter that had committed this atrocious crime? He did not want to think about how the old lady had died in the first place.

“How could you?” Tim struck out at Sarah, for the first time ever. Sarah cast her eyes down to the floor. She did not make an attempt to deny or argue.

Tim dragged Sarah into her bedroom and locked her in there. He sat down in front of the dining table, his face buried in his trembling hands, as the sound of Sarah banging on the door persisted.

“Papa! I'm hungry! Let me out! I want to eat! I want meat! I need to eat meat!” Sarah's voice continued to haunt him. He sat stiffly and did not move.

The banging on the door grew weaker and weaker, and finally stopped. Tim stood up and found himself still shivering, despite the fact his shirt was soaked from his sweat.

His cell phone rang again. Tim almost jumped. Breathlessly, he answered the phone without checking who was calling. Veronica's voice came through. "I want to speak to Sarah."

Tim looked at the locked door of Sarah's bedroom. Veronica pressed further, "Where is she? Tell her Mummy is calling. I miss her so much!"

Tim took a deep breath and said firmly, "Not here." He hung up on Veronica. He let his cell phone fall to the floor. How could he let Veronica talk to Sarah now? Now that Sarah had changed—changed into something he couldn't recognise.

Rain and wind continued to drum on the window. Tim composed himself, and walked towards Sarah's bedroom. He knocked. "Sarah?"

No one responded. Drawing a deep breath, he unlocked the door. Sarah was no longer in front of the door. She was lying on her bed, staring at the ceiling. The blood on her face had dried. Her chest was rising and falling steadily.

He sat down on the floor beside her bed. She turned and looked at him. Slowly, she spoke again. "Papa, I'm hungry." Her soft voice echoed in the stifling room.

Tears rolled down Tim's face. "I'm so sorry, Sarah," he said as he shook his head, his heart gripped by pain.

Sarah gazed into his eyes and repeated, "Papa, I'm hungry."

"No..." Tim continued to shake his head as he started to sob helplessly.

"Papa," Sarah pleaded tirelessly, "I'm hungry. I'm so hungry, Papa. Hungry..."

He had no choice. With a shaking hand, Tim caressed his daughter's face whispering, "Papa knows."

Sarah looked at him, her green eyes filled with a mixture of fear, disbelief and tenderness. She sank her teeth into his hand. The burning pain was intense, rising to a peak as she tore away a chunk of his flesh, but it was all nothing compared to his broken heart.

Twins

By Andrew Lennon

"Quick! Call an ambulance!"

The two girls just stood staring at the woman on the floor, who cradled her son's bloodied head.

"What are you just standing there for? *Get some help!*" The girls didn't move. Their eyes were blank, empty.

"*Help!*" the mother screamed.

A man, hearing the screams, ran across to the park from the other side of the field. "What's happened?" he asked. The girls glanced at him and then returned their gaze to the boy on the floor.

"I, I don't know," the mother cried. "I turned away for a second and then, when I looked back, he was on the floor. I think he might have fallen."

"From up there?" The man pointed, his face awash with terror as he looked up at the treehouse. He took his phone from his pocket and dialled 999.

The treehouse wasn't an actual treehouse. It was more of a climbing frame in the shape of a tree. The outside was plastic. From one branch hung three metal swings, from another a climbing rope. The centre of the tree was made to look like a giant face. Perhaps, to children, it looked like an inviting, friendly tree. To adults, who no longer had the innocence of a child's mind, the tree looked terrifying. It was the face of nightmares.

The mouth formed an entrance hole in which children could enter and play with the different toys and activities fitted to the walls inside. They could look out of the trees eyes and wave to their parents down below. The mouth entrance was around fifteen feet high, very high for a children's playhouse, especially when there was no way up or down other than a rope ladder.

The mother stared up at the haunting face of the tree. Her boy had been spat out of that godawful mouth. She turned to the girls. "Did you see what happened? Do you know how he fell?"

Neither of the girls spoke a word. They both slowly just shook their heads from side to side, signalling a "No".

"You must have seen something! *What happened?*"

No response.

By the time the ambulance arrived, a small crowd had already formed around the injured boy. Everyone pushed and shoved, just to try and see what was going on. One paramedic took the mother aside to talk to her as the others loaded her son onto a stretcher, and into the back of the ambulance.

"Ok, so did you see what happened?" he asked.

"No, I think he fell, but I didn't see. I think those girls may have seen something."

"Which girls?"

"Those two, the twins." The mother turned to point.

The girls were gone.

***

"Nicole, Georgia!"

The two girls ran into the living room, where Tom, their father sat on the couch. They were both dressed the same. Both wore pink and white summer dresses, white frilly socks, black patent leather shoes, and a red bow in their matching blonde hair. Their mother always dressed them the same, it's what some parents do when they have twins. It's supposed to be cute. They both stood facing their father.

Two identical peas from the same pod.

"Yes, Father," they said in unison.

"Ah, there are my girls. So, how was your day? What have you been up to?"

The girls smiled and looked at each other mischievously.

"What's so funny?" he asked.

"Oh nothing, it's just that we had fun today. We went to the park."

"Really, and what did you do at the park?"

One of the twins ran to her father and jumped on his knee. He glanced at her for a second. It was Nicole. He could always tell them apart, but it did sometimes take a second glance. Other people struggled to tell the difference. Being identical twins, the girls had a lot of fun with this. They would swap names and places all the time. This trickery was made much easier with their parent's wardrobe choice.

"So, Nicole. What did you do at the park?"

"Well, there was this boy," Nicole said.

"A boy?" Tom looked surprised. He wasn't expecting this for another few years, the girls only being eight at the moment.

"No, daddy. Not like *that*," Georgia said as she jumped onto his other knee.

"Well, did you play with this boy?" he asked.

"We played *Visiting the Darkness*," Nicole answered.

"Shhh," Georgia rasped.

Tom coughed. "What is it, Visiting the Darkness?"

"It's just a silly game," Georgia answered. "Come on, Nicole. Let's go and play in our room." The two girls left the room side by side. Tom watched them go, his mind filled with horrible thoughts.

Visiting the Darkness, that's one of the creepiest games I've ever heard of. Who the hell is this boy, teaching them things like that?

He walked to the kitchen where his Sue, his wife was preparing dinner. "Oh – hey, honey," she said.

"Hey." He gave her a kiss on the cheek. "So the girls tell me you went to the park today. Who's this boy they were playing with?"

Sue glanced at him with a worrying look and carried on preparing dinner. She spoke into her chest. "They weren't playing with him. They were just there. The boy he just fell. The girls had nothing to do with it."

"Whoa, hang on a minute here, calm down. What do you mean the boy *fell*?"

"The girls were playing at the park and while they were there a boy fell from that big ugly tree thing. That's all. They didn't have anything to do with it."

"Is the boy okay?"

"Yes, well, I think so. The girls looked like they were in shock so I brought them home. I didn't want them seeing any horrible stuff like that."

"You didn't even check to see if the boy was okay? Do you know how he fell?"

"Are you suggesting the girls did it?" She glared at him.

"No," he raised his hands in defence. "Of course not. I'm just concerned for the boy is all."

"Well, when we left there were people taking care of him. He's fine, I'm sure."

Tom left the kitchen shaking his head. *Either the females in this house are going crazy, or I am.*

***

Nicole and Georgia were playing in their bedroom with their friend, Olivia. The three girls were class-mates at the same school. The twins didn't have many friends; they enjoyed each other's company more than the company of strangers, or outsiders. Today, however, Olivia's mother had been called into work, and she couldn't organise a baby sitter, so she had arranged with the twins' mother for Olivia to play at their house for the day.

"My mum goes to work and earns us lots of money," Olivia boasted. "Your mum just stays at home with *you* two."

"Our mother does a very good job at maintaining our house," Nicole said.

"And she takes very good care of us," Georgia followed.

"You two are creepy, you know that?"

Nicole rose to her feet. "How about we play a new game?"

"Yes," Georgia said. "Let's play Visiting the Darkness."

"What's that?" Olivia asked.

"Well," Nicole answered, "it's a new game. First you have to look into my eyes. Keep staring. Don't look away. No matter what you do, you have to keep staring into my eyes. You have to remain as silent as possible."

Olivia could hear Georgia hurrying around the room, throwing things from boxes and drawers.

"Where are they?" Georgia sighed.

"What's she looking for?" Olivia asked, glancing to the side.

"Never mind that," Nicole said. "Keep your focus on my eyes. This is all part of the game. You can't look anywhere else and you can't talk."

"Yay, here they are." Georgia called with excitement.

"Okay, now close your eyes and stick out your tongue." Nicole spoke with a calming aura.

"My tongue?" Olivia said. "What is this stupid game?"

"Just trust me."

"Yes, trust her." Georgia giggled. "It's a really fun game."

Olivia closed her eyes and stuck her tongue out.

"Now remember, you have to keep them closed tight."

A shot of white-hot pain shot through Olivia's mouth. She opened her eyes to find blood sluicing down her front. She looked down to see her tongue lying on the carpet in front of her. Georgia stood to her side with scissors in hand and an evil smile on her face. Olivia tried to scream but Nicole pulled a plastic bag over her head. Georgia yanked her to the floor and sat on her, legs straddled. Using her knees to pin down the girl's arms, Nicole crouched behind still holding the bag tight in place. She watched as the girl struggled, gasping for air. The bag began to fill with blood.

"This game works better if you can't see either," Georgia giggled.

She stabbed the scissors into each of Olivia's eyes, puncturing the bag. Olivia tried to scream, but the sound was muffled by the plastic and blood, which now filled her mouth. Nicole held the bag in place until Olivia stopped struggling. Both girls left her on the floor and continued to play with their toys.

When Sue entered the room, she almost fainted, her eyes wide as she gazed upon the gruesome sight in front of her. The child lay in the middle of the room surrounded by a pool of red, a blood smeared, plastic bag wrapped around her head. She looked to her daughters. Both of them playing nicely with their dolls. Both girls were awash with blood. It was on their hands, their knees, and in their hair. Their dresses were smeared in crimson.

Sue began to cry. "What have you done?"

"What do you mean, Mummy?" The girls asked in monotone unison.

"What...what are you?" She put her hand to her mouth to hold in a scream.

The two girls slowly walked towards their mother.

"We were just playing, Mummy." They spoke in sync. "Olivia lost that game and we don't want to play it anymore."

"You. You've killed her!"

The girls began to cry. They ran to their mum. Hugging one side each. "We didn't mean it, Mummy. We were just playing and..."

Sue felt a searing pain as Georgia stabbed the scissors into her lower back. Nicole started to giggle. "Yaay, now we get to play with you, Mummy."

Sue fell to the floor, her body doubled in agony. Nicole snatched the scissors from Georgia's hand. "You did it last time! It's my turn now," Nicole hissed. She thrust the scissors into her mother's back over and over again. She screamed out in pain, but no one, apart from the girls, was there to hear it. Nicole kept going with the stabbing motion, moving up the back as she went, over and over again, until – eventually – she stabbed her mum right in the base of the skull. The scissors stuck a little bit. Nicole didn't strain to pull them loose, she left them were they were. The mother lay motionless in a fresh pool of blood.

***

"Honey. Nicole, Georgia! I'm home!" Tom called.

The two girls ran to the living room where their father sat on the couch. They were both freshly washed and changed.

"Ahh, there's my girls," he said. "So, what have you two been up to today?"

Both the girls giggled and ran to sit on each of his knees. Their usual tradition. "Hello, Daddy. We're glad you're home."

He laughed. "I swear you two must practice that. How do you manage to speak at exactly the same time?"

"We're twins, Daddy. We do everything together."

"Yes, I suppose you do."

The girls giggled again.

"So what fun filled activities have you had today?"

"Well, we played with Olivia, then we played with Mummy." More giggles.

"What?" he laughed, puzzled.

"Well, now we want to play with you."

Out of the corner of his eye, he saw a glimpse of light reflecting from metal just before the scissors skewered his eyeball.

***

Olivia's mother pulled her car into the driveway. She had called ahead to ask Olivia to be ready, since she was in a rush to get home after a long day at work, but there had been no answer. She beeped the horn. Usually, she would go to the door, but she really didn't want to be held up in a really long conversation. She just wanted to get home.

After a couple of minutes of waiting and beeping the horn, she stomped to the front door and rang the bell. She waited. Again, no answer.

"Hello?"

Losing patience, she tried the door. It was open, so she stepped into the hallway. Stood facing her were Nicole and Georgia. "Didn't you hear me calling? Where is Olivia, and your mother?"

The twins giggled.

"What's so funny?"

"Oh, nothing. Olivia and Mummy are upstairs, resting."

"Well, it's time for Olivia to come home. I'm late. *Olivia!*"

"We've had a fun day playing with Olivia, and Mummy. Even Daddy played."

"Well that's very nice, but really I have to be going. *Olivia!*"

The girls walked slowly towards her. "Now it's your turn to play. Close your eyes."

The Ladder

By Pete Clark

I write this (what... confession? Yes, confession fits), sitting at a desk, foreign winds whispering serenely about me, clouds forming and unravelling in beautiful shapes above me. You are forgiven if you don't see the shakes in my hands, or notice the hurried scrawl of my writing. I write fast as I have no idea when he might come back to me. According to my watch, it has been three days and roughly six hours since I last saw him, and fourteen hours since I last heard his voice. *I'll be back, Dad,* he said. And I believe him.

There are unfamiliar and frightening noises in the far distance. The wind smells faintly of cut grass and faintly of rot. I do not know which I prefer, because cut grass reminds me too vividly of home, and sunny, perfect days on the lawn with my son, throwing Frisbees and kicking balls. I can close my eyes and imagine the silk of his translucent yellow hair. I don't close my eyes too often here, because when I do, the sounds and smells become too real, and that brings the very things I am trying to avoid all the closer.

My son has been gone for over three days. I heard him speak those final words after two and a half days searching, and as I called out to him, spinning to look in every possible direction, I was sure I caught a glimpse of his bright red t-shirt. Then it was gone and I'm now not so sure I saw anything. *I'll be back,* he said. And so I write, waiting for some sign. Waiting for the courage to follow those sounds into the far distance and find my boy.

***

He first showed me the ladder on the day after his eighth birthday. We have a large oak tree at the bottom of our garden, standing monolith-like on the edge of a large, unkempt lawn. All other plants and ornaments seem placed in such a way that they draw the eye to it, although this is wholly unintended. This particular day, my son was standing in front of the tree, looking smaller than ever. I can still see the way the dappled sunlight played on his face, soft ripples of light turning his hair white and then darkening, to a [illegible] blonde. I loved him more than ever at that moment, I think.

Around the tree was an old garden seat, its deep green paint so weather-faded that it almost seemed part of the tree. It curved about a third of the way around the tree, and as I watched, my son stepped up on it, reaching to touch the ladder that folded itself around the front of the tree. It followed a curve around its massive girth, ever upwards. It vanished from sight into the branches around the back.

I had never seen the ladder before.

I stared. My son turned to face me, a look of wild excitement on his face, and even across the distance I could see the sheen in his eyes and the wind in his hair. I think that the look he had is saved specifically for eight-year-old boys, when every event becomes adventure, every darkness a monster-filled cave, and every anomalous ladder simply another thing to climb because it is *there.* The look said, *Can I climb it, Dad? Can I?*

I approached the tree, ruffling my son's hair as I passed and I looked closely at the ladder. As I think back on it, it is a surprise even to me that I felt no shock at seeing it there. It was as if I had convinced myself it had *always* been there. I had just never seen it.

It seemed to begin at the back of the tree, out of sight, its rungs organic and woody, laced with delicate ivy, slick with old moss. I stepped slowly to the side and followed it around. It seemed to curve forever upward and as I stood at the back, it yet again disappeared out of sight, this time around the front of the tree.

And there was no sign of its beginnings.

I told myself I had just been at the front of the tree, and the ladder did *not* reappear there as it surely must, looking at it from this angle. I hurried around the tree, following the ladder as I went, and I found myself again at the front, seeing the original perspective. Then again, around to the back. It seemed that wherever I began following the ladder, its origins were out of sight, and it disappeared into the branches at either side. It was the most perplexing optical illusion, and I followed it two more times, coming up with the same conclusion each time.

What is it, Dad? my son asked. I grinned at him (and that grin I now feel was the start of it all, as if I had given his excitement fuel and permission. God, had I but known), and shrugged, feeling like an excited child myself. I had an idea, and I asked my son to run in the house. He did, dutifully, and I spent the time he was gone walking round and round the tree, following the ladder with my hand, losing it as it became too high, but marking the height of its disappearance. Time after time I marvelled at the way the ladder just seemed to begin again at that height without being visible on the opposite side.

My son returned. In his hand he clutched a red crayon, and I took it from him and began to retrace my steps, this time running the crayon along the edge of the ladder. When the ladder became too high to comfortably reach, I marked the height by running the crayon along the trunk itself, picking up the ladder again at the front, impossibly at the same height as it always had been. By the time I had walked around the trunk a further four times, there were five clear lines of red following the ladder's progress. *I must be stooping as I reach the front*, I thought as I made a sixth journey. But, no. I wasn't. I dropped the crayon. I had the sensation of running my hand around the sharp edge of a giant screw that was boring its way into the earth, so that, give or take depending on my speed around the tree, the height of my hand on the leading edge of ladder remained the same. But the tree was not boring its way into the earth. I was stumped.

You may think that the next logical step was to mount the thing. But we didn't. Not then anyway. I ushered my son away from the tree, distracting him with promises of ice cream and movies and for a day or two, we almost forgot about the ladder.

And then he climbed it.

***

He was up it and gone before I knew what was happening. He had a glazed look on his face as if something had called him, hypnotising him, and as I ran towards the tree, calling his name so loud that my throat was still hurting three days later, I saw him turn to me. The look I saw there chilled me. He looked at once as if he knew exactly what he was doing, and yet his face screamed at me to stop him. It forced my own legs into a paroxysm of power and I cleared the distance to the tree in seconds.

But I was too late.

As I reached the trunk and followed the spiral steps around it, I caught a glimpse of his shoe as it disappeared into the leaves. I circled the tree in the vain hope that I would see him up in the branches, a cruel trick. Of course, I saw no such thing.

The ladder ascended terminally onwards, ever spiralling. Of my son, there was no sign. It was as if he had vanished. I screamed his name up into the branches, scanning their depths for a sign of him. The leaves continued their soft waving, and the breeze sighed through them. For a moment I imagined his voice calling me. I thought my heart would break. I gathered myself for the ascent, and had even stepped onto the bench at the tree's base, when I heard a soft step. I saw one foot, then the other and I stood paralysed, waiting.

His hair looked ruffled and was flecked through here and there with seeds and grass. There was a flush to his cheeks, the exuberant glow of a child at play. I reached up to him, snatched him off the ladder and threw us both to the ground, sobbing and clutching him tightly. He was silent, and he shook, I presumed, with fear. As I separated us, and held him at arm's length for the admonition that had to come, I saw he was shaking with laughter. He seemed paralysed by it, tears coursing down his grubby face, his teeth shining through the redness of his moistened lips. His silence ended suddenly in a gasping inrush of air, with the familiar cackle of his laughter. Despite myself, despite the fear and chill that still caressed me, I smiled. The smile grew and I laughed with him, caught up by the infection rather than with any genuine humour. I felt his admonishment dissolving in that sound, and I hugged him close.

"What happened? Where did you go?" I asked him.

"Dad, why didn't you come with me?" was his reply. "It was fun. Loads of fun!"

"What happened up there?" I asked again.

"I just played! But it was so much fun, Dad!" he replied. The chill of fear began to return, and God help me, for an instant I looked at my son and I swear I had to stop myself looking for the birthmark at the crown of his skull for proof that it really was he who had returned.

"But you were only gone for seconds!" I said feebly.

"Don't be silly, Dad," he said as he walked back to the house. "It was hours. Two at least! Why didn't you come, we could've played together!"

He left me standing at the base of the oak tree, speechless.

***

In a fit of foolishness, of reckless curiosity, I asked him that night of what he had seen, of where the ladder had ended.

"It doesn't end, Dad," was all he said. I asked him what he meant.

"I mean it keeps going. It just carried on until I couldn't see it anymore. Round and round and round the tree. Do you want to come with me, Dad?" he asked. I said no, and that I never wanted him to go back there. He reluctantly agreed, and yet his next words confirmed to me that it would be hopeless trying to keep him away.

"Okay, Dad. I'll see if he can come to play down here." I stared at him.

"Who's 'he'?"

"My friend," he said.

My God, I remember thinking. *Just how long was he there? For me it was a matter of agonising seconds, but he is talking like he had hours to play and to even make friends. Just who the hell was up there? Is up there still?*

That night, after my son had gone to bed, I took a glass of wine outside and sat looking at the ladder in the failing light. I walked cautiously down to the tree, and felt immediately foolish doing it. I shut my eyes, reliving the afternoon's events. I found that the panic and fear I felt was slipping away (although I wasn't sure that it wasn't the wine helping me in that regard). Had my son really been gone for hours, instead of the seconds I had experienced? I even contemplated the notion that I had had some kind of seizure or mental block.

I drank and as the sun set and the darkness really set in, I heard the noise. It was like the soft hooting of an owl, which would have been no surprise, but it sounded like… I can't describe any of it without sounding like a mad man. It sounded so ethereal and distant that it could have been coming from another dimension. It didn't sound like it occupied the same space as the other natural sounds around me, the cars and the wind and the rustle of leaves above my head. I shifted my position so that I half faced the tree and I looked upwards into its darkness. I could see almost nothing. I shook my head to clear it and moved to go inside, but not before the faint hooting startled me again. This time it was accompanied by other sounds, hissing and whistling voices. Despite myself, by the time I reached the back door, I was moving at a healthy jog.

***

At breakfast the next morning, my son had a wild-eyed look about him, as if the dreams of the night were with him still. I asked him about them and he said nothing. I saw him glancing past me, through the open kitchen window. Down the length of the garden. I said nothing of my experiences of the previous evening. As I cleared away the breakfast things, I watched my son play in the garden, thinking that to deny him access to the garden and the ladder would only increase his desire to get there. I did not fail to notice the looks he shot towards it. I wasn't so far away that I could not hear him catch his breath each time he came within four feet of the tree. My heart caught at each of his stopped breaths and I imagined myself running from the kitchen, just too late to grasp his heel as he disappeared into the tree. He showed no inclination, however, of climbing again. I began to relax and brewed some tea.

I carried the drink into the garden, along with my usual weekend newspaper, and selected the bench at the top of the garden to begin my weekly perusal of it. I had been reading for perhaps ten minutes when I sensed, rather than heard, a change in the dynamic of his playing. My heart stopped and I stood suddenly, lukewarm tea spilling into the grass. I stared at my son.

He stood at the base of the tree, one hand resting casually on the leading edge of the ladder. His hair blew in a wind, but the wind seemed to blow *downwards*, as if it was coming from directly above him. He nodded slowly, and a wide grin split his face. He spoke, but the words were lost to me. Given the distance, they should not have been. I started towards him, shouted his name,

"Walk towards me!"

It seemed he heard me at the last moment, turned to me, and as I saw the look on his face, I broke into a run. It was the look I had seen the last time he had climbed. Pure fear. He seemed to be imploring me to catch him, stealing glances up the ladder so that I was sure he was seeing something up there. He spoke a word, and for the life of me, I was sure it wasn't English. I haven't heard its like before or since that moment. Its guttural bubbling sound was utterly alien coming from my son's mouth. I saw his eyes roll upwards until they were white, and as he started to slump forward, I threw myself at him in a vain attempt to catch his fall. I was beaten to it.

A long arm snaked downwards, fastened on a shoulder, and pulled sharply on my son's body. The hand at the end seemed too long, and thinking back now, I know that I had convinced myself that I saw pink flesh and a dark dusting of hair on the back of it, and not that dark indigo scaled horror. I know now that it was no human hand that snatched my son. I collapsed onto the grass and stared weakly up into the depths. I saw nothing.

The worst of it all, perhaps, is that apart from that crawling malevolent word he uttered before he fainted, my son made no noise. There was no cry as he was taken, no sign that he even knew what had happened. I sobbed into my cupped hands and raced back to the house, my first instinct to phone for help. I stopped myself with my hand in the receiver of the telephone. What on earth could I tell the police?

I walked in a daze back to the tree, fearful now that I would see my son's slumped body at its base, drained of life, and the creature crouching above him. The area around the tree was free from such visions and that was somehow worse. I reached the ladder and craned up into the darkness. Nothing. I started back to the house, desperate to do something, knowing there was only one thing that I could do. I fought with myself for minutes, precious minutes that I knew could mean the difference between finding my son or not. I curse those wasted minutes now.

Fast, so as I could not stop myself, I rushed back to the start of the ladder, and leapt the first three rungs, running up it using feet and hands. At first I did not take in my surroundings, but it soon became clear that

I should have easily cleared the height of the tree, and hadn't. I slowed my ascent, and looked to either side.

What I saw was so alien to me that I nearly lost my balance. Unthinking, I stepped from it and the ground beneath my feet seemed to thrum as I made contact with it. The earth here was a deep shade of ochre, nothing strange in that, but the grass shooting through it was the colour of spun glass, transparent and yet catching the dull light and throwing out spirals of twisted rainbows. I reached my hand to it, and snatched it back quickly as the edges parted my skin like razor blades. No playground this, then.

As much as I wanted to stay and explore (despite the obvious challenge), I knew (and prayed) that my son was not here and so moved on up the ladder. There seemed no end, each rung a door to as new and equally alien a landscape as that first. A breeze ruffled my hair. I smelled something in that breeze, familiar. It smelled faintly of ice cream and heat and joy, and I recognised the scent of my boy. I shut my eyes to focus on it, and stepped off the ladder.

***

It felt like stepping back onto the land around my house. Smelled the same, too. There were noises here, as those I had heard from the base of the tree, hooting and exuberant whistles. I opened my eyes, and saw the table off to one side, the one I am sitting at right now, on a patch of bare ground. The earth was the red colour of the Australian outback. To all sides, I saw fields upon fields of deep yellow corn, alongside tall trees that stretched into infinity. Beneath all of it, the redness of the earth looked like sunburned skin from which the corn grew like hair. I thought I saw movement in the corn, shadows and flitting shapes that leaped and cavorted among the dusty stems. I stared harder but this only served to blur the edges of my vision and so I looked away.

On the table I saw a pen and paper. Hooked over the back of the chair that accompanied the table, as casually as if it had been at home, was my son's jacket. I rushed to it, expecting to find something, some warmth in its cloth that would give me a clue. It was cold, and as I drew nearer, I saw splashes of mud coating it. I grabbed it up and crushed my face into it. I shouted my son's name again and again until my voice cracked and failed me. Clouds of dust and dried corn husk rose from the fields as if in response to my calls, but I neither received, nor expected, further reply.

My legs weakened suddenly, and I collapsed into the chair, feeling it creak under my weight. I spread my son's coat out in front of me and absently picked at the flecks of dried mud, thankful it was not blood.

I looked down at the red ground, not wanting to see the way my hands shook. My mind was filled with voices, all clamouring to be heard, all saying one thing or another, all mine. I bit down hard on my lip to snap myself out of this destructive thinking. Blood slowly filled the gap between my lower lip and my teeth and as I tasted the bitterness of it, my eyes found something on the ground at my feet. A tiny depression in the hard soil, no more than a finger's length. A swirling pattern in the middle of it, concentric circles the size of a small coin. I jolted in the chair so hard that my thighs caught painfully on the underside of the desk. I stood suddenly, tipping the chair backwards, and still clutching my son's jacket, I sank so that my face almost touched the earth. The voices in my head quietened suddenly. I knew this pattern. I had seen its like rendered numerous times in mud on the floor of my kitchen. It was my son's shoe print, I was sure of it, and now that I had seen one, I seemed to see them all.

Some were only traces of the print, some more full, and they led in a weaving pattern away from the desk and into the cornfields. What my eyes also found, and what I tried to not see, were the prints next to them, crossing them, scuffing them out. They looked vaguely bird-like, long and slender with three distinct trailing scratches at the front of each, as if made by three claws dragging with each footstep. Without stopping to think, I tucked the arms of my son's jacket into my jeans and started following the footprints.

The going was hard, strangely so, as if the very ground was holding me back. When I looked down at my feet I saw that the redness of the earth had crept up the legs of my jeans almost to the knee. I thought (no, I knew) that when I looked away the ground would be reaching up, grasping my legs, slowing me. I called out my son's name suddenly, not liking the hoarseness of my voice. A flock of birds exploded from the cornfield, black as crows but twice their size, oily blueness shimmering from their wingtips in the low sun. I allowed myself to think that the noise they made as they flew, the barking calls they made unlike any crow I had ever heard, the hissing as their wings exited the dry corn, completely masked the call made by my son as he answered me. Despite their racket, I almost heard him, I am sure of it. If I had made the sound up in my head, would I have added details like the obvious sound of his distress, and the low guttural rumbling that could only have come from his captor?

I began to run then, mimicking the birds' flight with my own, obliterating the footprints and the claw prints, tearing my legs through the grasping soil, seeing a red rain of dust flick from the ends of my shoes as each left the ground. The low rumble that I imagined was the voice of my son's kidnapper grew louder and I almost thought I saw a flash of indigo scales as it sped away through the corn field. I screamed as I ran, the name of my son morphing into a single strained syllable of wrenching pain. I thought I heard him again then

I urged my legs to move faster and sensed the ground under my feet responding to this as the creeping redness reached to my knees and then further, clawing at my thighs. Still I ran. Hours passed, or seemed to. My watch was still running but I wasn't sure I could trust its timing. In the blink of an eye, hours would pass, and then time would slow so that I seemed to cross vast distances in mere seconds.

I heard the shuffling steps of the kidnapper at every twist and turn of the corn plants, and as they slowly merged and then vanished into forests of deep green trees, the sounds grew quieter and eventually stopped altogether. I slept when I literally had no strength to stand, but the sleep was fitful and seemed to last no more than minutes. My watch said differently however, and a day, and then two, seemed to pass. I felt time's progress in the growth of stubble on my face, but in nothing else. I did not eat and I drank what water I could find in the forests, praying I would not sicken before I had found my son.

It was perhaps two days, or maybe two and a half when I eventually saw him. I was so shocked that for a moment I didn't recognise him. I was close enough to see streaks of tears cutting through the dirt on his face. Close enough to smell him. He stood with his head bowed, and as I scanned around for his tormentor,

I saw nothing. I looked back to my son, heart racing, words drying in my throat. He caught my eye suddenly, and the look in his eyes stopped me cold. It was blank fear, and yet he seemed to be telling me something with tiny movements of his head, shaking this way and that. He looked to his right and then left and again shook his head. I saw a grimace of pain cross his face then, and he crumpled slightly. As I looked to either side of him, and he was lost to the periphery, finally I saw what he was telling me.

The creature was not gone. It stood, its many-jointed, bowed legs dripping moisture and a glistening swollen sac of a body depending from them, its scaled hands at his throat. It shrouded itself somehow, so that when I looked back to my son, it vanished. And yet now I had seen it, I couldn't *un*-see it.

I gagged with the fear and revulsion, with the pain of seeing my boy harnessed by such horror. The thing tugged at him and he stumbled against the soft body. From it issued the same gargling word I had heard from my son. I wasn't sure if it was talking to me or my son, but I saw him nodding gently, and I sensed his fear subsiding, both in his eyes and the set of his body. His hands, that had been fisted tightly this whole time, slowly unclenched.

"Go back, Dad," he said, and my heart stopped at the sound of his voice. "Go back to the ladder and wait for me."

I began to protest, but days with mere mouthfuls of liquid had turned my voice into a silent scratch and I'm not sure he would have heard even if I had continued. As it was, he held his hands out and implored me.

"Dad, please! Go back. Wait at the ladder and I will find you. I'll be back, Dad. I promise. I love you, and I'll be back. Now *go*!"

The creature wrenched my son onto its back. I started running towards the spot where they had been standing, but I was too late. They vanished in a cloud of red dust, and I heard him shout as they went.

"I'll be back, Dad."

I sank to my knees and watched them leave, the dust settling just enough for me to glimpse the bright red of his t-shirt before it was shrouded in distance and mist and dry, cracking corn plants. My raw cry of loss followed them where I could not.

* * *

And so I wait for my son as any father would. I hold in my mind the sound of him and the sight of him and the smell of him, and I know he will return to me. He promised and I believe him. The sounds in the distance seem to be getting closer. I had a moment of inspiration and tied his jacket, which miraculously remained with me this whole time, to the last rung of the ladder that I stepped off. I think I might search for him on further rungs and in further worlds, or even go home. I know that I can find my way back here.

I have written my son a note explaining what I have planned, but he promised me, and I believe him. "*I'll be back*", he said. I need to be here when he does.

The jacket, still tied to the ladder, is flapping in a soft breeze. It reminds me of home, and the sound, like a kite or a flag in summer, comforts me. Every few minutes, I leave off writing and walk a distance and start calling my son.

So far I have heard nothing, but he promised.

Born Bad

By Mark Parker

1.

"Goddamned kid!" Claire Comstock muttered, as she continued to fill her basket with plump heirloom tomatoes from her garden. There were two rows of plants hanging low beneath the relentless rays of the July sun. She wanted to hurry up and get as many of them picked before the fully ripe ones had a chance to go to rot. It was Independence Day weekend; any excess would definitely go to use somewhere. She distributed among her friends for their backyard cookouts, if nothing else.

"What's that kid think he's doing, anyway?" Joanie Randall asked, wiping beads of perspiration from her furrowed brow with a gloved hand. "I mean, is he actually *trying* to hit us with whatever it is he's throwing over here?"

"All I can say is, he'd better not!" Claire shot a warning look over at the mangy-haired boy, who was digging in the threadbare strip of brown lawn fronting the Breslow house. The place had been an eyesore ever since the family had moved in. "If he so much as *nicks* us with anything, I'll show him some of my own fireworks… mark my words!"

No sooner had Claire gotten the words out of her mouth, when she felt something hit her on the left side of her head—just above the ear—and *hard.*

Momentarily stunned, she fell back onto the ground and reached up to slip a finger beneath the rim of her well-worn Red Sox ball cap. When she brought her hand away, there was a glistening slick of blood on it. Shocked that the kid had actually hit her, she could feel herself filling with a lancing chord of noxious rage. Like a shot, she was on her feet, as if someone had rear-ended her with a blazing hot poker.

"That little *sonofabitch*," she growled, dropping the plump tomato she'd been clenching so hard that it'd burst in her hand to the ground with a thud. Without giving a moment's thought to what she was about to do, she took off running across the street, shouting as she went.

"Don't you dare let me catch you, you little *brat!* If I do, I swear I'll skin you alive."

Still seated cross-legged on the ground, Joanie watched in stunned silence as her friend chased after the boy, who was now running around the corner of his family's dirt-streaked house, headed for the rutted driveway filled with so many rusted out cars that it looked like a makeshift junkyard.

As Claire reached the corner, right on his heels, she stopped dead in her tracks when she heard the loud metallic creak of an unoiled screen door opening and shutting behind her, followed by heavy footsteps, shuffling their way toward her.

"Whadd'ya think you're doin' yellin at my boy like that, you crazy old bitch?" Dan Breslow closed the distance between them in a matter of seconds. "If I *ever* hear you threaten my boy like that again, believe me when I say, it'll be *you* who gets skinned alive. Do you understand me?"

Suddenly feeling frightened by his father's presence, Bobby Breslow ran the rest of the way up the dirt driveway and hid behind the dilapidated barn at the back of their property.

"Who are you calling *crazy*?" Claire shouted, spitting her words up into her neighbour's unshaven face. "That little *spawn* of yours was throwing things up in the air, then he whipped *this* across the street and hit me in the head with it." She held up a medium sized wrench, its red paint long since worn off. "As hard as the little cretin hit me, I'll most likely need stitches. And don't you dare think for a second that *I'm* payin' the bill!"

Dan stood in front of her, slack-jawed for a moment, either shocked by her unexpected show of bravado, or simply proving that he was just as weird as his own son. With another loud creak and clatter, the front door opened and slammed shut again, and a rail-thin woman wearing a stained housedress and a pair of greyish-pink bunny slippers came scuffling across the yard with a jelly-faced toddler, hoisted on the protruding blade of her right hip.

"Danny, what's goin' on out here? I thought you said you was gonna make us some lunch. If you wait any longer, I'm gonna dry up and blow away."

Too late…Claire thought, looking at the woman's wisp of a frame, which was lopsidedly topped by a mass of dirty-blonde curls, limply framing her gaunt, greyish face. Dan looked at his wife and shooed her away like an annoying fly. "Get back inside, Gracie. Can't you see I'm takin' care of sumthin' out here?"

Without as much as a huff, Grace Breslow turned and shuffled back inside, slamming the screen door behind her.

Before Dan could say anything else, Claire was already walking back across the street, coming to a stop next to Joanie, who was still seated on the grass, looking up at her with an unabashed look of astonishment on her round, sun-reddened face.

Although there were still plenty of tomatoes left to pick, Claire had all but lost interest. She could actually feel herself trilling with a kind of fury she had never before felt—and wasn't at all comfortable to be feeling now. Turning back toward the street, she shouted, "You better get that boy in line, Breslow. One of these days, he's going to do the wrong thing to the wrong person… and there'll be *serious* hell to pay!"

Dan was still standing with his mouth hanging open in the middle of his yard, looking as if he had no clue what to say—or do—next. With a guttural clearing of his throat, he reluctantly shrugged his broad shoulders and pulled the front screen door to his house open with such force that it nearly tore right off its hinges. The sound of it slamming shut behind him reverberated down the sun-washed street like a deafening gunshot.

Glancing down at Joanie, Claire motioned for her to follow her inside. In her uncharacteristic show of anger, she'd nearly forgotten about her bleeding laceration. She needed to get it cleaned up and see if she would in fact need stitches or not.

2.

The following morning, while sipping coffee and nibbling on a home baked blueberry muffin, Joanie smiled across the kitchen table at Claire, brushing a thick red curl out of her face before saying, "Hon, you do realize he's only a boy, right?"

It was no secret her friend felt regret over how she'd acted the previous day—coming unglued as she had—especially in front of the whole neighbourhood. But Bobby Breslow clearly had a negative effect on her.

Claire doubted it was the kid's odd behaviour alone that had sent her so uncontrollably off kilter. What mostly got to her, was the way he leered at her from beneath those stringy bangs of his, defying her to say or *do* anything by way of retaliation.

"I hear what you're saying," Claire said over the rim of her coffee mug, "but he's certainly no child, Joanie. The boy's sixteen years old, for chrissakes. That's old enough to know better than to throw things at people. And that miserable father of his is certainly no help, constantly coming to his defence rather than teaching him the difference between right and wrong, only reinforces his absurdly disrespectful behaviour, as if it's of no concern whatsoever—which we both know is nothing but a load of bullshit."

Claire broke off a piece of muffin and took a nibble before washing it down with another sip from her coffee. "Besides, you've known me long enough to know I would've never made good on my threat to skin the kid alive! I was just trying to put the fear of God in his scrawny ass."

Joanie laughed. "And there's that…"

Claire dabbed at her mouth with a napkin, and then continued on. "Every time I see him, he's sneering at me through that filth-streaked bedroom window of his, or out of the toy-cluttered front bay window, like he's not-so-secretly plotting my goddamned death or something. The kid freaks me out, plain and simple. Especially when Mitch is on one of his long-haul trips, and I'm home alone with the cat. No doubt my Murphy is sizeable in cat terms, but he's a momma's boy. He'd be no help whatsoever with guarding the house. I mean, he's no Rottweiler, for godssake! If Bobby Breslow really had it in for me, I'd be in big trouble, teenager or not."

Joanie stood up to refill their coffee mugs. "I suppose you have a point, but still, that doesn't give you the right to go screaming and running after him like that." Friends for nearly twenty years, Joanie understood how Claire felt. She could remember times when she'd caught Bobby glaring at her with that same *dark* look on his face, like he was seeing her without really *seeing* her. It was like he was looking right through her. Just thinking about it caused a coil of icy fear to race up her spine.

"I know. I've seen him look at me the same way," Joanie said. "I guess I never really gave it much thought until now. I just figured he was always off on some sort of daydream or something, drifting off in space as a way to escape his crummy home life."

"While that could be true," Claire said, taking her refilled mug from Joanie, "it still doesn't give the little creep permission to hurl things at people. He's lucky I *didn't* catch up with him! With the foul mood he had me in yesterday, there's no telling what I might've done if given half a chance. He pissed me off something fierce, I think we can both agree on that. I've just never seen a kid treat someone with such blatant disrespect. If I'd done that when I was a kid, my parent's would've killed me and buried the evidence."

"Well, I'm just glad you're feeling better today, hon," Joanie said with a smile. "Now I suppose we should figure out what we're gonna do with all these friggin' tomatoes!"

They both looked over at the baskets filled to near overflowing on top of the kitchen sideboard. Claire laughed. "Well, I figure once we've taken the ones we want," she said with a wink, "we can try to sell the rest at the Farmer's Market, although I don't know if they'll be open, it being a holiday weekend and all. If not, maybe that vegetable stand over on Old Dunlock Road will be set up. We could take a drive over and see if they're open if you want."

"Sure," Joanie said, taking her half-empty mug over to the sink to rinse it out. "And then maybe we can go check out that used bookstore I was telling you about. They just opened for business last week. It might be fun to see what they have on their shelves. I'm already finished with the bag of mysteries you gave me to read last month. With Paul locked away in that man cave of his most of the time—watching ball games and drinking beer—I'm always looking for something to pass the time. With all this heat and humidity, there's only so much knitting I can do before my fingers start to ache. Even the softest yarns feel like rope in damp weather like this."

They both chuckled.

Picking through the baskets of tomatoes, they each put the ones they wanted in reusable canvas grocery bags, and carried the excess outside to Claire's brand new Honda Odyssey; a gift from Mitch for her fiftieth birthday.

Standing next to the SUV, Claire looked over at Joanie before shooting a sideways glance toward the Breslow place. She was relieved to find none of the house's front-facing windows framing Bobby's leering stare. Instead, the house stood in a curious kind of silence. Perhaps Dan had finally put the fear of God into that boy himself. Whatever the cause for the silence was, Claire was thankful for it. She was anxious to get the day's activities started without drawing any unwanted attention from across the street.

3.

When they returned several hours later, Claire became visibly nervous when she pulled into her driveway to see a car from the sheriff's office parked there.

"God… now what?" Claire looked past Joanie, taking her time to turn off the SUV's ignition. "I know Dennis loves my tomatoes, but something tells me he's not here for a friendly visit—call it a hunch."

"I'll bet that jerk Dreshaw called and complained about the way you spoke to his son yesterday. If you ask me, those two deserve each other!" Joanie smiled supportively, her face flushing bright red. "You know what they say. *Like father, like son.* To be honest, it wouldn't surprise me at all if he did call Dennis. He's the sort to cover his own ass, rather than do what's right."

Before they even had time to get out of the car, Dennis Frates was climbing out of his own department-issue brown and gold sedan, heading over to greet them. He was flashing his customary photo-ready smile, but it was no satisfactory ruse. Claire could easily sense the professional guardedness behind it.

"Good afternoon, ladies. How are you both enjoying this steamy July weather we're having?"

"Looks like it's gonna be another July 4th scorcher, Sheriff," Joanie said, stepping out of the car to retrieve her purchases from the back.

"What's going on, Dennis?" Claire asked, closing the driver's side door before taking a step toward him. "What brings you out to the sticks on a sweltering day like today? Did someone tell you I'm overrun with heirlooms again this year, or is your visit of a more *official* nature?"

The sheriff flashed another broad smile at her before going on. “Well, we all know how well-oiled our gossip mill is around here… But that isn’t why I stopped by.”

“By the clipped edge to your voice, something tells me you’re not here to chat about tomorrow evening’s fireworks,” Claire said, grabbing her own bags out of the back. “Let me guess… Dan Breslow called your office to complain about me. I should’ve known he would.”

“What’s this about Breslow?” Dennis asked, a confused look creasing his face. “Complain about you for what? The calls I generally get, are more *about* him than from him. You know, folks calling to say he’s being drunk and disorderly again. I had to warn him just the other night that the next time I get a complaint about him, he’ll have a chance to get well acquainted with one of the holding cells down at the station.”

Claire shot Joanie a questioning glance over the roof of the SUV. “I’m happy to say I don’t see him all that often, really,” she said, shrugging, taking her bags from the backseat. “And, whenever I do, he always seems put out by my presence somehow, like I caught him with his pants down. Yesterday, we just had a disagreement about his boy, is all.”

“He’s probably drunk when he sees you,” Joanie said. “I’d sidestep my neighbours, too, if I was always getting caught staggering around the yard, yelling at my family. And don’t even get me started on that weirdo kid of his! He may only be a teenager, but he’s one creepy kid. Every time I see him, I turn and run into the house, before he has time to put some sort of hex on me with that damned *look* of his. He gives me the heebie-jeebies."

Dennis followed the two women up the back stairs and into the house. "I know what you mean about Bobby Breslow. I hear all sorts of things from the folks around town. Mostly from the staff over at the school he was going to. His parents were forced to start home-schooling him, after he was expelled for giving his teachers so much trouble. Apparently he was getting physical with the other kids in his class."

"Physical?" Joanie asked, taking a long swig of water from the bottle she'd brought in from the car. "How do you mean, sheriff?"

"Well, apparently he was caught hitting on some kids who were giving him a hard time at school, calling him names. I'm told he even threw a full can of soda at a girl in the lunchroom, because she wouldn't let him sit with her. The cut was so bad, the poor girl even had to be rushed over to Doc Daniels' office, to have the damned thing sewn up."

Joanie pulled out a chair for the sheriff, which he took with a nod and a smile. After a moment of silence, he added, "I suppose it's like you said, Joanie. That odd way he *stares* at folks is off-putting—even unsettling to some. Especially the older female teachers at school who haven't had much experience with such outbursts. I'm guessing it was a much different world when they first began teaching. These days, teachers don't know what they're going to be confronted with when they walk into their classrooms."

"Just last week," Joanie said, sitting in the chair next to his, "I heard on the news a girl had been caught bringing a Taser into class. From what the news reporter said, she even set the damned thing off…just to prove to her friends it was real."

"So, what *did* bring you here, Dennis?" Claire interjected, as politely as she could manage. "Not, of course, that it's not always a pleasure to see you."

"Well, I actually *did* get a complaint call from the Breslow family, but it wasn't Dan who called in the complaint. It was Grace Breslow. She called, ranting about how you chased her son and threatened him, after he'd accidentally hit you with a wrench he'd been playing with. I'm guessing it's difficult to keep a home-schooled boy like Bobby entertained, especially having to grow up with a man like Dan for a father."

"*Accidentally* hit me?" Claire said, suddenly fuming. She looked down at Joanie for reinforcement. "Joanie was there when it happened, Dennis. I warned the kid to stop throwing things across the street at us, but he wouldn't stop. He wasn't *playing* with the stuff he was throwing. He maliciously kept on doing it, until he actually hit one of us. *Me*, to be exact! Just like that poor girl at school, I, too, had to have stitches put in. Doc Daniels couldn't believe it. He said I was the fourth person in the last week who'd been in to see him with the same kind of laceration. When I told him what'd happened, he couldn't believe it. He just shook his head and said, 'Kids today…' Although it wasn't all that deep of a wound, the damned thing bled like a sieve… ask Joanie. That little brat's lucky I didn't make good on my threat and kick his butt all the way to next Sunday!"

"I get what you're saying." Dennis nodded, taking a sip of the iced tea Claire had poured for him. "Really, I do. But I think we all know if Child and Family Services gets as much as a whisper about this, we'll have a far different problem on our hands. One that I'm sure none of us here wants. Besides, Grace said your threat was that you'd skin the boy alive. That's a pretty nasty thing to say, Claire. Even if you wouldn't've made good on your threat."

Claire shook her head. "I'm sorry, Dennis. The boy just had me so angry. I acted in a way that isn't like me at all. Joanie and I were saying as much over coffee this morning. I do regret letting him get under my skin the way he did. It won't happen again."

Finishing his tea, Dennis stood up and offered a half-hearted smile. "It can't, Claire. It simply can't. I have to insist you both keep to yourselves… and avoid the entire Breslow family whenever—and wherever—possible. And, whatever you do, keep your shouting to a minimum, especially if it's directed toward any of your neighbours. If you're outside and Bobby starts up again, come inside and call *me!* Let *me* be the one to take care of things. If it would make you feel more secure, I can have one of my deputies drive by every couple of hours, to make sure things are under control."

"That would be great, Sheriff," Joanie said, reaching over to touch him on the arm. "We'd really appreciate that."

"Well…" Claire huffed. "All I can say is, if he ever does anything like this again, I'll press charges, underage or not!"

"Let's just take things one step at a time," Dennis advised. "We don't want to go off counting our chickens before they're hatched. If anything happens—anything at all—I want you to call me, is that clear? I can be here in a matter of minutes."

Joanie giggled like a star struck schoolgirl. "Look at you, getting all *sheriffly!*"

"I'm serious, Joanie. This *cannot* happen again."

He turned and headed for the door.

"Did you want to take your tomatoes with you, Dennis?" Claire asked, walking over to the sideboard. To say there are plenty is an understatement, as you can see. Or would you rather I bring some along tomorrow evening, when we head down to the harbour to watch the fireworks?"

Dennis flashed a mouthful of white teeth again, to at least somewhat take the sting out of his earlier warning. "If that wouldn't be too much of an imposition that would be great." He tipped his hat toward her, more out of habit than anything. "I'm afraid they might just explode in the car before I got them home. I still have several hours left of my shift."

"Tomorrow it is then," Claire said, reaching over to give him a hug before he walked back outside, into the sweltering afternoon heat.

4.

Twilight came early the next evening, as the whole town made its way down to the waterfront to take in the July 4th festivities. Each year the fireworks committee went all out to celebrate the holiday in style. It'd become their aim to make each year bigger and better than the year before. And this year it was proven in spades.

The entire fishing fleet was decked out in red, white, and blue bunting, along with flags and lights, which added a festive shimmer to the surface of the surrounding waters.

"Doesn't everything look beautiful?" Joanie asked, as she and Claire—flanked by their husbands—stepped down onto the newly replaced town pier that stretched the full span of the harbor on all three sides.

"I think this is the first time I've seen the boats lit up like that," Joanie's husband Paul said, putting his arm around his wife's shoulders.

"No," Mitch contradicted, disputing his friend's claim. "Don't you remember they do the same thing every year for the Blessing of the Fleet?"

"Not in red, white, and blue, they don't," Paul retorted.

"S'ppose you're right there," Mitch teased. "They *don't* use red, white, and blue lights to mark the Christmas season."

They all laughed as they took their seats next to Dennis Frates and his wife, Nancy.

When the fireworks began to light up the darkening sky, Joanie leaned over and tapped Claire on the leg. "Don't look now, but Breslow and his brood just showed up."

Claire felt an instant knot of apprehension well up inside her at the mere mention of the man's name. Acting as if she didn't know they were there, she leaned against the reassuring strength of Mitch's shoulder, and looked up at the exploding spectacle overhead.

Thankfully, the rest of the night went along without incident. After the fireworks and concert, they leisurely made their way home, enjoying the ocean breeze drifting through the open car windows, as they took the winding back to the house like a group of seniors out for their Sunday drive.

When they finally pulled into the Comstock's driveway, and all four of them climbed out of the car, Joanie was first to let out a loud gasp, when she saw that the windows of Claire's new Odyssey had all been smashed in.

"That little *fucker!*" Claire spat, glaring over at the Breslow place, which stood in total darkness, beneath a gauzy thread of moonlight.

“When did you start talking like a truck driver?” Mitch teased, pulling his wife toward him. “We don’t know it was the Breslow kid who did this… or any member of his family for that matter. To think along those lines would be us giving into speculation, which isn’t good for anyone involved.”

“Speculation my ass!” Claire said, shrugging out of her husband’s embrace. Heading toward the back door, she said, “If you aren’t going to do something about this, Mitch, I will. And, believe me when I say, I won’t be quite so forgiving with that little bastard this time around!”

Not knowing exactly what his wife meant by that, he and their friends silently followed Claire up the back-stairs and into the house, carefully shutting and locking the kitchen door behind them.

“What’s it gonna take, Mitch?” Claire shouted, her voice trembling with anger. “You’re gone most of the time. How would you feel if something truly terrible happened to me while you’re away on one of your long haul trips, huh? You won’t be satisfied until that boy has me dead and buried….”

“That’s ridiculous, Claire! Must you always make things so dramatic whenever you talk about that damned kid? Instead of taking things one step at a time, looking at things logically, you always go for the worst possible case scenario, as if Bobby’s the goddamned devil himself!”

“Well, one of us has to see things for what they are. You’re never around when that kid stares at us with that *insane* look of his. I’m not the only one who’s freaked out by him. He has Joanie frightened to leave the house when he’s around.”

Paul looked over at his wife, worry creasing his deeply tanned brow. “Is that true, honey?”

"Yes," Joanie said, wrapping her arms around herself. "He *does* look evil, if you ask me."

"It's like I told Dan yesterday when his son threw a goddamned wrench at me, that boy's clearly his father's spawn. Loins like his can only produce a boy like Bobby. But, with an abusive drunk for a father, what chance could the boy possibly have?"

Joanie nodded. "If someone doesn't straighten that kid out soon, God only knows what'll happen next."

"I don't know about the rest of you," Claire said, "but I don't plan to wait around to see. I'm going to do as Dennis asked, and call his office. I'll be damned if I'm going to take all of this lying down. You're right, Mitch, we don't know if it was Bobby who smashed in the windows of my new SUV, but the sooner we get the sheriff's office involved, the sooner we can put all this bizarre crap behind us. I don't know about you, but I'd prefer to not be another newsworthy casualty. Like I said before, you're not always around."

5.

When Dennis's car pulled into their driveway twenty minutes or so later, Claire didn't know what to think when she saw the blanched look on her friend's face. Opening the kitchen door, she asked, "What is it, Dennis? What's happened?"

"I see Mitch's here. I need you both to come outside into the backyard with me. There's something I need to show you."

"We've already seen the smashed windows," Mitch said, crossing over to where his wife and Dennis were standing.

"No, it's much worse than that, I'm afraid. I need to warn you both, it's not something either of you are going to want to see."

Joanie and Paul walked in from the living room. "Is everything okay, sheriff?" asked Paul.

"Oh, hello you two. I'm sorry… I didn't know you were here. I need to take Claire and Mitch outside for a moment. I apologize for the interruption. It shouldn't take long."

"Claire called as you asked," Joanie said.

"I know, but this is about something else, I'm afraid."

He turned toward the door and waited for the couple to follow him outside.

Training his Maglite beam onto the ravaged body of their cat, Murphy, Dennis apologized for having to show them something so painful. Claire and Mitch gasped at the sight of their pet, who might as well be their son, laying in a blood-soaked patch of grass, reduced to nothing more than a heaping clump of innards and fur.

Grief stricken, Claire fell against Mitch's chest in a fit of agonizing sobs.

"What the fuck—" Mitch started, but his words were cut off by his wife's sudden screaming. "Dennis, I need to get her inside. She doesn't need to see all of this."

Mitch walked Claire back inside the house, hugging her tightly before handing her off to Joanie and Paul, who pulled her into the kitchen with them. Joanie ran over to the kitchen window and drew the curtains shut while Paul closed the door.

Hurrying back down the stairs, Mitch asked Dennis, "What do you make of all this? Claire is convinced the Breslow boy is responsible for her smashed car windows… but *this?* Do you honestly think a boy Bobby's age could have the stomach to do something this horrific?"

"Well…" Dennis said, choosing his words carefully, "from everything that's happened in the last twenty-four hours, it would certainly *seem* like he could've done it. But I'll have to get some tech out here to process the scene before we can draw any real conclusions one way or the other. Once we have proof, we'll know better what we're up against. I'm so sorry for your family's loss. I know how much you both loved Old Murph."

Mitch looked down at the cat's remains once again. He'd been a part of their family for so long, it was unbelievable to think he wouldn't be around anymore. Mitch knew his wife's reaction was only the beginning of what was to come. Claire loved Murphy as if he was her child. This was undoubtedly going to hit her hard, she'd been the one to pick him out from the litter he'd come from, and had immediately bonded with him from the start.

Once the cat's remains had been removed from their property, Mitch would replace the grass and have a small monument and memory garden put in.

As he and Dennis waited for the crime scene techs to show up, Mitch heard shouting coming from the top of the stairs. Racing toward the sound, Mitch and Dennis stopped halfway up the staircase when they saw who was causing all the commotion.

Grace Breslow was talking animatedly to whoever was on the other side of the kitchen door. As always, she had her diapered daughter perched on her hip.

Drawing closer, Mitch heard Grace say, "Dan and Bobby are gone! I need the sheriff's help. I know he's here…." Her words hung in the humid night air like an unveiled threat.

"What do you mean they're gone?" Paul asked, opening the kitchen door a few inches.

"Missy and I were taking a nap after the fireworks, and when we got up, the house was dark and empty. Dan didn't mention anything about going out nowhere. I figured he'd plant himself in that recliner of his, drink a few beers, and fall asleep watchin' the Sox game or somethin'." She took a moment to shift the toddler from one hip to the other before continuing on. "And of course that damned son of his is gone too. But that's no surprise. I can't ever seem to keep a short enough leash on that kid. He's always runnin' off or gettin' himself in some sort of trouble. I once found him under one of his dad's rusted out jalopies in the garage… just staring up like the goddamned mysteries of the universe were written on the car's floorboards or somethin'. That kid sure acts odd sometimes. No matter what Dan says!"

When Dennis reached the top of the stairs, Grace turned around and said, "There you are, Sheriff. I need help. Dan and Bobby are missing!"

Obviously exhausted from the long day he'd had, Dennis asked flatly, "Is there anywhere you can think they'd go at this hour?"

"I wouldn't know, Sheriff. Dan hardly checks in with me about anything he does, least of all where he's goin' or when. And, as for Bobby, that kid could be anywhere. Your guess is as good as mine. I'm thinkin' it must've had something to do with all that crap Bobby was spouting on the way home from the fireworks."

"How so?" Dennis asked. "What was he saying?"

Grace shrugged. "Oh… he was goin' on about how Claire had it comin' to her for the way she'd yelled at him yesterday over the whole wrench throwing thing. At one point, I caught him starin' at me in the car's side mirror, and he was wearin' that *dark* look he gets when he's really upset, so I didn't say anything at the time. Folks generally get the situation between him and his dad all ass-backwards. They think the boy acts up because his dad's a miserable drunk and beats on him all the time, but it's the other way around. Dan gets drunk because his son's such a weird kid. I know that's a terrible thing to say, but he's been that way ever since he was born. He came out nasty, and has been ever since. That's why we had to start home-schoolin' him. Even his teachers couldn't drill any sense into him. And things have only gotten worse since he was expelled. He hardly talks anymore, and when he does, he says things that don't make any sense. He mumbles in some kinda gibberish I can't understand. I'm always havin' to ask him to repeat himself. And then he just gets madder and runs into his room and slams the door in my face."

Dennis took off his hat and ran his fingers through his thick hair. "I had no idea all this was going on. Why didn't you call me, Grace? I could've come out and helped you and Dan get things sorted out with the boy."

Grace didn't say a word. She just stood there shaking her head, tears streaming down her face.

6.

Once the techs had showed up and removed Murphy's body from the backyard after processing the scene, Dennis headed across the street to check if Dan and his son had made an appearance yet.

When Grace opened the door to him, he told her he was going to check around outside and see if anything looked out of place.

She just nodded and shut the door quietly.

He walked around the parameter of the sad looking house, careful to take note of everything his Maglite beam showed. After making a second pass, he noticed a weak thread of light coming from beneath the barn's weathered doors.

Walking quietly over to it, he clicked off the flashlight and slipped it back into the metal ring hanging from his gun belt. As he drew closer, he heard muffled sounds emitting from the gaps in the walls of the sagging structure.

One of the voices sounded like Bobby's, but as low as it was, Dennis couldn't really tell with any certainty. It wasn't until he had his gun drawn and had pushed the barn door open an inch that he saw Bobby's hooded figure standing next the rusted out body of a car, hunched over someone tied to a chair, who could only be Dan Breslow.

In the stale humidity of the barn, there was a menacing edge to Bobby's voice when he murmured something to his father seated in front of him. Grace had been right; the boy's words didn't seem to have any noticeable logic to them. It *was* as if he was speaking a language that only he seemed to know. But what caused Dennis even more concern, was how it sounded like the boy was speaking to someone other than his father, even though he clearly faced him.

Easing the door shut, Dennis crept around to the side of the barn and peaked in at Bobby through a gap in the wall. From this angle, he made out the black expression that was spread across the boy's face and the sight sent a chill through his body. It was as if someone else had taken control of him and was acting *through* him. The absolute darkness of the look wasn't due to the pool of shadows Bobby was standing in, either. It was more a kind of darkness coming from within him. The crazed look had Dennis frozen to the spot in the sweltering heat of the heavy, still night air.

Dennis couldn't help wondering how Bobby could've gotten his father—who was easily twice his size—tied to a chair in the barn. But when Dan's head lolled slightly to the right, Dennis could see the unfocused look on the man's face. Either he was drunk or high on something, or he'd been drugged.

After a dizzying moment, Dan tried to say something but nothing came out. As his head lazily slipped further to the right, Dennis could see that Dan's mouth had a thick strip of duct tape stretched across it. Unable to utter a word, his slowly shifting eyes said everything his mouth couldn't.

Dennis quickly surveyed the gloomy space. There was a rusted fuel can at Bobby's feet and he held a box of wooden matches in his left hand. As he stood there glaring down at his father, the indecipherable words he muttered grew even louder. It was as if whatever darkness resided inside of him wanted out, and was doing its best to find a viable way.

Dennis noticed something else he hadn't seen at first. He originally thought the fuel can at Bobby's feet was there to taunt Dan… but as his eyes continued to adjust to the tenebrous light of the barn's shadowed interior, Dennis could see that Dan's clothing was sodden and dripping onto the dirt floor beneath him—no doubt wet with fuel from the can.

With an almost electric shot of adrenaline, Dennis ran back to the front of the barn, and slammed his shoulder against one of the two sagging doors. Hit by his full weight, the door flew wide open, followed by the echoing sound of falling tools.

"Bobby!" Dennis shouted, holding his gun out in front of him. "Whatever it is you're thinking of doing, believe me when I say, you don't want to do it. Now, step back from your father, and toss that box of matches over to me!"

Spinning around to face Dennis, the expression on Bobby's face had grown even darker. The muscles in his face twitched, taut with anger, giving him an admittedly demonic look.

And then, he spoke...

"The question really should be, what do *you* think you're doing, *Dennis*?" The sound of the boy's voice was much deeper than that of a teenager; it carried a dark taunting quality to it, making everything all the more unnerving. "For fuck's sake, Sheriff, even with that gun of yours pointed directly at me, it's you who appears to be the weaker one of us at the moment, wouldn't you say?"

"Not by a longshot, son. Now, do as I instructed, and toss that box of matches over to me."

"Wouldn't it be funny if it was *your* gun instead of *my* matches that ignited the fuel my dear old dad here is doused in?" Bobby taunted. "I mean, consider the irony there."

The words that came out of his mouth were clearly not those of a sixteen-year-old boy—they had a kind of confident maturity to them that no teenager would be able to manage on his own. "You don't sound like yourself, son. Has something happened to you that you'd like to tell me about?"

A sinister chuckle rose up from Bobby's throat, dark and guttural. "And what might that be, *Dennis*? Are you referring to the shit everyone says about me? You know, about me being *born bad* and all. Even that cunt mother of mine says that shit about me! And we all know how reliable *her* word is, now don't we?"

Dennis couldn't believe what the boy was saying, referring to his mother by such a derogatory term. But clearly, the boy in front of him was no longer Bobby. This was an entirely different entity altogether. "It doesn't matter what anyone says, son. It's what's happening *now,* in the present that really matters! If you don't do as I say and back away from your father, you're going to leave me no choice but to shoot you. And neither of us wants that."

"I wouldn't be so sure . . ." the gravelly voice said, using Bobby's mouth.

"Don't you feel any guilt about the things you've done?" the sheriff asked.

There was that mocking chuckle again.

"Guilt?" Bobby's mouth said. "Are you fucking *kidding* me? What would I have to feel guilty about? If you ask me, I've brought a little excitement to this boring-ass neighbourhood. That Comstock bitch and her rosy friend think they've seen the worst of their *weird little neighbour*, but those two haven't seen anything yet. Even this little standoff of ours is lame compared to what I'm really capable of. But folks will see soon enough. Now, is it gonna be *your* bullet or *my* match, that gets this blaze started?"

Slick with sweat, Dennis's gun hand trembled. He fought hard to refocus and steady it, but his whole body was amped with conflicting emotions. A moment of sour silence played out between them, before the first shot rang out.

Dennis was both frustrated and relieved to see that his shot had gone wide.

Bobby chuckled maniacally, mocking the sheriff's poor aim.

"I would've thought you'd be better at your job than that, Sheriff. Surely you can hit *some* part of my body from that distance, can't you?"

Dennis heard a loud clattering sound coming from behind Bobby. It was Dan thrashing frantically in the chair he remained tied to. His eyes searched the shadows of the barn wildly, with a look both horrified and hopeful.

And then there was a terrifying *whooshing* sound…

Bobby had struck a match and dropped it in front of him. In a matter of seconds, the interior of the barn ignited in gas-fuelled flames.

Holstering his gun, Dennis ran toward the boy and his father, thankful to see a gleaming red fire extinguisher standing on the workbench next to the rusted out car frame that was up on blocks.

Racing for the extinguisher, Dennis heard a low roar emit from Bobby's throat. He turned toward the boy and watched as his slender frame swayed with the growing coil of flames surrounding him.

Grabbing the extinguisher from the workbench, he pulled the release pin from the handle and pointed the nozzle at Bobby's feet while simultaneously engaging it. The boy was immediately engulfed in a cloud of powdery white. Once Dennis was sure he had the fire put out, he ran toward Dan to repeat his actions.

Again, a roiling cloud of white.

And then… nothing but silence.

7.

After what felt like hours had passed, the night air was suddenly filled with the welcome sound of sirens.

Dennis looked up and saw Mitch walking up the driveway, pocketing his cell phone. "They should be here any second," Mitch told him.

"Thank you for calling them."

"Did everyone get out safely?" Claire asked, stepping out from behind her husband.

Dennis nodded. "Thankfully, yes."

Claire wanted to say something else, but instead she just stood next to Mitch, who was now seated atop a metal garbage can, looking down at the ground in silence.

As Joanie and Paul walked across the street to join them, Claire felt the anger she'd been carrying toward Bobby and his father ease up slightly. It would undoubtedly take a very long time for her to get over what they'd both done to her—especially Bobby. The crime scene technicians had found the sledgehammer he'd presumably used to smash in her SUV windows, and decimate the cat she'd loved so dearly.

She watched as a blur of activity unfolded around her. And when Bobby was wheeled past her on a stretcher, her eyes locked with his, and for the briefest of moments she felt a wild sense of triumphant satisfaction in knowing he would be out of commission for a while.

And, at least for now, that was enough.

Milk

By Michael Bray

1.

September 1986, and England has been treated to the rarest of things; a good summer. Days had been hot, nights long and warm, the air filled with the smell of barbequed meats and freshly cut grass. Mike Tyson became the youngest world heavyweight boxing champion, capturing the imagination of the sporting world. The space shuttle Challenger exploded on take-off, killing all on board, the harrowing footage played on television screens worldwide as the investigation into what happened begins.

Nintendo finally released their NES entertainment system in Europe, its lead game, Super Mario Brothers, featuring a mushroom eating plumber looking to rescue a princess proving to be all the rage with schoolchildren the world over. Movies which will go on to be iconic are screening in theatres. Top Gun featuring a young Tom Cruise and Val Kilmer is getting rave reviews. The sequel to the Karate Kid is also showing, once again featuring a fresh faced Ralph Macchio in the lead role as he plays the humble, but talented, Daniel La Russo.

Television too is seeing a surge of new and colourful programming imported from the United States, from George Peppard leading his band of mercenaries called the A-Team in their weekly exploits against evil, to light hearted family comedies like the Cosby Show and Cheers.

As the August days began to shorten and the oppressive heat had started to fade, bringing with it the first slight bite of winter, thoughts for many of the children who had enjoyed one of the best summers on record turned towards the dreaded return to school.

For most, the first day back was something to dread. It meant that winter was on its way, and as the summer had been a spectacularly good one, the majority of the pupils at Evanshaw Middle School were not happy to be back. Nine-year-old Dillon Thomas, however, was looking forward to it. He walked towards the red bricked building, hands thrust in jacket pockets, last year's Transformers lunchbox nestled in his school bag, his Teenage Mutant Hero Turtle toy figure hidden amongst his school things, despite his mother's insistence he leave them at home. Dillon didn't like to go against her wishes, but he had been playing with them all summer and it seemed a shame to leave them at home.

Things in the house had been difficult since his father had left them. Although his mother didn't know it, sometimes Dillon could hear her crying on a night when she thought he was asleep. If she came into his room to see if her cries had woken him he would lay perfectly still, eyes closed and pretending to be asleep. He thought it was better that way. Easier for them both. He didn't really remember much of his father anyway, and whenever he tried to ask about him, all she would tell him was that he wasn't a good man and that they were better off without him. Dillon had seen pictures of him though, and his mother reluctantly admitted that the two of them looked alike, both slim with blonde hair and sharp, inquisitive blue eyes.

His mother did her best to run the household on her own, working part time at a restaurant in town, but times were hard and money in short supply, so Dillon was forced to go without the latest things. His shoes were battered, beaten, and had been repaired more times than he could recall, his jumpers and trousers were years old, and were already starting to get too short in the arms and legs respectively. By no means popular anyway, Dillon was constantly teased by his classmates about the circumstances at home and the way he was forced to live. They were absolutely merciless, picking out his tatty shoes, frayed sweaters and repaired trousers as valid reasons to tease him. As a result, he had few friends, most of the other pupils shunning him for fear of being seen as a sympathiser and, by default, picked on too. This is the dog eat dog world of mid-eighties middle school in the U.K.

The one exception to the rule was Billy Lawrence, who was a year older than him and, like Dillon, was the butt of most of the jokes in his class too. Either by necessity or a shared need for companionship, the two had become friends, helping each other through what had proved to be a turbulent two terms at school. Because of his lack of other friends, Dillon always went out of his way to seek approval from his classmates and change their opinion of him. He tried to be nice, tried to offer help to them, but nobody wanted to be seen with him. He had, it seemed, already been singled out as the unpopular member of the class, and had also now attracted the attention of Ron Spengler, who although the same age as Dillon was much taller and already had a reputation as a bully. At the end of the previous term he had shoved Dillon down the steps leading to the playground, the fall causing him to tear his school trousers on the knees (the same ones he was wearing now, complete with patches to repair the damage). As angry as he was, he, like most of the other kids, was afraid of Ron, and the best way he had learned to deal with it was to ignore it and hope it went away. For a while, that had worked, but Ron, it seemed, had marked Dillon out as a long term target for his humiliation and bullying.

Dillon approached the school, its reddish walls contrasting against both the concrete playground in front and the fields and trees behind where they would play sports during P.E.

Dillon's excitement about the new school day halted as he walked through the gates. Ron was standing with his friends by the entrance, yellow Sony Walkman earphones hanging around his neck. For a split second, Dillon wanted to turn and run, maybe enter the school by the side entrance, which would take longer but prevent a confrontation. It was too late, however, as he had already been seen, and Ron and his friends were watching like a pack of hungry lions as Dillon walked towards them.

"Still not got any new trousers have you, tramp?" Ron asked, enjoying the chuckles of his companions. He was big, his chin seeming to morph straight into his shoulders where his neck should have been. He had a buzz cut, and his face was littered with spots.

Dillon said nothing. He knew that to answer would only provoke them more. Instead, he did the same thing as always in situations like this. He lowered his head and tried to shoulder past them and into the relative safety of the school.

"Wait. I'm talking to you," Ron said as his friends closed in around him.

Dillon sped up, scared now about what they might do and desperate to get inside the building. Someone stuck out a foot in front of him and before he could stop himself he stumbled over, crashing to the ground on his hands and knees.

Laughter.

Pointing.

Not just by Ron and his friends, but others in the yard too. As he knelt there on the floor, the embarrassment far more painful than the sting in his palms, Dillon's excitement for the new day was gone. Now, he wished he was anywhere else in the world. Maybe at home playing with his Masters of the Universe figures, or at Billy's house, although he was also probably on his way to school now too, so that was a non-starter.

He started to get up, feeling sick, afraid, and unsure how to react.

Ron, it seemed, could smell the fear and with a growing audience watching to see what would happen, shoved him back down. "Nobody said you could get up." He grunted, looking around for approval.

Dillon didn't fight it, and waited on all fours as the laughter continued.

Always the laughter.

Never any offer of help.

They just watched and let it happen.

"You stay there like a good dog." Ron said, clearly enjoying the attention. He was everything that Dillon wasn't.

Popular.

Confident.

Strong.

A bully.

Dillon could taste it in his throat, something he was all too familiar with.

Fear.

Bitter and strong, intense and all consuming, it hovered there, making him incredibly aware of everything around him. He could feel the blood surging around his body as his heart thumped its high tempo rhythm. He hated that taste. He had started to forget its flavour over the summer but now it had come back stronger than ever.

It was more than just teasing now, more than just verbal jibes. The new school term had brought with it a new, more physical side to Ron. It seemed that, for whatever reason, verbal taunts didn't cut it anymore and he was looking for new, more physical ways to get his kicks.

"Kiss my shoes, Dog," Ron said, grinning at his friend, a short, greasy-haired boy called Damien. "Kiss them and you can get up."

Dillon shook his head, wishing the others weren't watching, wishing they couldn't see him crying. Most of all, wishing they would stop laughing and *help* him.

"Kiss them or I'll make you sorry."

He knew he would have to do it, and then they would have something else to tease him about. He could only begin to imagine how it would be if the rest of the year went on like this. He squinted up at Ron, the sun for a second masked behind his head so that his form was a shadowy, featureless mass against the pale morning sky. He leaned close to Ron's outstretched shoes, the bottoms caked with mud, the tops wet and covered in tiny blades of grass.

Of course.

Ron walked across the fields to get to school from the council estate where he lived. Dillon could smell that wet grass and fresh dirt smell, which as strong as it was didn't overpower the fear which seemed to be hanging at the back of his throat. There was no way out of it now. He would have to go through with it and deal with the aftermath later.

"What on earth is happening here?"

The laughter stopped, and just like that, the spell was broken as those watching dispersed, leaving just Ron, his friends and Dillon behind. Mr Ashley, the head of science, stood at the entrance, hands on hips, tweed jacket open and exposing his gut, which strained against his slightly yellowed shirt and threatened to pop off the buttons holding it back. The little hair he had was combed over, a salt and pepper series of strips pasted from left to right across a shiny dome of a head, in what looked to be a failed effort to cling on to a long lost youth

He looked from Dillon to Ron, then back to Dillon. "Well?"

"Nothing sir," Ron said, hiding away the bully everyone knew was there and trying to play nice. "We were just playing a game."

"Is that true, Thomas? Were you and Spengler playing some kind of game?"

Dillon got up, checking his knees and brushing the grit from his pants.

"Well?" Mr Ashley said, his coffee and tobacco breath pungent.

Dillon shrugged, which was all Ashley needed. He turned towards Ron. "I've told you about this before, Spengler. See me in my office after school."

But sir," Ron started, glaring at Dillon. "It was just a game it was just -"

"I don't want to hear another word. My office, after school. Understood?"

"Yes." Ron mumbled.

"Yes what?"

"Yes, *Sir*."

"Good. Now get to class, all of you."

With that, Mr Ashley was gone, perhaps to grab

another coffee or quick smoke before the school day started. Ron's friends too dispersed, glad to have been let off the hook. Ron looked ready to explode. His cheeks were spotted red, eyes cold and emotionless. He walked past Dillon, pride bruised but lesson learned.

As he walked past he leaned close, eyes sly and full of venom. "I'll get you for this, Tramp," he whispered.

Dillon didn't reply, he simply watched as his bully disappeared into the building. He wasn't quite sure how to react to the threat. He was sure that Ron would soon find something else to focus his attention on other than him, even so, it still didn't stop him from feeling absolutely terrified about whatever Ron might do to get his revenge. The first bell rang, and the other children started to filter into the school. Dillon tried to shake off how afraid he was, then picked up his bag and went into school. He had started the school year hoping to have a better year than the one before. Already, he was just hoping to get by without getting a beating.

2.

It was three weeks later, during Friday morning registration, that Dillon received both good and bad news almost at the same time. The bad news was that Ron was due to return to school the following Monday after being suspended for fighting with another pupil. He had already been given a weeks' worth of detention after the incident outside the school with Dillon, and the word amongst the pupils, if you chose to believe it, was that he was waiting for the opportune time to get his revenge and beat Dillon to a pulp.

For a few days, Dillon was sick with fear, but if

the rumour was true then Ron didn't show any signs of living up to it. If anything, he mostly left Dillon alone, which in itself might have been just a ploy to make him lower his guard. Despite the reprieve, Dillon still expected that one day soon, Ron would take his revenge. Of course, just because Ron was currently enjoying a quiet phase, didn't mean that life was perfect for Dillon. No matter what he did, people still laughed. They still pointed at him and insulted him. They still called him the same hurtful names and laughed at the way he was dressed.

"You're an easy target,", his mother had said when he'd told her what was happening. "You need to stand up for yourself and show these people you won't be bossed around."

He couldn't explain to her that it wasn't like that. He couldn't make her see how cruel a place the school yard was and how, no matter how hard he tried, they wouldn't accept him for who he was.

He was sitting in class, thinking about his mother's words when his teacher, Mrs Simons, called out his name. He looked up at her, eyebrows raised, ignoring the whispers and chuckles aimed at him. The seven words she said next were ones he'd been waiting to hear for what felt like an eternity.

'Dillon, you're the milk monitor on Monday.'

It took all of his effort not to scream in delight. This was what he had been waiting for. This was the opportunity to prove to his classmates that he was more than they thought he was. He smiled, and even the whispered insults combined with the way John Groves kept snickering and kicking the back of his seat seemed distant.

Milk monitor.

To Dillon it was a massive responsibility and one he was looking forward to completing as best he could. The rest of the day went by like a hazy half-dream. At lunch, he sat on the table with the other children who were shunned and ridiculed for various reasons, eating his sandwich from the tatty red Transformers lunch-box with the broken handle. The job of milk monitor was one of responsibility. Whoever had that job would command the respect of the other students. He would be in charge of distributing the morning milk to the rest of the class and anyone who misbehaved wouldn't get a bottle. It was a school rule. His mind tried to turn its attention towards Ron's imminent return, and what that could mean to the period of relative peace. For Monday morning at least, Ron would have to do as *he* said. Accept the milk that *he* chose to hand over and be nice about it, or go without.

Power.

Finally a sense of worth.

The idea alone excited him.

Monday couldn't come quickly enough.

3.

The weekend was spent mostly thinking about his special task on Monday morning.

He had spent Saturday riding his BMX with Billy, both of them making sure to avoid the places where they might bump into other kids from the school (Ron especially). They had talked as always about their favourite shows, the cartoons they liked, the action figures they had and wanted, but Dillon was never quite engaged in the conversation, his mind fixed firmly on Monday.

They had talked about the latest episode of the

A-Team, and who their favourite characters were. (Billy couldn't look past B.A Baracus, whereas Dillon was more of a 'Howling Mad' Murdoch fan). They had swapped a few *Star Wars* figures, Dillon reluctantly trading his Luke Skywalker in Storm trooper disguise for the Yoda figure from *The Empire Strikes Back*, which he had wanted for a while but didn't have the heart to ask his mother for.

On Sunday, after eating dinner, Dillon sat outside on the back step, enjoying the solitude of the overgrown yard as day melted into night. The sky was clear as the fading day finally revealed the first stars. It was perfect. He was excited, looking forward to what the next day would bring. It seemed like he had been waiting for this forever, for this one opportunity to show that he was something special. The idea of Ron coming back didn't even bother him, not anymore. He could handle whatever he wanted to dish out, just like he always had.

Dillon pulled his knees up to his chin and smiled.

Nothing was going to ruin his big day.

Nothing at all.

4.

He woke early on Monday morning, setting his alarm for five thirty. Daylight was already bleeding into the sky, and as he looked out of the window he was sure it was going to be a perfect day. Dillon decided to leave for school early for the simple reason that he wanted to avoid any kind of run in with Ron that might ruin his day. He had kissed his mother goodbye and set off on the ten-minute walk to school. Being out so early was bliss. There were no other children around, none of those who laughed at him or pointed. None of those people who used him as a way to make themselves feel better by insulting his clothes or his hair. It was almost like it was a secret time of day designed just for him, the perfect start to his perfect Monday.

He approached the building, hands in pockets, loose sole of his shoe slapping against the concrete. He would have to have his mother glue them again as he knew she didn't have the money to replace them yet. The building had a very different feel when its yard was devoid of children. It was strange to see it so bare. It almost made him feel like a trespasser as he walked towards the entrance. He could see a scattering of cars in the car park, Mr Ashley's Ford parked close to the gates. Dillon wondered if he'd made a start on creating his uniquely pungent morning coffee and tobacco breath for the day. He smiled at the idea of his teacher standing in front of the mirror and brushing his teeth with coffee flavoured toothpaste. It was funny, and he reminded himself to tell Billy about it later, if he remembered. He entered the school, the cavernous corridors long and quiet, polished floors echoing as he walked them, loose sole slapping a unique rhythm.

Click slap.

Click slap.

Click slap.

He went first to his classroom, poking his head into the door. Mrs Simons wasn't there, but her red coat was hooked over the back of her chair. He counted the desks, mouthing the numbers to himself as he tallied up the numbers. Twenty-three pupils including him. He repeated the number over and over in his head, committing it to memory. The last thing he wanted to happen was for him to miscount and for someone to have to go without. Not after he had waited for so long to do such an important job. He took a deep breath, inhaling the slightly musty, polish smell of the room. To see the building so quiet was almost like exploring a place for the first time. It was like the time he and Billy had wandered the woodland behind the school pretending to be explorers like Indiana Jones, only this time it was a solo mission for him alone. Billy was probably only just getting up to start the day anyway. Dillon nodded to himself then closed the door and walked down the corridor towards the dining hall. Like the rest of the school, it seemed so much bigger than he remembered. Empty tables and circular desks waited for children to inhabit them. He glanced at the spot where Ron had knocked his food tray out of his hands, spilling gravy and potatoes all over the floor. The laughter then had been awful, amplified by the high ceilings. He had gone hungry that day, but the pain inside had been worse.

He shook it off, determined not to let anything ruin his good mood.

The kitchen was at the back of the hall behind the serving area. He walked there, sole of his broken shoe still flopping against the floor. The clock on the wall said it was just after eight thirty. School started at eight fifty-five. Plenty of time. The kitchen was cool, and other than the buzz of the fridge, was silent and deserted. The crates of milk were on the table, one for each class. He wasn't sure what time it was delivered, but assumed the caretaker, Mr Ruddock, let them in. The dinner ladies wouldn't be in until at least mid-morning, meaning that, for the time being, the kitchen was his alone. He walked around the table, running his hand across the crates, each containing the miniature bottles of milk, one crate for each class in his year. On the counter top beside them was a bulk pack of blue straws. Dillon went to these first, recalling the number he had memorised and counted out twenty-three of them, taking them to the first crate. He paused, flicking his top lip with his tongue as he counted the bottles, lips moving in silence. There were thirty bottles in the crate, and so he removed seven of them, putting them on the counter top.

Satisfied, he shrugged out of his backpack, set it on the floor and took out the box he had brought from home. He set it on the counter and opened it, removing the syringe and one of the bottles of liquid that were packed along with it. He traced the word on the bottle with his finger, struggling to spell it in his head.

In-su-lin.

His mother had to have it when she was feeling weak. The doctor had given her it as he said she was dibetric, or maybe it was diabeteric, he couldn't recall the right word for it. He remembered the way she had taken him aside and shown him how to use the syringe, and said that if for any reason he came home and she was asleep and couldn't wake up, that he had to inject her with it. She had, of course, warned him that it was dangerous, and that he wasn't to touch it unless it was in an emergency. She made him repeat it, to tell her he understood. He had asked her how dangerous, and she had told him that if it was given to someone who didn't need it, they could die. That had scared him, and he hadn't touched the box that was kept in the fridge until that morning.

He took the syringe and pierced the lid of the bottle, pulling up the plunger and filling the tube with the clear liquid. He held the syringe up to the light; unable to believe it could be so dangerous.

It looked just like water.

Carefully and methodically, he injected the syringe into the silver foil cover of the first milk bottle and squirted it inside, the insulin mixing into the milk without any trace. He nodded, satisfied. It was all going to work out exactly as he had planned it. There were three bottles of insulin in the box he had taken from the fridge, and he used them all. When it was done, he took the pack of blue straws and pushed into each of the puncture marks he had made, hiding any evidence of what he had done. He was calm as he worked, humming the theme from *The A-Team* as he carefully arranged the bottles, setting his own, unspoiled milk towards the back of the crate and away from the others.

When it was done, he put the syringe and empty bottles back in the box, then the box back in his bag. He stepped back and admired his handiwork. It was perfect. And although the wait to do it had been long, it was worth it. He stood in silence, watching the clock and waiting. At eight fifty-five, the bell rang, and he listened to the thunder of feet and chatter as the school was filled with pupils.

Normally, he hated that sound.

Today, it filled him with joy.

He thought about them, the people who had let him be bullied, the people who had laughed at him and called him worthless. There was a sadness in him, but no regret. None whatsoever. He heard the other milk monitors coming towards the kitchen, chatting and joking, ready to count out their straws and prepare the milk for their classmates.

Colin Decker was first through the door, followed by Laura Perkins and the other five milk monitors, one selected from each class. They gave him that look, the one he was used to.

Distain.

Hate.

Repulsion.

None of it mattered anymore. Dillon picked up his crate and walked to the door.

"What happened here? Did you do this?" Decker said as he looked at the table. Dillon followed his gaze. Each of the crates had already been prepped, each bottle of milk pierced with blue straws. He locked eyes with Decker and nodded.

"Oh," Decker said, glancing at the others. "Thanks, Dillon."

He nodded again. It was always this way. Laughter and jokes, finger pointing and ridicule when there was a crowd, but fine and civil when there were less of them. He had seen the pattern. Dillon walked out of the kitchen, pushing it open crate first and headed through the hall. He could hear the other milk monitors laughing at him as he left, but it was okay. Let them laugh. By the end of the day, he was sure he would be laughing too.

He walked through the dining hall and out into the corridor. He paused there for a second, taking it all in, savouring the moment, then set off, milk bottles rattling as he walked towards his classroom. He started to hum the theme tune to the *A-Team* as he entered the classroom and gently nudged the door closed behind him.

Anna

By Matthew Hickman

1.

Some people say that being a parent is the greatest gift on Earth.

I would agree, but being a single parent can be twice the hard work, sacrifice, effort, commitment and pain, but upon reflection I believe it has twice the rewards. Two years ago, when Anna was just eleven years old, my husband, Stuart, was involved in a serious car collision on the journey home from work late one evening. The head-on collision had left both cars a complete mangled mess of steel, broken glass, flames and limbs on the country lane, just four miles from our family home in the rural countryside of North West England.

We were alerted by a uniformed police officer at the front door of our country home, informing us that Stuart had been rushed immediately to the hospital in the village, after 8:30 pm. Still in shock, I jumped into my car with Anna and headed to the hospital, every type of panicked thought running through my mind. Upon arrival, we were informed by the doctor that, despite their best efforts, his injuries were too severe and that he had died shortly after admission. Immediately, we both broke down in tears. Just like that, we were left heart-broken and alone, mother and daughter, by some other faceless driver who was killed upon impact. This faceless driver who was suspected to have been under the influence of drugs and alcohol. I made a promise there and then that Anna was my sole responsibility and I would do anything I had to do to protect and nurture her.

The following months proved a very difficult time.

A battle with the insurance company over a technicality in Stuart's policy initially delayed the pay-out. This, coupled with the costs to cover his funeral and attempting to satisfy any other outstanding creditors meant that it was nearly six months before we were financially settled. This time had been a rough ride for Anna, having to try to come to terms with her loss and varied emotions whilst attempting to offer love and support really took its toll on the girl. I had seen her teacher, Miss Hughes, a few times about her changes at school, not in the way of ill behaviour or standards of work slipping, more in the way of becoming more withdrawn from her usual group of friends and quieter in general. I'd spoken to Anna following these meetings with her teacher and she shrugged it off as just feeling down. Sometimes, she just preferred her own company. Accepting that she had been through so much, I agreed that maybe she just needed her own space and didn't push the issue.

A couple of weeks went by and I received another phone call from her teacher asking if I could pop into the school to see her. Upon chatting with Anna's teacher she informed me that, in registration that morning, Anna had run out of the classroom in tears and did not return until after the lunchtime break. When questioned by her teacher about her actions, she claimed that Jonathan, a boy in her class, had taken a broken chair with a faulty leg from the back of the classroom and swapped it with the chair at her desk. As she sat down, the chair collapsed and she ended up on her back, the laughing stock of the classroom. I promised Miss Hughes that I would speak to Anna that evening and try to get to the cause of the problem. It didn't seem too difficult to work out in my mind, it was obvious: Anna was being bullied.

2.

I waited around after seeing the teacher, to pick Anna up after school. She exited the school gates as usual, with no indications of anything wrong, apart from being a little quiet. As we drove home she sat in the passenger seat beside me, staring blankly out of the window, her mind on things other than answering my questions.

"How was your day?"

"What did you have for lunch?"

I resisted the urge to probe further.

I held back my tears at the thought that she couldn't confide in me about her problems, she couldn't bring herself to tell me about the incident in the classroom this morning, or where she had spent the rest of the day. I knew one thing; Anna was my daughter; she had already been through a great deal of heartache and pain, and one of the boys at school was not going to continue to make her life hell. When we get home, we were having this out.

Upon arrival, she went to dart upstairs into her bedroom, but I asked her to sit down in the living room with me. A puzzled look, but she obliged. Not knowing where to start, I blurted out, "Where did you go after registration at school this morning?"

A look of shock appeared on her face, followed by realisation of that fact that I knew. Initially, she tried to bluff and claim that she'd been feeling ill and had gone to see the school nurse, until I informed her that I had spoken with her teacher and she had told me about the boy and the prank. She still refused to give anything up for a few minutes until I pleaded with her that, if something was going on, I need to know so that I could help.

After a short while she sat in my arms sobbing, tears running down her pink cheeks, telling me about the events that had been going on at school. There were three boys in total; Jonathan Willis, Max Bennett and Richard Banks. Their abuse had ranged from the odd name calling like 'orphan' or 'Annie' while she sat in the lunch hall, to tripping her up in corridors or stealing her bag and throwing it down the stairs. Each incident resulted in a mass eruption of laughter and cheers from the other pupils, and utter humiliation for Anna.

Heartbroken and deflated by Anna's confession of these cruel pranks led to anger that the teachers in the school had allowed it to get to this point, and guilt that I had not seen any of the signs and been able to act sooner. Questioning my integrity as a parent, I wiped the tears from her cheeks, kissed her forehead and explained to Anna that I would be seeing Mrs Maguire, the head teacher, at the school the next day, and that I would get things straightened out. She smiled and thanked me, but she didn't look convinced.

The following morning, I sat opposite Mrs Maguire, a stern-looking character with piercing eyes and a strong jaw, and retold the events that my daughter had poured out to me the previous evening. I gave the names of the boys that Anna had stated, their taunting and details of the verbal, physical and intimidating abuse. I explained about Stuart's death and the subsequent struggles, and how Anna had been affected by it all. She took various notes and explained that she, and indeed the school, did not take bullying lightly and that appropriate measures would be taken with the boys and to form an appropriate course of action for prevention. I left her office feeling relieved and satisfied.

Well, until I went to pick Anna up from school.

3.

I sat in my car at the school gates twiddling with the radio, trying to find a decent station. I glanced up as Anna walked down the driveway towards me. Even without speaking to her, I could see that something was wrong; her eyes were puffy as if she'd been crying and her brown curly hair was a total mess on top of her head. Without a word, she climbed into the car and threw her bag into the foot well with a huff. I was about to question what the hell had happened, when I noticed that she was missing her coat. I asked her if she'd left it in the cloakroom and she replied that Jonathan, Max and Richard had cornered her behind the science block. They had all been told off by their form teachers, so said that she had to pay. They had threatened that every day, they would take something from her and dump it in a bin or bury it somewhere on the school grounds, as a punishment for being a 'grass'. The coat was just the beginning. Anna burst into tears.

The following morning, once again, I sat opposite Mrs Maguire in her office and told her about the coat and the further threats to Anna and her property. "These boys are getting worse," I added. Once more, I was assured that this would be looked into and dealt with, but this time she added that she'd personally spoken to the boys involved and that they'd categorically denied any of the accusations made by Anna, claiming that it was attention seeking on her behalf, and that if there were no evidence provided or unless they were caught in the act, there was little she could do. "Would there be any reason for Anna to want to seek attention?" she asked. I shook my head in disbelief. "Just do your job and sort these boys out," I replied.

I stood up and stormed out of her office, this time, feeling annoyed and let down.

That afternoon, I sat in my car as Anna walked down the driveway toward me. I squinted, not quite believing what my eyes were seeing. I jumped out of the car and ran towards her, panic and revulsion in my stomach as I quickly approached; she was absolutely covered from head to foot in blood.

I reached her within a few seconds and she was, once again, sobbing uncontrollably. I grabbed her to see where the blood was coming from. It clotted in her mangled brown hair, streaked her uniform and skirt, and ran down both sides of her legs. I frantically searched her all over before breathing a massive sigh of relief that it wasn't her blood.

Apparently, the three boys had decided that they were going to assault her on the way home with water balloons filled with red paint. Furious, I asked her to show me who these boys were, but they had apparently sneaked through the fence at the back of the school and over the railway to avoid being seen. This was starting to get out of hand. I would give the school one last chance to sort this out and then I would take matters into my own hands. The next morning, I supplied the head teacher with photographs of what had been done to Anna, and advised that if something wasn't done, I would consider going to the police.

She took the photographs and looked at them in pure revulsion and shame. She assured me that enquiries would be made.

4.

Home time once again and today was different; today Anna skipped down the driveway towards my car, full of joy and all smiles. She jumped into the passenger seat and immediately gave me a hug and a kiss. Dumbstruck, I asked her what had happened. She replied that it was fantastic, two people had witnessed the paint attack and had reported it to the school authorities. The three boys had been called into the office that morning and had been indefinitely suspended from school. At last, it seemed that a little bit of justice had been served our way.

I breathed a sigh of relief and gave her a hug. Hopefully, this would be the start to the end of her ordeal. Happier than I had been since I learned of all this mess, I decided to treat us to McDonalds on the way home. We sat in the restaurant, talking away happily and eating our burgers, when Anna suddenly stopped talking.

"What's the matter?" I asked, but she didn't respond. Her gaze was fixed on something outside in the car park, she started to shake and turned pale. Asking what the problem was, I followed her line of sight and saw them; three boys outside on their bikes, grinning at us. "Anna, is that who I think it is?" I asked, no response came which confirmed my suspicion. I grabbed her by the hand and dragged her out of the seat, through the doors of the restaurant and quickly over to the three boys.

"*Are you the little bastards that have been picking on my daughter?*" I screamed at them. "You're lucky you got away as lightly as you did."

The largest of the three stepped forward, a skinny looking kid with blonde spiked hair and blue grey eyes.

A hint of bum fluff sat on his top lip, in lieu of a proper moustache, to complete his scowling little face. A rolled up cigarette sat burning away between his fingers.

"As we said to Maguire, love, we ain't done nuffin', it's her that's attention seeking. I mean, just 'cos her old man snuffed it…oh, we're sorry, *love*, forgot it affects you an'all." He smirked. Suddenly, I saw red. I don't know how I mustered the strength to keep my hands off him and suppress the urge to throttle him there and then in the car park.

"Stay away from my daughter or, I swear to God. *I will kill you!*" I screamed at him

All of a sudden, the other two reprobates joined in with a chorus of "Ooooooh!" before an outburst of laughter. I considered punching the ring leader, which I assume was Jonathan, in the mouth, but it would only lead to further trouble.

I grabbed Anna by the arm and pulled her towards the car, glancing quickly over my shoulder as the three boys continued to goad. "See you around, *Annie*," shouted one of the boys from the rear while the other two were blowing kisses and throwing hand gestures.

In the car, I told Anna to belt up and sped off, wheel spinning from the car park. I felt an anger running through me that I'd never felt before and Anna was sat beside me in floods of tears. The journey back home was spent in silence aside from the odd sob and sniffle coming from my little passenger. These boys had no respect at all, not one slight bit of remorse for their actions, such hatred at such a young age. I pulled from the road into the long driveway of our property and continued slowly through the trees into the clearway of the main building, which is when I saw the damage.

Two of the windows on the front of the house were shattered, presumably smashed from outside by a brick or similar object being thrown through them. In two-foot-high painted graffiti across the front door, the word 'GRASS' had been sprayed in red paint.

5.

I sat in the police station opposite the officer who had been assigned to take our statement, running through the details of the subsequent events leading up until now; the name calling, the physical abuse, the stolen property, the paint attack and violent damage to our property, the desecration of our home. He took my statement down in writing, asking a few questions along the way and making further notes while remaining fairly impartial. "Are you sure you have included everything that you feel is necessary?" he asked.

"I think so, are you going to go and arrest these people?" I asked.

He mumbled something vaguely about the families in question being known to the police, and assured us that someone would be going round and having words.

"*Words?*" I screamed. "These animals should be *locked up*."

He asked me to remain calm. They would continue with their enquiries, question the neighbours to see if anyone witnessed the criminal damage, speak to the families, the boys in particular, and warn that they stay away, but as there is no evidence at this point, they would be unable to take things any further. I tried to reason with him, stating that I knew it and he knew it, but he remained adamant that he had to follow procedure. I should go home and contact them if anything else should happen. They would be in touch in due course.

Anna cried all of the way home from the police station, clearly upset by the lack of justice and action from our law enforcement. I tried to reassure her that everything would turn out okay and that the police would do their job, it just may take a bit of time.

She continued to cry softly. "I will never be free of those boys, I hate them." I held my breath and squeezed her knee. I felt utterly useless.

Sudden dark thoughts started to enter into my mind. "One way or the other, you will, sweetheart, even if I have to get rid of them myself." I winked at her and she gave me a puzzled look, then started to laugh.

Upon arriving home, I called the local glazing firm to come and patch up the two broken windows and paid them for their job once completed. Time was getting on for 7:30 pm. I asked Anna if she would like to take a bath before me, and she told me to go on ahead. She would go in next as she sat on the sofa in the living room, headphones plugged into her laptop. I slowly climbed the stairs and ran a hot bath, filling the room with hot steam, and slipped in. For a few seconds, in the pure bliss and relaxation, I completely forgot about the awful events leading up to now, but shortly, those dark thoughts started to enter my mind again. She was my daughter, I'm all that she has, I can't let her down, and I can't expose her to danger like this.

If I need to, I will do anything to protect her.

Anything.

I must have stayed in the bath for about twenty minutes, the stress of the day slowly soaking away, but struggling to stay awake, I decided that it was best to get out and refill the bath for Anna. It had been a long day for her too.

I quickly threw on a dressing gown and wrapped a towel round my head. The water had drained by now, so I started to fill the bath with fresh water. I walked to the landing and shouted downstairs for Anna to come up and take her bath. A few seconds passed, with no response, so I shouted for her again.

Again, no response.

Kids and their music, it's a miracle that she wasn't deaf.

I walked downstairs and into the living room where she had been sat, the sight of unimaginable horror before me turned my stomach. I screamed at the top of my lungs. Anna lay on the sofa unconscious, her white school blouse soaked in blood, her right arm, slit at the wrist, hung down over the side of the sofa. A pool of blood had gathered below and started to congeal on the carpet.

Her left wrist, also slit and rapidly leaking blood, rested on her chest, the fingers of the hand curled round a large butcher's knife from the kitchen. I rushed into the kitchen and grabbed a handful of tea towels from the drawer. I began desperately wrapping them around her wrists to try and stem the bleeding, whilst speaking to the emergency services through sheets of hot tears, giving them the details of the emergency and our address. I sat hugging Anna, rocking back and forth, her pulse was still there – albeit very weak.

My poor baby. I knew things had been bad for her, but to try and take her own life?

I sat holding her, waiting for the ambulance to arrive. Just then, I glanced over to the screen of her laptop, open at the message section of her Facebook page. The screen displayed a message, from Jonathon Willis, that read: *"You fucking grass, we're cumming for you and you're bitch of a mother 2nite. We will rape and kill you both.*"

I sat in the hospital in the intensive care unit with Anna. Her condition had been stabilised and the doctors told me that she had lost a lot of blood, but the cuts had not been fatal as the wounds were not deep enough. I leaned over and stroked her curly brown hair, a peaceful look on her pale face as she slept in the hospital bed. I looked down at my clothes; covered in dried red stains, as were my hands.

That's my daughter's blood on them, I thought.

My thoughts returned to Jonathan Willis, Max Bennett, and Richard Banks.

This would be the first blood spilled.

6.

"Wake up," I said to him.

There was no response, so I gave him a few gentle slaps on the cheeks to bring him back around. He groggily looked round the room, observing the plastic sheets that had been roughly pinned to the walls and floor, for ease of being discarded later.

I had kitted out one of the rooms of the house for my little acts of revenge on these three.

A mere forty-watt bulb hanging from the ceiling offered sufficient illumination for my needs, two extra strong hasps had been connected to the outside and the inside of the door, with two padlocks ensuring that once someone was in the room, they were not getting out. Well, not in one piece anyway. Albeit a situation born from necessity, I must admit that I'd gotten things down to a fine art now, and my little hobby had become a thing of morbid enjoyment.

He continued to glance round the room, a look of confusion upon his face, confusion that quickly turned to fear when he saw me standing before him. His eyes widened like an animal about to be hit by a car, and he shouted something, something that was muffled by the duct tape covering his mouth. He looked down, trying to move his arms and legs that had also been strapped to the chair; he was going nowhere and he knew it.

Suddenly, a wet stain started to appear from the front of his grey boxer shorts, and started to drip down his leg.

"Jonathon, you dirty pig. At least your friends had the dignity to hold themselves, well at least until I started working on them." I smiled, and gave him a quick wink.

Again, he pulled at the restraints and tried to move. I continued to explain that he wasn't going anywhere, and that he was going to be spending the last moments of his life in absolute agony. The aroma of fear emanated from him, and began to fill the room.

As with his two predecessors, I started with his legs, there's less chance of them getting away if they cannot walk - it's a solid safety precaution.

Max, my first victim, didn't get away. He got a leg free and managed to frantically kick out at me, causing mild annoyance until I managed to smash his kneecap in with a lump hammer. For old Jonathon here, I tried something a little more inventive. I picked up the large G clamp from the table beside me, the type with the adjustable thread, which allows devices to be clamped between the jaws. I calmly hooked it over his kneecap and tightened until I heard a slight cracking noise, then looked him in the eye. "This may sting a little."

I grabbed the handle of the clamp and violently twisted it as far as it would go, in a single twisting motion. It gave off a satisfying *Crack*.

After one quick movement, the kneecap popped off and hung beneath the skin. He threw his head back, and his first scream was muffled from beneath the duct tape. It was ignored. One knee down, one to go. As I attached the clamp onto his second knee, he started to hyperventilate and closed his eyes in preparation.

I gave him a minute, which must have hurt a little, judging by his attempts to struggle free and the tears running down his cheeks. I selected my hammer from the table of items, this was always one of the funnier parts. I walked over to him and knelt down on one knee, hammer in hand.

I danced my fingers through the air. *Eenie meenie miney*… and on *moe*, I smashed the hammer down to his foot and two of his toes exploded, offering no more resistance to the hammer than if they were eggshells. Blood and flesh squirted out, and a little landed on my knee, along with a nail. Most of the time, you can get two in one shot, followed with a single shot for each big toe. Another six blows with the hammer and Jonathon had no toes left. Again, with the screaming, he was sweating all over and his eyes rolled back in his head. "Don't you get passing out on me yet," I warned.

My next preference is the fingernails, at first I struggled as they kept snapping off, leaving parts behind. The trick is to have a good solid grip on the pliers and give them a sharp tug outwards, as well as upwards. I grabbed his hand and extended his index finger forcefully between my fingers and thumb, the filthy nail aiming towards me. "Do you never wash your hands, boy?" I gripped with the pliers and pulled. A slight spray of goo, and it was off in one clear motion. I repeated this another four times, after which, he looked like he was getting weaker.

I took a look at him. Pathetic, the big bully. I ripped the duct tape from his mouth. “Anything you want to say before you die, you little bastard?”

“Please… please,” he began groaning. I couldn’t believe it; did he really think that I was going to *let* him go?

“K... K… Kill… me,” he finished. I smiled. *Oh, don’t worry, you can bank on that.*

I swaggered back over to my table of tools with a smirk on my face. After a few seconds, torn between my remaining choices, I selected the corkscrew.

With my first victim, Max, I had used a Stanley blade to cut across his torso and chest with large, ugly, ragged cuts, unfortunately, it caused him to bleed out too quickly. The corkscrew, to the same effect, leaves a nasty wound, but less blood. I wanted these bastards to suffer as long as possible. I raised the corkscrew and Jonathon’s eyes went wide before I brought it down and struck it into his chest, just below his shoulder. He let out a deafening scream, loud enough to make his throat bleed, I yanked it back out, a satisfying popping sound as the coil retracted, dragging little clumps of flesh and skin with it. The ugly opening that was left gaped, spewing a thick, steady trickle of blood. I flicked the end of the corkscrew to clear the fleshy debris before smashing it into his stomach; each time the same result, his screams echoed around the room. By the time he was hit with the fifth blow, his screams had died down to a mere sobbing sound.

I checked the time, I had ten minutes. “Is there anything that you would like to say at this point, Jonathon?” I looked down at him but he didn’t reply, he barely had any strength left in him, but there was still a shred of life. I selected the large butcher’s knife from the table, and with no word of warning I thrust it down, way into his thigh, then through it, the tip of the blade embedding into the seat below. A howl of pain ensued. Blood squirted across my body and smiling face.

I asked him; "Do you know, Jonathan, they say that the eyes are the windows to the soul? Have you ever heard that saying?" I held up the corkscrew so that the very tip caught the light and gave off a little reflection in the glare. He gave no response, his eyes looked straight at me defeated, dying. With all the strength I could muster, I thrust the corkscrew point straight into his eye, as far as it would go, his head buckled back, and tried to jerk forward a few times, he coughed up a mouthful of blood and his head dropped back, hanging over the top of the chair. He was dead.

At that moment, to my surprise, I felt the strangest thing. It was a feeling of guilt. I looked down at the boy and the spoilt mess of his young body. I held up the back of my hands, looking at his blood and gore slowly running down my forearms. The moment lasted only a few seconds. I turned my hands over to see the pink ragged scars running across both of my wrists, the everlasting reminder of the cruelty subjected by the actions of these boys. The feeling of guilt quickly turned to feelings of satisfaction.

7.

I turned my back, he was going nowhere.

I opened the door from the summer house, and walked down the corridor toward the kitchen. I stuck my head through the gap in the door, looking for signs of movement. Satisfied, I proceeded, nobody in sight until a few seconds later, when Mum walked in with an empty coffee cup and started to move toward the sink.

She froze on the spot, a surprised look in her eye.

"Hi, Mum." I said.

She stood rooted on the spot, offering no reply. As I started to run towards her, my arms thrown wide open ready for an embrace, she stumbled backwards three steps, doubling back, almost falling over her own feet.

"*Don't come near me!*"

I halted my approach, surely she knew that I meant her no harm? I stamped my heels down on the kitchen tiles attempting to halt, and skidded on the trail of blood that had been dripping from my arms and legs, then fell flat on my arse on the floor. I started to giggle.

I gazed down at myself, covered in blood, gore, and parts of Jonathan. Mum shook her head and then started to laugh. "I just changed my dress," she said, "looks like I will have to mop again, and it looks like you've had had twice as much fun with him than with the last two. Get your arse upstairs, girl, the bath is running. I'll put the taxi back. You've got ten minutes."

As I ran upstairs to the bathroom, I heard my Mum's parting remark.

"Kids."

Dig

By Alice J. Black

"Ben," Connie called from her stance at the kitchen sink. "Ben, come here."

The sound of his loping steps came through from the front room as his slippers dragged on the tiled carpet. He made his way across to the window [illegible] a man accustomed to keeping his wife happy, Connie turned and answered, "Yes, dear?" Pushing his glasses up his nose, Ben leaned on the sink, where Connie was washing up the last few dishes, and peered out of the window alongside his wife.

As she glanced down, Connie noticed the bulbous veins on the back of his hand, the papery-thin skin stretched tight. Looking up, she noticed his whiskers coming in grey around thick jowls. *When did we get so old?* She felt it too - the constant weighing of age on her bones, her joints, making her sag. She saw it in the mirror every day when she put on her moisturiser. It sure hadn't done her skin any favours judging by the wrinkles that seemed to multiply overnight. Shaking herself, Connie thrust the thoughts from her mind. Now wasn't the time to contemplate getting old, it was the time to appreciate youth.

Nodding to the window, she spoke. "Young Jessica has been digging in the garden all day."

The pair stood at the window and watched the next door neighbour's little girl as she worked in her garden over the fence. It seemed that she was digging a trench of some sort right in the middle of their lush green lawn.

"I hope her mum knows about that," Ben commented. "Imagine what you would think finding your lawn in that state?" He shook his head as wiry arms crossed over his wilting chest.

Connie nodded. "I know. Perhaps we should mention it to Pauline?"

"I don't know." He sucked in a deep breath. "She might see it as interfering."

"Oh relax, Ben. She's just a child and it's just a voice of concern, is all. Imagine if one of our lot had been doing that without us knowing. I would have gladly listened to the neighbour."

Ben shrugged. "I see what you mean, but then, back in our day, the neighbours knew what community spirit was. Just be careful, if it comes back on you, don't say I didn't warn you." He wiggled his greying eyebrows.

"Maybe I'll just go talk to Jessica." She glanced at the girl again. The ten year old wore plain blue jeans and a t-shirt that rode up her back each time she thrust the shovel into the hole she was creating. Her brown hair was tied back in pigtails and dirt marred her pale skin. Her brow was creased as she worked, determined.

"You never used to be so bothered about neighbourly activities." He turned from the sink and turned the kettle on. "Tea?"

"Coffee, dear. And you never used to drink so much tea either." She winked.

"Look what retirement has done to us, Connie. I think we need to go back to work."

"Speak for yourself." She tutted.

"Would you settle for a trip out?"

Her pursed lips melted into a smile. "Sure, what have you got in mind?"

***

When Connie and Ben returned from their trip, the sun was setting across their back garden, the warm orange rays a welcome sight. “Want a cuppa?” Ben asked as Connie instantly moved to the back door.

She dropped him a knowing smile before responding, “Yes, please.” Unlocking the back door, Connie stepped into the golden rays of light at the back of the house. Bees buzzed across the flower beds on the right and the bird feeder in the centre was still thrumming with life. But that wasn't what caught her eye.

As she glanced to her left across the small brown fence that bordered each of the gardens in the estate, she caught a glimpse of something moving. Creeping forward, she watched. With each step she took, more and more came into view. First the top of a head, then the shoulders and then the shovel. It was Jessica still hard at work. As she took another step the hole came into view. By now, it was so big it could have been a small pond.

“Hello, Jessica,” Connie spoke.

The girl whipped around, startled, but on seeing Connie, a smile curved on her lips and she dropped her shovel. Climbing out of the hole with a boost on stick-thin arms, Jessica heaved until she was standing straight and dusted herself off. Connie finally got a proper look at the girl. Mud smeared most of her denim jeans and her t-shirt was caked with sweat and streaks of dirt. Her hair was still in pigtails but they were loosening, hair becoming frizzy in the heat. “Hi, Mrs. Dowins.” She stepped up to the fence, hands pressed behind her back as she grinned.

“Have you had a nice day?”

“Oh yes, I've been out in the sunshine all day.”

"I can see that." Connie nodded with a smile. "What on earth are you doing?"

"I'm just digging." She offered a simple shrug, her smile expanding.

"Digging for what, dear?"

"Just digging," the girl repeated. Connie noticed she had a tooth missing.

"I see. Did you lose your tooth?"

"Yesterday." She nodded definitively. "I put it under my pillow just like mummy said and I got a shiny fifty pence."

"Wow, that's brilliant. Did you put it in your piggy bank?"

Jessica shook her head. "I bought an ice cream when the van came around."

"I see."

"All this digging is hard work."

Connie couldn't contain the chuckle that escaped her mouth. *Children say the funniest things.* "I dare say it does look exhausting. Is your mum around?"

"She's asleep," Jessica shook her head, pigtails flying. "She's not very well."

"Oh, perhaps I should come in and see her."

"No, that's okay. She doesn't want visitors. I've been looking after her."

Connie bit her lip. Pauline was a single mother and was usually on hand to steer Jessica in the right direction. She wondered whether digging a giant hole in the back garden would be considered normal in their household. Still, as Ben would say, it wasn't her right to meddle. "Okay, dear. Well you let me know if she needs anything at all. I don't mind."

"Okay. Thank you, Mrs. Dowins, I'll tell her."

Instead of going back to her digging, Jessica made her way back inside the house, closing the door with a soft click. All Connie could think about was whether the girl had wiped her feet on the mat.

***

The next day, as Connie rose early like she usually did, she made her way into the kitchen and put on a pot of coffee. Ben was still in bed and while tea was his favourite beverage, she couldn't say no to a nice coffee. As she waited for the percolator to brew, she shuffled across to the sink and gazed out into the garden. It was shadowed in darkness and would be until the sun came around later that afternoon, yet she still loved her slice of solitude.

As her eyes scanned the garden, taking in the flowers blooming — *which reminds me I need to go out and water them* — and the trees lining the back of her property, she sighed. Retirement suited her well, despite the old age that seemed to go with it. Every morning as she got up now, it seemed that she had grown older in the night. Her muscles screamed, her body always finding new nuances to deal with whether it be a creaky hip or a faltering knee. Having worked her whole life and being kept young, Connie felt that she was getting old. Not that she would let it stop her.

A sudden movement caught her eye and her head snapped to the right. It was Jessica. *What is she doing out so early?* A frown formed on her face as she leaned forward, knobbly hands resting on the window sill to balance her so she could see a little better.

The girl looked almost identical to the day before, except she had on a pair of shorts and a t-shirt. Her hair was still in the same pigtails judging by their straggled look and there was still dirt smudged across her cheek. With a grin, she picked up a shovel and began to dig.

"What on earth?" Connie's words were a whispered monologue to herself.

Behind her, the coffee began to drip into the pot, bringing a fresh aroma wafting across the kitchen. Shaking her head, Connie turned and stepped across to the bench. It was too early to be questioning the motives of a little girl.

After finishing her coffee and enjoying a light breakfast — everything seemed to be light or fat free these days, apart from her weight — she decided to go and give her garden the attention it deserved. Dressed in pants kept for the occasion and a straw hat to ward off the early rays of the sun as they peeped over the roof of the house, she made her way outside. The air was chilly, especially where it was doused in shadow but that didn't matter; she would soon warm up.

Grabbing the rail, she stepped up the small paved path next to the flowerbeds. Some of the dirt beneath the flags had shifted, causing a balance issue and some were cracked and worn with time, but she loved them anyway. It was her garden with her very own hand-made path crafted by Ben. Now, he would struggle with the lifting, but just a few years ago he would — and did — do anything for her.

As she reached the end of the flowerbeds, Connie turned the tap on the hose and it sprung to life in a spray of ice cold water. Some of the splash-back caught her off guard and she yelped in surprise, almost dropping the hose.

"Are you okay, Mrs. Dowins?" a young voice called to her.

Turning, she caught a glimpse of Jessica, hands wrapped around the top of the fence, head popping up like a meerkat.

"I'm fine, dear." Connie nodded, forcing a smile on her face despite the fact her hands felt like ice. "This water is just very cold."

Jessica nodded sagely. "Yes, it is cold this morning."

Connie, her attention now distracted, laid the hose at the base of the bed and stepped from the flags across to the fence. Grass poked her in the feet through the gaps in her sandals, sharp and unwelcome, yet she barely felt it as she stared at the girl. Her hair was frizzy beyond recognition, snapped strands sticking out at every angle from her two plaits. Rosy patches lit her cheeks from her exertion and not one speck of her was clean. Connie couldn't recall ever seeing the child so dirty before. *Pauline must really be unwell.*

"How is your mother?" Connie asked, leaning on the fence.

"Still sleepy." Jessica shrugged. "She'll be okay when she gets a good rest."

A frown crossed Connie's brow. "How bad is she? Do you want me to call a doctor?"

"No, that's okay." Jessica shook her head and her plaits went swinging around her head. "She's still asleep now anyway."

"So how are you? Are you eating okay?"

Her small head eagerly nodded. "I sure am. My mummy lets my make my breakfast everyday now."

"That's nice, dear." Connie smiled.

"Anyway, I better get back to work." Jessica dropped from the beam on the fence and hopped back across her own garden. Connie watched as the young girl picked up her shovel and jumped back into the hole. She almost disappeared, only the top of her head visible. She dug right in, shoving the flat blade into the soil, lifting it with a heave and throwing it across her shoulder with a grunt. She was already breathing heavily.

Connie stood on her tip-toes and watched as the girl worked furiously, determined, throwing dirt over her shoulder in a rhythmic motion. Connie's eyes widened as she took in the extent of the girl's work. The hole had to be at least three feet deep and longer in length, probably by double. It was square in shape and Connie had to admit she was impressed with the way the young girl had cut the ground so precisely, and squared it off.

"Jessica?" Connie called.

Her head popped up and brown eyes spied the woman out. "Yes?"

"That's going to be a mighty big pond."

"It's not a pond, Mrs. Dowins." She shook her head.

"It's not?"

"Nope." Bending down she scooped up another shovel of mud and thrust it above her head and behind her where the mound was growing larger and larger.

"Then what is it, dear?"

"I told you yesterday, I'm just digging." The words were full of pre-teen attitude.

"I'll leave you to it then. Give me a shout if you need anything." Connie ambled from the fence and back to her hose, yet her mind never left that hole.

For the rest of the day, each time she looked through the window, she would catch a glimpse of the girl still digging. The mound of dirt grew and grew until it started sliding towards Connie's own fence and slipping through onto the small patio.

"Ben," she called as she washed her hands at the sink, rinsing off the last of the suds. "*Ben.*"

"Yes, dear?" He slid into the kitchen as amiable as ever.

"Jessica is still digging."

"She's a child, Connie. She's just keeping herself occupied."

"Pauline will go mad when she gets better and sees the state of her lovely garden."

"She isn't well?" His head cocked.

Connie shook her head. "No, Jessica says she's not feeling too good. I offered to go around or call the doctor, but Jessica said she's okay."

Pursing his lips, Ben considered the situation for a moment. "Maybe if you don't see Pauline tomorrow you could pop in?"

"Yes, I think I will." Connie nodded definitively. It wasn't like Pauline not to be seen, even just across the gardens for a few minutes as she put her washing out. Yes, Connie would check on her tomorrow.

***

It was in the dead of night when Connie heard a thump that woke her up so rapidly that sleep was gone in an instant. Startled, her eyes flicked open in the darkness and as she scanned the room, the immediate panic gripping her mind began to subside. She was in her bedroom and safe and nothing looked out of place. Her voile curtains let in the moonlight as it danced across the sky. It lit her room in a violet-white glow, glinting in her vanity mirror.

Then she heard it again. A loud thump followed by the sound of something heavy — possibly something being dragged. *What if we're being burgled?* Connie flung herself up in bed, her nightgown sticking to her chest as her hand went to her heart. "Ben," she hissed in the darkness. He moaned and turned over. "*Ben!*"

"What?" came his harassed reply.

Ignoring the anger in his voice, she reached over to him, his warmth comforting her. "Did you hear that?"

"What?" he snapped again.

"A thud. I'm sure it was outside." Glancing to the window behind the bed, she peered out into the night sky.

"Then it's outside and nothing to worry about. Go to sleep, woman." He shrugged her hand from his arm and pulled the blankets closer to his chin.

Connie was too scared to be angry. There was something wrong.

Swinging her legs from the bed, her bare calves met the chill of the bedroom. Shivering, she stepped into a pair of slippers and pulled on a thin robe, tying it tight across her stomach. Shuffling from the bedroom, she made her way down the stairs, ignoring the aching in her hip with each step she took. Her hand gripped the rail tightly lest she take a tumble in the middle of the night.

Reaching the bottom of the stairs, she took a sharp right and moved down the hallway, her slippers gliding across the laminate floor. In front of her, she saw the garden from the kitchen window, sheltered in shadow and streaks of light where the moon reached through the trees at the edge of the garden.

On she crept, through her kitchen in the darkness, heart hammering against her chest and there she paused, silent, listening. Only the sound of her heart pumping blood through her body assailed her ears. Her hands clenched the fabric of her dressing gown and her legs trembled.

Then it happened again. One last, final thud and then the sound of something being dragged. A gasp died in her throat as she pressed her hand to her mouth. Her brain screamed. She wanted to run to the phone and ring the police but something stopped her.

Something of an insecurity that made her doubt her fear. She always had been a worrier. It could be nothing and then she would look like the ridiculous old woman who cried wolf.

Instead, she made her way to the source of the noise. Outside.

The key in the lock snapped as she unlocked the back door. Wincing, she bit her lip, hoping the noise had not been loud enough to be heard, before stepping outside. The night air was frigid, peppering her legs with cold kisses. Shivering, she wrapped her arms around her chest, holding herself tight as she began her journey to the back of the house. Her breath heaved from her lungs — whether from fear or exertion she wasn't sure — as she made her way to the corner. Her slippers dragged on the concrete and she cursed, finally deciding to step out of them. Her bare feet fell on the flags beneath and a cold train shot through her legs, tingling at the base of her spine. Yet, despite the coldness, she carried on, glad to have quiet on her side.

Sneaking to the corner of the house, she grasped the brickwork with her fingers and peeked around the side. In the shadows of the night she saw nothing. No movement, there was no noise, nothing. There was just the moonlight and the darkness.

Then a small grunt caught her ear from across the fence. Her head snapped up and she took a few quick steps forward, forgetting her self-preservation. Another grunt and something fell into the hole that Jessica had been digging. Something big.

The girl stood straight in the darkness, stretching her back out and wiping a forearm across her brow. Her pigtails were silhouetted against her shoulder. "Jessica?" Connie called out in a hissed whisper.

The girl's head turned. "Mrs. Dowins? What are you doing up?"

Her words caught Connie off guard. There was no fear, no shame in being up past midnight, despite being only ten, and there she was questioning Connie about being up. "I heard a noise, dear," she stuttered. "It woke me."

"Oh, sorry – I didn't mean to. I was trying to be quiet."

"What's in there?" Connie stepped forward, hands resting on the fence. She nodded to the hole in the darkness

"Want to come see?" Jessica asked, the smile on her face widening, white teeth glistening in the moonlight. Shadows fell across the girl's complexion as the trees waved in the cool breeze.

Something in Connie's mind screamed. Something told her to get out of there and call for help, like she wanted to originally. But she didn't. As she gazed at the child before her, she rationalised. The girl was just that, a child. Innocent, pure. There was nothing to worry about except perhaps her mother's view on curfew times, but she would deal with that tomorrow.

"Okay."

Stepping over on light feet, Jessica unlatched the small gate that opened in the fence and Connie walked through. In her bare feet, she crept over to the hole and peered down into the square — *or is it a rectangle?* Her eyes squinted in the night. It was hard to make anything out but the never ending darkness itself. It swallowed everything, but as her eyes adjusted they made out a shape, big and bulky taking up most of the room.

"What is it?" Connie asked, bending lower.

"Mummy," Jessica answered with a keen smile, rocking on her feet at the edge of the pit.

"W… what?" Connie swallowed as she swung up to look at the child.

"Mummy went to sleep and wouldn't wake up."

"Oh, God." Connie's hand flew to her mouth.

"But, I thought if I planted her like you plant your flowers, Mrs. Dowins, she would grow again, all new." Her teeth were stark white against the black night.

"Oh, honey, no that—" Connie lost her trail of thought as she stared down at the mound lying at the bottom of the shallow grave. The longer she looked, it seemed the more she could make out. The outline of her body, small and slender. Her limbs were splayed across the dirt, her left arm curled up to her chin. A wave of nausea rose in her throat and she felt glad she wasn't able to make out the dead woman's face.

"She just needs a little rest, that's all." Jessica thrust her hands on her hips and gave a definitive nod. "And maybe some water too. That'll help her re… jurenate."

Rejuvenate. The bile rose in Connie's gut. *The girl thinks she can plant her mother.*

A sharp pain stabbed her heart. Her hand flew to her chest as she moaned in pain, doubling over at the belly. Her mind span. She couldn't believe what she was seeing — hearing. This couldn't be happening. She had to get help for the woman. Pauline wasn't moving but maybe it wasn't too late. Maybe they could save her.

Spinning, she tried to thrust herself away from the grave. She had to get help. The only thing that flashed through her mind was the phone on her kitchen table. In the darkness, her bare feet caught on the shovel on the grass, almost invisible, and she stumbled forward and fell. A dull crack fell on her ears and an arc of pain shot through her left leg. Through gritted teeth, Connie glanced down at her leg and saw her ankle twisted at a funny angle, foot sticking out backwards. She suppressed a groan as the bile in her stomach finally rose, vomit hitting the grass with a soft splash. Coughing, she wiped her mouth with the back of her hand and fought to turn her body as much as she could to face Jessica.

"Jessica, honey, go phone an ambulance for me," Connie asked, forcing a smile on her face despite the pain that blasted her leg.

"I have a better idea!" A grin lit the girl's face. Leaping forward, her hands wrapped around Connie's ankle, now swelling profusely, and yanked her a few inches towards the grave with a deep grunt.

Connie screamed as she felt her body shifting. "No, Jessica, no!"

"You can rest with mummy." She yanked again and Connie was powerless to stop, to do anything. Slicing pain cut up her leg with each minute movement and she could only watch as the girl continued her journey to the grave.

"Jessica… It doesn't work like that," Connie stuttered, trying to catch her breath.

"And then I will get you both back up." Another heave and a huff of air as the girl dragged her another few inches. Connie was teetering on the edge now, her legs splayed across the vast empty void of earth. This time, Jessica changed her stance and moved behind Connie, pushing with both hands on Connie's hips and heaving with all of her might. Jessica strained as she thrust Connie forward. She was almost there, her legs dangling with nothing to grab onto. Then, with one final thrust, Connie was caught by gravity as she balanced on the edge. It pulled her downwards where she fell into the abyss. Her foot scraped across the wall of dirt on her way down and she wailed in agony. The wind flew from her chest as she landed on top of the dead woman — now Connie was sure she *was* dead after feeling the stiffness in the body — and stars spangled in front of her eyes. They faded into a dull black warmth.

When she regained consciousness, her legs were already buried to the hip in dirt and a huge mound of dirt was already compressed over her torso, arms by her sides. Her head was lying just on top of Pauline's, the stench of the woman almost overpowering. Bile rose up her throat once more but she swallowed it back down. Now wasn't the time to panic. Now, she had to rationalise. "Jessica, listen to me!"

From above, the girl's head peered down at Connie and she grinned. "It's time for you to regrow, Mrs. Dowins."

Another scoop of dirt landed on top of her, crumbs of mud dropping on her face, flaking in her mouth. Spitting, she coughed and appealed to the girl once more. "Jessica, please!" Her wail was a failing siren in the night as more dirt was shovelled into her grave, cutting out the last of the moonlight.

Omens

By Chantal Noordeloos

Kazakhstan 1338

The fires flared brightly in the cold, dark night, and the frost made us huddle close together. We'd picked a spot for the winter where the snow was light on the ground, where yellow grass still peeked above the white, so that our horses, camels and sheep could still eat. This winter had been harsh, but as always, our livestock had been strong and fat enough to withstand the frost.

Sparks flew up from the flames like dancing fairies escaping from their crackling prison. I could taste the ashes on my tongue, and the heavy scent of burning wood filled my nostrils. The bright contrast of the fire against the velvet black backdrop hurt my eyes, but there was something magical about these cold nights. It was as if the cold bought the tribe closer together… as if we were more a part of each other, somehow.

I looked at all the faces illuminated with a soft orange glow, faces that peered out through thick fur rims that topped their sheepskin coats known as Ton. There was love in our midst, especially for me. My mother died when I was eighteen months old. She had been a special woman, who knew much about medicine, but more importantly, she possessed 'the sight'. Mother knew things that common people couldn't possibly know, and her predictions always came true.

Our people considered her to be a blessing to the tribe, and believed she was a token of good luck. The tribe prospered when she joined them. The animals seemed more fertile, and there were no more miscarriages among the sheep. Mother knew how to deal with illness in both humans and animals alike. The people followed her as loyally as they did my father. When I was born, my people called me a 'golden child'. I inherited my mother's strange sixth sense, and the people felt safe near me. When my mother was taken from us by illness, one that not even she could cure, I–in some ways— took her place. The tribe grieved over our loss, and the people turned to me for comfort, even at a young age. Not that I was aware of it until years later, but as long as I was near them, all would be well; my people were convinced of this. They believed that touching my hair would bring them good fortune, and so I grew up having my dark locks stroked often. I never lacked for attention or kind words growing up, and I was allowed to do things that were forbidden for other girls, like join the men when they would go on their eagle hunts. My father was a great hunter, and I enjoyed riding with him during the day. It was my favourite pastime aside from gathering around the campfire at night.

This night was special, for we had visitors from another tribe. The eldest of the newcomers was my grandmother, Sezim, who was my father's mother. Sezim was a tiny woman, with a wrinkled face. Her clothes were old and faded, the *Shapan* – a traditional dressing gown – she wore had once been beautiful and a vibrant orange. Now it was weather-stained and most of the stitching had come loose.

Sezim had sixteen children, most of them living in different tribes, who she visited throughout the year. Every year she would tell us it was the last time she would visit, that she was getting too old to travel, but the next year she would be back. I enjoyed it when she came to our camp.

Despite her old age, she still had a sharp mind – unlike some of the elders in our small tribe – and her stories entertained the children. When the fires were lit high that night, I quickly claimed a spot next to my grandmother, in hopes that she would tell us a tale or two. The old woman had been rather quiet that day, and I wasn't the only one who noticed.

"What's the matter, *Ejee* (mother)?" Nurzhan, my father, asked, as he put his hand on Grandmother's fragile shoulders. He was a tall and handsome man. "You usually speak fast enough to quiet evil spirits, yet tonight you seem so solemn."

"It's the omens, my boy," she said – her voice raw and deep, like that of a man.

"Omens, Ejee?"

The old woman shook her head, her breath escaping like a long wheeze, and I leaned closer not to miss a word.

"These are dark times." One gnarled hand reached out to me, and caressed the dark locks on my head. A few strands of hair escaped the ties of my bun as a result. I didn't mind, I was used to people stroking my hair.

Grandmother sighed. "There is much evil lurking, and I fear none of us are safe."

"Evil? What sort of evil?" Father's eyebrows shot up, disappearing into his *Kamshat Boryk* –a beaver skin hat.

The others around the fire moved in closer, curious to hear what the old woman had to say. Their faces were filled with tension, though Father seemed calm. He wasn't easily stirred by stories of evil, and often didn't share the people's superstitions.

"Have you not heard the tales?" Grandmother looked up at him in surprise. "They're all around these lands. All the tribes speak of them." Her hand moved back to her lap, where it rested. I stared at the thin fingers; the light of the fire cast shadows on them, and they looked almost like the claws of a bird.

"I've heard of no tales that should worry us. Tell us what we need to know, Ejee." Father sat down, the smile on his face faltered a little.

"There are many tales of the Dokhio."

"Dokhio?" Father asked. "Hatlingu[illegible]?"

"Indeed." The old woman coughed, her shoulders shaking. She wiped the spittle from her lips into a faded blue rag. "They roam these very lands, in the form of young children, seeking a sacrifice. They come for what is most loved, and they'll tear it to shreds before your very eyes." Another cough escaped her cracked lips. Her eyes shone with the firelight, and she pointed with a shaking digit at our goats. "They came to your sister's tribe and took all their livestock. All of it… the children just devoured them alive, while the tribe watched. Your sister still has nightmares."

Around the fire, the people expressed different reactions. Most were shocked, some looked angry. Anxiously I looked at my father's face, but I couldn't read his expression. He seemed confused, perhaps angry… I just couldn't tell.

"My sister… *saw* these Dokhio?" Father's words were slow, and he looked at his mother with narrowed eyes.

"She wasn't the only one. I came to their settlement only days after the Dokhio left." Grandmother spat on the ground. "I saw the blood of the animals… and the bones."

"They witnessed it? They saw children devour their livestock? It wasn't just wolves who killed the animals?" Father rubbed the back of his neck. His movements were fast and betrayed his irritation.

"I looked into your sister's eyes, Nurzhan… I know my child. She saw what she saw, and so did the rest of them." Grandmother challenged my father, and though she was only half his size, he respected her enough to trust her word.

"What are these Dokhio? Ghosts?"

"No one knows. All I know is that they took the form of children." Grandmother shuddered, pulling her furs tighter across her frail shoulders. "Your sister's tribe has nothing anymore, and they're struggling to survive."

"We can't help them, Ejee. We don't have enough to share." Father's hard face betrayed his determination. We were a fortunate clan, richer than most, and we had some excess food to give away. But it wouldn't be enough for the other tribe to survive, and if we would split our livestock in half, we would struggle. My father wanted to protect us, and he would take no risks... not even to help his own sister.

"I'm not here to ask for your help, my son." There is a hint of bitterness in my grandmother's voice. "I wouldn't dream of it. I know what you are like."

I felt shame for the way my father declined to help those in need. I couldn't remember my mother, but I was sure she wouldn't have approved. I thought of speaking out against my father's decision, our people would surely listen to me… but I feared my father's discontent too much. He could be frightening when he was angry.

"You said these Dokhio are just children?" Father stood up to throw more wood on the fire. "Why would the tribe accept the children to take their livestock? Why not stop them?"

Grandmother pulled back from him, her hand shooting up to her mouth and her eyes were round with shock.

"It's bad luck to deny the Dokhio their tribute."

"Bad luck? Would you say it's worse luck than losing your livelihood?" Father tossed a second branch on the fire, and the embers shot up again, dancing elegantly in the air. "Worse luck than having people starve? I don't see the logic in that, Ejee."

"You do not deny the Harbingers, my boy."

"Says who?"

"These are the laws we live by. We are granted much in this mortal world. We humans take animals and plants for our food, water and milk for our drink, and wood for our shelters. This is our way of life. Like fleas, we suck the blood from Mother Earth. She expects us to repay her for the bounty we claim by making sacrifices. The Dokhio are here to collect our atonements."

"Nonsense and superstitions," Father said, crossing his arms like a headstrong child.

"This is not how I raised you," Grandmother chided, "I taught you to respect all omens, not just the good ones. You didn't mind them when they came to you in the shape of a blessing, like your beautiful wife, who brought you luck."

"You forget that my wife was taken away from me too soon." The firelight reflected in Father's dark eyes. "That was enough sacrifice on my part. Ejee, when the Dokhio come to our tribe, they will get nothing from us. We will send them away. We've worked too hard to offer anything to a stupid superstition."

A collective gasp escaped the lips of the tribe. They looked at Father as if he had gone mad, and when the initial shock wore off, protests erupted.

Father stood tall and listened quietly to the dozens of voices for several minutes. When he had enough, he held up his hands and commanded them to be quiet.

The shouts died down into whispers, which, in turn, ended in silence.

“Would you have them take the only thing that keeps us alive? Our livestock?” Father asked, his voice loud enough to be heard throughout the small camp. “Are your superstitions worth starvation?” He walked to one of the small boys who was sitting next to his mother, and lifted him up in the air. “Would you let these Dokhio take the food from the lips of our very own children?” His words hit a nerve with the people around him. He put the child down, who was immediately pulled into his mother’s arms. Others grabbed onto their children as well, and I saw some of the men ball their fist in anger. My father always knew how to sway the tribe’s emotions, that’s why they looked to him as a leader, even after my mother’s death.

“If you wish to believe in omens, believe in Aliya.” He pointed at me, the emphasis to his point, and the attention caused hot blood to rush to my cheeks. “She is proof of our fortune. She – like her mother – keeps us healthy, and keeps our animals fat and fertile.”

People nodded their heads. I was their golden child, they believed in me above all else.

“We shan’t let anyone take away that which belongs to us,” he said, his voice powerful. “We are better than that, and we have luck on our side.”

They believed him because he made them feel safe. Muttered agreements surrounded me like verbal shadows, and the spirit of the people flared as much as the flames do. Something about it, about the sudden anger, frightened me. I slipped my hand into my grandmother’s, and she squeezed it.

“Your father is a foolish man, Aliya. And an arrogant one,” she whispered to me. “He has never understood the importance of sacrifice. Not even as a small boy. I had hopes that your mother would teach him, but she was taken from us too soon. Let us hope he will never encounter the Dokhio, or bad things are sure to happen."

***

After my grandmother's visit, there were many more reports of the Dokhio claiming an offer from different tribes. The sacrifices were often cattle or goats. Sometimes, the Harbingers would ask for other tributes that were a far greater sacrifice. We ran across forlorn travellers who told us stories that were so horrible, they gave me nightmares. One woman told us that her tribe had fallen apart after the Dokhio demanded one of the newborns. The people of the tribe obviously refused, and so, as a punishment, they took all the children under one year of age. The mothers were forced to watch as these strange children killed their babies with their bare hands and sharp teeth.

Father was appalled by these stories, and swore to the people of our tribe that not one hair on the heads of our children would be harmed. Despite my disagreeing with Father's passion, I wanted to keep our children safe as much as everyone else.

We came across many more disheartened tribes, and lone travellers. The Harbingers were on our minds and on our lips. I dreamt often of the Dokhio. In my dreams they were not children, but the monsters who lived in the shadow, and who visited the people for a reason. What that reason was, I didn't know, but I always woke up with a sense of unease. In my dreams there was always one figure who stood out. Though I couldn't see her face, I knew it was a girl. She was the leader, and she was on a mission.

The Dokhio frightened, but also fascinated me. Like everyone else, I wondered where they came from. Why would a group of children just wander around the lands? Who were their parents, and why were they alone? These were all questions we asked each other quietly, when my father couldn't hear, for he chided anyone who was led by fear of the Harbingers.

***

We broke camp to travel to better pastures. The winter was almost over, and, if we wanted to cross Lake Balkhash before the ice would be too thin, we had to move fast. Spring would make the large frozen lake too dangerous; it couldn't be trusted to hold our weight.

Father had told me of the different places that were suitable for us, and he asked me which one I believed was best. He drew symbols for each place in the snow, a ritual he would perform with me each time I had to make a choice, and one he had performed with my mother before I was born. With one long, gloved finger, he drew a line from each of them, right to the spot where I was standing. I waited silently as he worked, concentrating on the three drawings in front of me.

One I immediately discarded; a dark shadow covered it. Whether it was a cloud that covered the sun, or something only I could see, I didn't know, but I knew how to read the omens. There would be a drought there in summer, and we needed water and grass for our animals.

The second two were more difficult. They were both very fine choices, but after a bit of concentration, I realized one would be the better of the two. A ray of sunlight shone on my choice.

I smiled at Father and stepped onto the path that led to the drawing on the right. As soon as my foot hit the snow, I stopped dead in my tracks. A milky grey haze loomed up, clouding my vision. I knew what that meant; the spirits were trying to tell me something.

"Aliya?" Father's voice sounded so far away; it only just pierced the mist of the other world I was in. Dark shapes moved around within the grey. At first, only one revealed itself, then two, and soon there were at least a dozen. Footsteps echoed through the fog, and children's laughter surrounded me. The sound was not sweet and joyful, like the way the children from the tribe laughed when they played. It was hollow and filled with menace. My heart turned to ice as I listened to them. The scent in the air made me nauseous. Metallic, like the smell that lingered after one of the animals was slaughtered, interlaced with something else that I couldn't identify; it reminded me of a combination of rot and urine. Bile rose in my throat when I looked down at my Shapan. It was covered in blood. I held up my arms and hands, and they too were drenched. Every part of me, even my hair, felt heavy with blood.

I screamed.

My father's hands grabbed me, shaking me away from the realm of mist. His voice and his touch were my anchors, dragging me back into reality. My heart was filled with panic and I grabbed my hair, but it was clean. I ran my fingers over the fabric of my Shapan, but not a trace of blood remained.

"What did you see, my daughter?" Father kneeled in front of me, and his eyes were filled with worry.

"I saw the Dokhio," I answered, hardly able to get the words out, for my teeth were chattering too hard. "If we take this path, we shall run across them."

Father stood, his face filled with determination. "Then we must take this path."

"No, Father…" I felt the tears well up in my eyes. "Please… You'll put us in danger."

"We're not in danger from a handful of children. I refuse to live in fear of them."

"Father… in my vision, I… I was covered in blood." Hot tears spilled over my cheeks. The memory was still so vivid.

"Don't be silly, your vision could mean anything. You've let these stories get to your head, Aliya. That's exactly the problem, and the reason why these children manage to terrorize us. We give them what they want out of fear, while what we should be doing is drawing them on our knees and spanking the insubordination out of them."

"No… I think…"

Father beckoned me to be silent, and I held my tongue. I was stunned that he didn't take me seriously. My father had always listened to my visions.

"You will not speak to anyone of your vision, Aliya. We don't want the people to panic for no reason." My father's dark eyes flared. "Do you understand?"

I nodded. Perhaps he was right, perhaps these were just wild children that needed to be taught a lesson. But my heart told me to avoid them at all cost. I had to trust my father; he knew what was best.

***

The next days I kept myself busy with the upcoming journey, and it was enough to distract my thoughts from the vision. Like most of the younger members of the tribe, I usually enjoyed moving. The journey was often interesting, and we were always excited to see new sights. The elders of our tribe struggled a bit more. Travelling was for the young, they always claimed, and I guess it was true.

I did my best to cheer up the elderly, which was always appreciated. My very presence would make a difference, since I was the golden child. Everyone knew that I would lead us to the best places, just like my mother had. My heart was heavy with my foreboding vision, and I felt like I was betraying my people by keeping silent.

We packed up all the dwellings and our meagre belongings. The camels, which served as our packing animals, were loaded up with the long poles, boxes and folded canvas. I watched as Father put our weapons within reach. This was not uncommon, we were always prepared to encounter wild animals along the way, but this time it felt more sinister to me. He had ordered me to keep a knife hidden in my skirts at all times. I hated the idea, but I obeyed.

One by one we mounted our horses. Some of the larger families had wagons, in which the little children were gathered. This was a journey we would take as a tribe, as one large family. I did my best to keep a smile on my face at all times but there was nothing genuine about it. I knew this journey would not be a pleasant one.

***

They came in the night, on the eighth day of our travels, right after we had crossed Lake Balkhash. We were huddled close together around the fire, still cold from crossing the ice. It was as if the frozen water had drained us of body heat as we crossed. None of us rode our horses, and the wagons were stripped of the heaviest goods to make everything as light as possible. The little ones had shivered all the way across. We had crossed the lake before, and I can't remember it ever being so cold. I guess I should have read the omen.

The Dokhio could be heard before we saw them. Their childish voices filled the air, and all who sat around the fire froze in fear. Through the smoke we watched as the dark shapes neared us. They stopped only a few feet away.

They were children of different ages. There were little ones, no more than two or three-years-old, and bigger children who looked on the cusp of adulthood. One child was obviously the leader, and though I had never seen her, I recognized her from my dreams. Unlike what I had expected, she turned out to be a girl of around my age, ten or maybe eleven-years-old. She was like no girl I had ever seen, and for a moment I wondered if I were looking at a child of flesh and blood, or at a ghost. Her skin was pale, like the colour of the moon, and her hair shone golden in the firelight, like the sun. In the darkness I couldn't see the colour of her eyes, but somehow I knew they were the same hue as the sky during the daytime. A dirty blue frock, exotic in make, covered her frame, and wolf-skins hung around her thin shoulders. Her hair and clothes were unkempt, but there was still something regal about her. She looked like the *Kahn* of this rag-tag bunch of children. All of them were malnourished and dirty. The children had deep, dark circles under their eyes, which looked menacing in the light of the fire. No one in the camp spoke. Even my father stared at them in silence; the sight of these children surprised us all.

"We've come for a sacrifice," the girl with the golden hair broke the silence. Her voice was very sweet, and had a thick foreign accent. Her words broke the spell that held my father's tongue, and he stood up, grabbing his spear.

"There will be no sacrifice," he said, holding the spear out to the girl.

The children responded to his movement, and slowly they began to spread out, surrounding our small camp. The women at the fireside cried out, and pulled their children close.

"Everyone must sacrifice, what makes you so special?" The girl's voice rang through our camp.

"Who are you to demand a sacrifice of us?" Father shouted. "I will not be commanded by children."

"You are an arrogant man. A perfect example of humanity." The girl looked at her fingers, and pursed her lips. "If you do not give us what we want, we'll take it."

"No, you will not." Father raised his spear. His action triggered the rest of the people around the camp, and one by one they grabbed their own weapons. More spears were raised, as were knives, and some grabbed their bows and nocked arrows, aimed directly at the children.

There were quite a few Dokhio, I counted at least thirty. Yet, though we were with smaller numbers, our tribe was well armed, and the children would be no match for us.

"Your threats do not frighten us. We shall take what we came for, and if you do not give it freely, we shall take much more." The girl cocked her head. I couldn't see any fear in her eyes, and that terrified me.

"What is it that you come for?" Dilnaz, a mother of three, cried. She sounded as afraid as I felt.

The girl turned to me, and pointed her finger. "We want the seer as a sacrifice."

My blood turned to ice, and my mouth filled with an acidic taste. *I will die this night, if these children will have their way*, I thought. My vision came to my mind clearly, and I remembered the blood. *Was it my own blood I saw?*

"You can't have her." It was Dilnaz who spoke again, and to my surprise I heard her words echo on the lips of others. My father said nothing, but his face betrayed the rage he felt.

"Others have tried to deny us," the girl said flatly.

"But were the others willing to fight you? Or were they too afraid of the myths that surrounded you?" Father countered. He balanced his spear in his hand. "Many believe that you are ghosts." He looked around the horde of children. "I don't… I think you are just mortal children. And I'm willing to bet my life on it."

"Bet your life on it you will," the girl said, her voice low and menacing. "The sacrifice we ask of you is little. Be grateful and give us what we want."

"No." Father's face was filled with determination. The fear I felt was overwhelming. I didn't want to die, but I didn't want my people to die either. Father was so sure these were just children, but what if he was wrong?

"Very well," the girl said, "then we shall take all your children, and your livestock."

"No, you will not," Father sneered at her, and that's when he threw the spear. He would have hit the girl if one of the other children hadn't jumped in the way. The girl, who was sixteen or seventeen at least, caught Father's spear right in the chest. She fell down with a meaty thud and for a moment everyone was quiet. I held my breath.

Father had been right… these were not ghosts, just children of flesh and blood. The girl with the golden hair looked at the child at her feet. There was no sadness in her features, but I did see a flash of anger. Around her some of the children moaned like wounded animals.

The girl looked up, the matted golden locks hanging in front of her face. She raised one hand, and clicked her fingers. At the sound the children moved as if they were one creature. They screamed as they ran towards us; the sound was the most terrifying thing I had ever heard. Their arms were outstretched, reaching for us, hands posed like claws. Bloodlust shone in their eyes, and the fire reflected off the sharp teeth they bared. Around me the people stood as if they were hypnotized. It was my father who broke the trance, he grabbed another spear and stepped forward. With one quick movement he impaled the nearest child, a boy of no more than eight, with a sickening crunch. As he pulled the weapon from the young flesh, I watched slippery entrails escape from the child's body, who sunk to the ground.

A shadow crossed over us, and an invisible force took over from the people of my tribe, a dark and murderous spirit. I stepped back, as far away from the skirmish as possible; I couldn't believe what was happening.

A few children jumped on one of the elderly men, tearing at him with teeth and nails. The man's screams were dampened by their frail bodies. Whilst in other places I saw the gentle-hearted Nuro, who always played with the tribe's little ones, bash in the skull of a girl who was no older than five.

The fight between the two sides was a bloodbath. I stood by in horror, just far enough to not be a part of it. The only other person who stood aside was the girl with the golden hair. She no longer looked like a ghost or a frightening omen, to me she was a wicked child now. Her people could bleed and die, just like the rest of us. My father had been right all along.

I ran to her.

"We can stop this… this bloodshed is needless. But we'll need to work together."

The girl turned to me, her eyes filled with hate. "I won't stop this. The blood needs to flow. If you try to intervene, I will kill you."

"But your own people are dying, as are mine."

"They should have made the sacrifice. Now more will die." The girl lifted her head, as an arrogant gesture. Her attitude infuriated me. *Who does this girl think she is? She's crazy.*

"But you will be alone, if all the children die," I grabbed her arm, her very human arm. *How could I have ever thought she was a demon?*

"I don't care for them," she shrugged, sulking like a spoiled babe. "When they are dead, I will find other children to join me. There are always others."

I turned to the fighting crowd, scanning the figures to find my father. He would be my strength; he would know what to do. It took me a moment to locate him, and when I did, I saw him engaged with three of the larger boys. One was hanging from his back, another held on to his right arm, but it was the third who worried me. The boy had a spear – it could have been Father's own – and he was feigning attacks against the bigger man. After several threats, the boy pulled the spear back, and as his companions pulled my father's guard wide, he plunged the weapon into his stomach. My father stiffened, and fell… the children still on top of him.

I wanted to wail, but instead, I turned back to the vicious girl, my rage pounding my heart like a drum. I had lost my father – my own blood.

"You are a wicked girl," I screamed. "And you must be stopped. There will be no more blood spilled in your name." Anger mixed with panic, and my hand reached for the knife in my skirts. All I wanted was to stop this child and all the cruelty clouding her eyes.

With all the force I could muster, I drove the knife into her stomach, avoiding the wolf skin. It didn't go in very deep the first time, so I pulled it out, and stuck her again. The girl's eyes opened wide, and her mouth was the shape of a circle. I pushed the knife in a third time, and blood poured from her pale lips.

"You have doomed us all," she spluttered, as she fell to the ground. When her body hit the earth, I heard a loud crash, as if a large boulder had struck the earth. Everything around me came to a halt. The Dokhio stopped attacking my tribe, and the adults lowered their weapons.

Beneath our feet the earth trembled. A bright light emanated from the snow-covered ground, and large cracks appeared underfoot, as if we were standing on ice, rather than frozen dirt. The ground rumbled with a thunderous noise, as the cracks spread into deep chasms, which intersected and collapsed together, forming a gigantic hole.

The girl's blood, still warm, dripped to the ground from my knife and hand. Each drop thudded like a heartbeat.

From the depths of the hole a creature appeared. Impossibly large hooves burst forth, and a gigantic horse stepped from the darkness. The horse itself was light, a yellowish hue, and on its back sat a rider dressed in a long black cloak with a yellow lining.

The rider was at least twice the size of a man. He steered his horse into the clearing, the light from the broken ground illuminating him. I couldn't see his face, and I knew I didn't want to see it. The horse was as commanding as the rider; two red eyes glared at its surroundings. The mere presence made me feel ill.

Something moved on his cloak, I couldn't make out what it was first, but the fabric pulsed and shifted as if it were alive. To my horror I discovered that it was. Hundreds, maybe thousands of small bugs crawled from the cloak – down the horse, and they scattered onto the ground. The black swarm spread as quick as wildfire, and I stood in terror as they scuttled towards the people in the camp. The mass of creatures flocked over my tribe and the children alike, covering them as if someone pulled dark silk across them. The victims tried to beat the bugs away from them, but there were too many.

Part of the swarm came my way, but they avoided the girl on the ground, and anything that her blood had touched, including me. Up close I could see that the bugs were large fleas, not unlike those I had seen on the camels and goats. Fat with the blood of their victims. They were gone as fast as they came. I looked back at the people of my tribe and the children, who stood around as if they were in a trance.

I saw them with my special sight, and I could see their futures. The small red marks that covered their skin now, had poisoned them. Black welts would appear on their skin, and a horrible death would follow. In my vision I saw the people wail in agony. There was no hope for them.

Another sound dragged me back to reality; it was the screams of frightened animals. I turned to see the tiny fleas feasting on the blood of our goats, our horses and our camels. Nothing was safe from them. My blood ran cold at the thought of how fast these things would spread.

The horse of the large rider whinnied, and I turned my attention back to the mysterious stranger. The rider kicked his heels and spurred on his mount, riding away from the camp in a fast gallop; his cloak still bleeding the deadly swarm of fleas.

The movement broke my trance, and I was once again free to act. I wanted to run to my people, but a hand clutched around my ankle. I looked down to see the girl bleeding at my feet. Taking a deep breath, I kneeled down next to her

"You… you must stop it," she whispered.

"What is that thing?" I asked, too afraid to cry.

"It… It's called Pestilence… and it will spread disease wherever it rides." Her voice was weak. "You must find it, and make the appropriate sacrifice. Only then will it return to sleep under the earth." She coughed and a gush of blood escaped her lips.

"How will I know what to sacrifice?"

"It will have to be something big, something terrible. I don't have the answer, but you will find it. You're special, just like I was when they chose me to fulfil my destiny."

I wanted to speak, but she put a finger to her lips.

"It's important to listen. Once it's asleep, your job is not done. Each lunar cycle something needs to be sacrificed to the rider. It needs to be of value to someone – anyone. Real value. Something that will be missed… something people will mourn." Her bloody hand touched my face, leaving traces. "You have the sight, when you visit people, you will know what to take."

"I… I can't…"

"You must. Or the rider will travel the world, and you don't want that." Her eyes looked glassy in the strange supernatural light. "Pestilence… what it spreads… it's called the black death. It will kill millions. And that's not all. The rider isn't alone. There are three others, and the rider will go looking for them. If all four of them ride, it'll mean the end of the world. There will be nothing left." Tears ran across her face, and I wondered if she could still see me. "You must put the rider back to sleep, or the whole world will die."

"How do I find this rider?"

"It travels the silk route. Follow that."

"But it's so fast…"

"Promise that you will never stop looking for it… Promise… that you'll stop it." Her hand clutched my T[illegible]

"I promise," I whispered.

She coughed again, but this time too much blood came out. Spasms overtook her body, and her eyes were wide, as she gasped her last breath. Her soul, a ball of many colours, escaped in that last exhalation, and with it a large invisible weight landed on my shoulders. *I alone bear this burden now.*

I could see it clearly, the path that the rider had taken. In my land of mist, I followed the rider with my third eye. I saw the spread of the fleas, and the damage they would do to the people of the world. Many millions would die before I found the rider, but I would find it, and I would stop it.

Not once did I glance back at my dying people, there was nothing more I could do for them. I cleaned the knife on the dress of the dead girl with the golden hair. I took the wolf skin from her, and placed it around my own shoulders. My heart as hard as a stone, I stepped onto the path that the rider left for me to follow. Along the way I would find my sacrifices, and I would demand them from people, in the same way the Dokhio had. If the people would not give me their sacrifice, I would take it… like the Dokhio, I would become a fearsome legend, a necessary evil, to bring about the end of this black plague.

The Box

By Gary Pearson

Oliver sat in the cold, damp, horrible room – which haunted his nightmares – with the darkness closing in around him. He closed his eyes, placed his hands over his ears and rocked slowly. It was the only thing that he had learnt to do to stop the horrors from coming out of the blackness.

He had been placed into 'The Box' once again.

This was out in the garden and had once been a regular garden shed. However, now it's where Oliver was taken to and locked in by his father, if he was naughty. Oliver had a tendency to be a brat at times, but he couldn't help himself, his parents gave him the opportunity and he exploited it. They thought there was something wrong with him; they had him tested for various illnesses and disorders to try and explain his wild nature over the years. Nothing came back as a reason, from the outside it looked like Oliver was a completely normal, ten-year-old boy.

His parents had adopted the method of taking him outside and locking him away for a while to let him cool down. This was on the advice of a psychiatrist, they had been told that he needs time 'to reflect on what he had done wrong' so that eventually he would not do it again. It usually worked as 'The Box' scared the hell out of him; he could feel the walls closing in around him, and the noises seemed to get louder each time he had been put in there.

During different visits, he was sure he could hear voices, but none of them ever made sense, just garbled words that drifted through the stale air. The normal time scale would be around thirty minutes. From the clock in his head, Oliver thought he must be nearly there. He felt a presence near and opened his eyes slightly, the darkness attacked his senses again, making it seem like he hadn't opened them at all. The padlock on the outside of the door was being undone and then it flung open. Oliver pushed himself back slightly as his eyes adjusted to the light again, seeing the outline of a large figure in the doorway.

"Have you calmed down yet?" his father asked.

Oliver just nodded furiously hoping it would be enough to get him out of there.

"Are you sure?" his father asked again.

Oliver nodded once more.

"Fine. Come on then. But anymore like that and you'll be back in here again. You understand?"

Oliver nodded, then rushed forwards, standing as he went, trying to push himself past his father and out of the confined space as soon as possible. His father grabbed him as he started running past. "Where are you going in such a hurry?"

"I don't like it in there, Dad."

"Then you know what you need to do, stay good."

"I can't help it."

"Don't lie to me!" His father's voice raised slightly.

Oliver shied away, praying he wouldn't be put back in there. His father kept a hold of his arm and started to drag him back to the house. As he entered, his mother sat at the kitchen table preparing vegetables.

"Have you learnt your lesson?" she asked not looking up.

"Yes, Mother," Oliver replied sheepishly.

"We don't want to take you out to the box, honey, but when you're naughty, you need to learn. Do you understand?"

"Yes, Mother."

"Okay. Well, sit down and I'll sort you out some dinner. Are you hungry?"

"Not really, but I'll eat."

His mother looked at him a little strangely, but set about preparing them some dinner anyway. His father re entered the house, this time with some logs for the fire. He walked into the sitting room and started stacking them up into the fire place. He spent the next couple of minutes lighting it until the flames started dancing through the logs and the heat crept out into the room.

"Son. You know we care for you right?" Oliver's father said as he approached the table.

Oliver nodded just staring straight ahead, not wanting to make eye contact with his father.

"Then you know why we put you in the box. We need you to understand that you need to stay calm."

"I told you. I can't help it."

"And I told you not to lie to me!"

Oliver pushed himself down into his chair, hoping that he could just run away from them. He'd endured this pain for the last year now, every time that there was a hint of him doing something wrong, he was taken out into the garden and placed into that hell. 'The Box' was more than anyone should ever have to deal with. It was cold, horrible, scary, damp, and full of things that gave him nightmares. Whenever Dad grabbed him and dragged him towards the kitchen door, he knew what was coming. Other kids didn't have the same kind of punishment, but then other kids were not as bad as him, *apparently*.

"John, leave him alone. He's learnt his lesson." His mother stepped in.

"No, Pam, he hasn't. If he had, he wouldn't keep behaving like he does."

Oliver's parents started to argue back and forth, each time getting louder until they were fully shouting at each other. Unfortunately, this seemed to be a recurring theme recently, and it was all his fault. His mum would fight his corner, say that he didn't mean to do it and it was all sorted with his time spent outside. His dad, unfortunately, never agreed. The current argument lasted a good twenty minutes, and his mother was in tears by the end of it, which infuriated Oliver. He could feel his blood boiling, the anger bubbling to the surface.

Eventually, he snapped.

"*Why can't we just be like a normal family?*" he screamed.

His father spun round to look at him.

"How *dare* you get involved in our argument! It's your fault that we are like this in the *first place!* If you could just be a normal child, we wouldn't have this problem!"

"I haven't done anything."

"You just can't do anything right. That's your problem."

Oliver just started screaming, it drowned out the sound of his father who was still shouting at him. His mother just sunk to her knees sobbing, her head in her hands. Oliver felt his cheek burn as his father slapped his face. The shock stopped his screaming straight away, but the searing pain then made him cry. He tried to fight the tears back to prove that he was stronger than that but he couldn't help it. His father grabbed hold of his wrist and dragged him back towards the door. Oliver's screams and tears intensified as he realised he was going back to 'The Box' for a second time tonight. This time, he wasn't sure that it was actually his fault. His father pulled him across the lawn, the whole time Oliver was kicking and trying to break free of his grip. He heard the padlock being undone, then he saw the bleakness through the open door. The next thing he knew, he was inside and the door was being closed again behind him.

As Oliver sat in the darkness once more he could feel the anger boiling over towards his father. Usually he managed to bury it deep down again but this time he'd had enough. He didn't like his dad having a go at his mother for something she had no control over. He knew he couldn't help the anger, and the outburst, but also didn't want to let his father get away with the way he had spoken to her. For the first time in a long while, he opened his eyes, the prison seemed to envelope him, the scary walls that had been clawing at him were not any more, the darkness was rushing into him and consuming him. He wanted to be let out, to confront his father, and tell him that it was not acceptable to speak to his mother in that way. But he was locked within the small confines of the four walls surrounding him. He sat looking around as his eyes started to adjust to the darkness. He could not see much but could now make out the outlines of the walls, he could see the slight light creeping in from the edges of the door in front of him. Oliver reached out and touched the wood of the door, he could feel the cold, dampness of it.

A voice whispered. "Do it."

Oliver jumped back in shock, looking around in the darkness to see if he could make out someone, but there was nothing. He shook his head to bring him back to reality, putting the voice down to just hearing things and moved forward again towards the door. He ran his hand around the edge and then pushed it, it recoiled slightly against the padlock that had been placed on the other side and then sat back in position. He placed his hand on the side where the padlock was and pushed again, harder this time; it didn't budge anymore than it did the first time. He tried opening the door as much as he could and slid a couple of fingers through the gap, trying to feel the lock, his fingers were not long enough and the realisation set in that he would just need to stay in and wait it out. Oliver sat back and stared at the door, waiting. He heard another whisper from the darkness.

"Soon…"

An hour passed and eventually Oliver heard noise from the outside, his dad crunching across the lawn to let him out. Many thoughts went through his head at that moment. *Should I attack? Jump forward and punch him? Do I try and kick him?* Ultimately, he decided to do what he always did and just hide those feelings, he realised he could do more damage from within the house than to try and do anything to him here. The padlock was removed and the door flung open again. Oliver's dad stood there once more, staring at him. He knew what was coming next.

"Have you calmed down now?" his father said.

Oliver did his usual and just nodded, his eyes fixed on his father.

"Are you sure?"

He nodded again and waited to be allowed out.

His father turned and walked away, leaving the door open as he left. Oliver stood and followed him back towards the house, his mind ablaze with thoughts of what he wanted to do to him. When they re-entered the kitchen his mother was nowhere to be seen.

"Where's Mum?"

"Upstairs. Leave her alone."

"Why?"

"I said, *leave her alone!*"

Oliver lowered his head slightly and wandered towards the staircase.

"Where are you going?"

"To my room."

Oliver's father just grunted as he walked back towards the front room, grabbing a beer from the fridge as he went.

As he reached the top of the stairs, Oliver heard a sniffling coming from the bathroom. He stuck his head round the door and saw his mother sitting on the toilet with her head in her hands, crying.

"Mum? What's the matter?"

His mother jumped, not expecting to hear the voice. She quickly rubbed her eyes and sniffed a few times.

"How are you doing, dear?" she asked with a croaky voice.

"Mum, what's happened?"

"Nothing. Have you calmed down yet?"

"Mum, look at me."

Oliver grabbed her chin and raised her head slightly. What he saw angered him more than ever; she had a bruise under her left eye and on her cheek.

"Did Dad do this?" he asked, raising his voice slightly.

"Shhh. I'm fine dear, don't worry about me. Have you calmed down? That's the main thing."

"Mum, tell me. What did Dad do?"

"Nothing. Now brush your teeth and go to bed. We don't want any more issues."

Oliver stormed out of the bathroom and headed back down the stairs to where his father was sitting in the front room.

"*What did you do to Mum?*" he shouted as he entered.

His dad spilt his beer in surprise as he got up out of his chair.

"You do not talk to me like that!"

"Did you hit her?"

"No. She hit her head getting out of the bath."

"*Liar!*" Oliver screamed.

"You ungrateful little shit! Clearly two times in the box has not been enough for you tonight! Well, third time's a charm I guess."

He grabbed Oliver by the arm. Oliver thrashed about as much as he could to resist, but his dad was far too strong. As he was being pulled out through the kitchen again, he managed to break free and swung his hand around, catching his father in the groin. His dad doubled over at the immediate pain that he had just suffered, but was quick to retaliate, hitting him across the face with the back of his hand. Oliver was stunned; it was the second time he'd been hit this evening by his father. He fell down onto his ass on the cold floor of the kitchen, and could feel his eyes watering.

"If you cry you will get another! *Understand?*"

Oliver turned away but felt a forceful hand on his arm once more. The pain as his father squeezed it caused him to try and furiously loosen the grip, but to no avail. He was put through the same routine again, being dragged out across the lawn and thrown into 'The Box'. When the door was closed and padlocked, he sat with his back against the cold wood, crying. His arm hurt from where his father had been so forceful, and his face was sore from the slap that Dad had given him. He lifted his knees up and placed his head on top of them, the tears streaming down his face and moistening his jeans. His father had not only hurt him, but had also hurt his mother. The anger started to build as he realised the truth. He knew his mother had been hurt by him before but never bruised, and he knew something had to be done. As the anger built, his tears slowly started to stop and he could feel a slow smile creep across his face. He heard a noise and looked up, struggling to focus in the bleakness. Oliver stared at the outline of the door in front of him, expecting it to open, but nothing happened. He put his head back down on his knees and heard another noise. This time it sounded like the voice he heard earlier. He looked up again.

"Hello? Is someone there?"

The whisper slowly gained volume.

"Do something. You must show him who is boss…"

"Who's there?"

"Listen to us. Do something. Hurt him."

"Who's saying that?"

"Embrace the darkness. Let us help you."

"Who are you? Leave me alone."

Oliver could feel himself becoming more scared, no matter how many times he had been put in there, he had never heard the voices like this before.

"Let us in. We can help."

"Who are you?"

"We want to help you. Let us show you."

"How can you show me?"

"Let us in."

"I can't. The door is locked."

"Not into the room. Into your mind."

"How can I do that?"

"Embrace the darkness. Let us help you."

"Go away. Leave me alone."

"We want to help you. Let us in."

Oliver placed his head back in between his knees and started to rock slowly.

"Don't be afraid. Embrace us. We will show you what to do."

He lifted his head up slightly and sat staring into the darkness, the walls which had previously seemed to close in around him, and the things that seemed to scare him, did not anymore. His mind was awash with thoughts of what he had to do. He knew that his father could not get away with what he had done. He had to be punished, had to be shown what would happen if he crossed the line. He stood up, felt the edge of the door, and pushed it hard. It bounced back from the stubborn lock on the other side, just like before. He raised his foot up and kicked it harder than he had ever done before. He heard a slight crack at the lower part of the door. He put all of his force into the next kick and put his foot through the door, cold air came in through the hole at the base.

Oliver crouched down and spent the next few minutes pushing pieces of wood out of the way, until there was a hole in the door big enough for him to squeeze through. He wriggled his way through until he was back out in the cold air once more. He stood up and turned towards his home, looked up slightly, and took a deep breath, filling his lungs with the pure air of the outside world. He knew what had to be done.

The voice came again. "Thank you."

He walked back towards the house, which was now shrouded in darkness. His guess was that they'd decided to leave him outside for the night and had gone to sleep. It wouldn't have been the first time. They used to call it the *ultimate cool down*, it made sure that he fully understood how bad he had been to deserve it.

He slowly approached the back door and pushed on the handle. It didn't move. He turned and scanned for the blue gnome which had a spare key hidden underneath for emergencies. He struggled to see in the black of the night, but eventually found it. He lifted it up and pulled the small silver key out from underneath. He placed it into the lock and turned the key, the barrels all clicked into place and he opened the door, stepping into the warmth of the kitchen once more.

He could hear the TV coming from the living room. His father would've either left it on or fallen asleep in front of it. He walked slowly through the kitchen, stepping carefully to miss all of the creaky floorboards, something he had taught himself to do years ago so he would sneak down and take cookies in the night. He reached up onto the counter and pulled a long knife out of the block, which sat in the middle of the work-top. He crept further onwards into the house. When he reached the doorway of the front room he peered in and could see that his father was not in there.

He turned and slowly headed for the stairs, almost trance-like. He mirrored what he had done in the kitchen, carefully placing each foot down on the steps as he rose through the house, not making a sound. As he reached the top of the stairs, he headed towards the bedrooms, stopping at his own and glancing in. Empty, as it should be. He carried on, the next was his parents' room, he quietly opened the door and looked in, his mother was asleep in the bed, but not his father. He left the door ajar and moved onwards. He reached the spare room. As he went to open the door, it swung open and his father jumped, startled to see him standing there. His eyes were instantly drawn to the knife.

"Oliver. What are you doing? How did you get back in here? Where did you get the knife from?"

"It's gone on for too long, Dad. I'm sorry."

Oliver swung the knife forward forcefully, catching his father across the stomach. His dad reeled backwards into the bedroom, falling slightly as he went. Oliver advanced into the room after him.

"What are you doing?" his dad screamed as he clutched his stomach.

Oliver kept moving forwards until he was standing over his father, looking down at him trying to stop the crimson from escaping his body. He pulled the knife up once more and thrust it down into his father's stomach again. He repeated the process over and over, the blood spraying everywhere each time he lifted the knife out from his father's wounds. After a while, the struggling ceased and his father lay motionless. Oliver stopped and looked down at the bloody mess of what had been the bane of his life for so long. He slowly raised his head up to the ceiling and closed his eyes.

The voice came once more. "Be free."

His peace was shattered by the horrific screams that came from behind him. He slowly rotated towards the door and saw his mother on her knees with her hands over her mouth, screaming. What his mother saw before her was her son, standing over what was left of his father, holding a knife and covered in blood.

"It's okay, Mum. He won't hurt us anymore."

"What… have you done?" she struggled to say.

"I've made things better. We can be free now."

"You've *killed him!*" she shrieked.

"He would have killed *us* eventually."

"No, he wouldn't! He never would have hurt us."

"He hit you. And me."

"He never intended to hurt us. You've killed him."

She was crying uncontrollably now, shaking in a heap on the floor. Oliver walked over towards her and sat on the floor next to her. He grabbed her arm but she tried to push away. He forced himself to be in a position where he was almost hugging her.

"Get off me," she cried.

"But Mum…"

"… You've ruined everything."

Oliver closed his eyes and then nodded to himself slowly. He tightened his grip around the handle of the knife before plunging it into her back.

"Be free."

Social Sacrifices

By S. L. Dixon

I hadn't finished emptying the boxes onto the shelves and into the closet of my new bedroom when the doorbell rang. I chased the sound, but my mother reached the door first.

"Well, hello there, boys," she smiled, obviously pleased to see the two boys standing there.

The last three places we'd lived, it hadn't been easy on me and was especially hard at the last place. We moved for my father's work, all over the country – we moved so he could redirect the ailing management teams of Peoples department stores. The last place we lived had a town full of jerks and I spent a year squashed to the bottom of the social totem; the kids with leg braces, children in ragged, outdated duds, the kids with lisps and stutters, I'd been below all of them. I've been the target of the frustrated low of low.

"I think it's for you, Sammy," my mother added and stepped aside.

Moving was always exciting, but it was also scary. What if it's just more of the same? What if I never have any friends? What if I get old and die alone with no friends?

Despite the trepidation, there was always hope with a move.

The boys were twins, close to identical, but not quite, although their mother dressed them as such. They both wore blue shorts and red t-shirts, sneakers and yellow Canucks hats.

"Hey, you just move in?" one boy asked.

I nodded, hoping that my skipping heart didn't show through my t-shirt like a cartoon horn-dog. I recalled a pair of twins from a past dwelling. They lived down the block, identical giants with ginger mops and big scaly hands. They used to dunk me into things just because they could. I told my mother one day after coming home, reeking of toilet and garbage. My mother swore vengeance and called the boys' mother. She was a police officer and said that her boys wouldn't do such a thing and said that my saying that was slander.

Luckily, we moved just a month later.

These boys weren't giants and they both had dirty blonde hair.

"I'm Walter, he's Greg," said one boy, he had a bigger nose than his brother and his head had a triangular shape.

"Yeah, I'm Greg, who're you?" said the second boy, smaller nose, but larger teeth, ovular head.

"I'm Sam," I said, forcing my words.

"We got toads, you wanna see?" asked Walter.

I looked to my mother, pleading that she let me go. Her smile didn't waver and I knew she wanted the same thing I wanted. I could unpack my stuff later.

But, there's always a *but* when it comes to mothering.

"Do you boys live around here?" she asked.

"Yeah-huh, next door," said Walter.

"You got a bike, right?" asked Greg.

I nodded and my mother continued, "Where do you keep these toads?"

"'Cross the bridge in our fort," said Walter.

"No girls allowed, not even mothers," Greg stated, arms draped across his chest.

My mother huffed a single syllable laugh and said, "Be back by supper."

It was so close to what I'd envisioned as the end point of my hopes: friends on bikes, a fort and toads.

My house and the neighbours' sat about sixty feet apart and a gravel path, overgrown with weeds and grass, ran between the property-lines back behind our houses. I followed, exhilarated, working hard to keep pace with the racing twins.

The path ran and shrank, barely wide enough for a bicycle, the grass on either side grown to three feet high. It smelled of dampness, the air was hot and sweat rolled from my hairline. For a second I wished I'd worn a hat, but I quickly forgot about it, happy to be around boys again. Real live friends in the making

The trail moved from the grass to the creek and we rolled over a dilapidated wooden bridge nothing more than planks dropped into position that had eventually fused into the path. The trees started out sparse, but thickened. I looked back over my shoulder, I suddenly seemed a long way from my mother; a woman who'd had to double as a friend when no other option existed. It felt great to be there, to be away for once.

"Up here," said Greg who rolled number two in our single-file trio.

"We need to catch more, got a new member," said Walter, I barely heard him.

He veered from the path and we rolled along to where the creek wound back around. The twins dumped their bikes with disregard. I always used my kickstand, but didn't want to look like a pussy, so I let my bike fall, tried not to wince at the sound.

It took almost no time at all. Walter and Greg knew the tricks and the sheer number amazed me. They'd catch and release, *too small, too small,* they say and let go of frogs and toads they'd pulled from the mucky edge.

"That's a good one," said Walter as he lifted the fattest toad I'd ever seen. "Here, take him."

I did and it peed in my hands and I almost dropped him.

The twins laughed and Greg stated, "They always piss, you get used to it."

The twins continued, Walter caught another, not quite as big, but of a good size, "Good enough," he said and looked at his brother and then to me.

I'd put most of my concentration toward not losing the creature in my hands. He was slick, his urine and my sweat doubled the slick effect. I silently begged Greg to hurry up so we could go with our new toads.

"Aha! Got you, bugger!" Greg jumped from the creek.

"We was getting' toads, not crays," said Walter.

"I wanted to show him a cray, you ever see a crayfish, Sam?" asked Greg as he held out a stick with a grey monster clinging on for life.

I shook my head, it was like a baby lobster and it was probably the most amazing thing I'd ever seen. I had no idea that kind of thing lived in creeks. The twins had moved from hopeful friends to boys of legend.

"Leave the bikes," said Walter and led us back out to the path. It was only a minute or two from the creek that we came upon the area cordoned off by small stones. Three trees stood as wall supports for the plywood walls where the twins had nailed shelves and drawn pictures in marker. In the centre was a spot for a fire.

"You like it?" asked Walter.

"You want to be a member?" asked Greg.

"Yeah, sure," I said, the toad and I had reached an agreement and he'd stopped moving.

"Gotta preform the ritual," said Walter.

Greg set the crayfish onto a stone and Walter lifted his toad into the air, both hands around its middle. I adjusted and mimicked him.

"You first," said Walter to his brother.

Greg picked up a stone, "The sacrifice," he said in a lowered tone and smashed the stone over the crayfish, careful not to ruin the claws.

"The sacrifice," Walter said and squeezed the toad.

It croaked and then its eyes bulged like water balloons. My heart thumped in horror when the toad's insides began spilling from its mouth in bright yellow strings.

"You go," said Greg; he and his brother looked at me expectantly.

I felt my mouth open to argue, but no sound came out.

"You go," Walter echoed his brother and stepped toward me.

"He's not going to go," said Greg.

"He's seen our ritual and he's not going to join. What will we do to him?" asked Walter.

They'd both crept close to me. They lowered their faces and I furrowed my brows. My fate felt sealed, like every unlucky toad in the creek, my time had come.

"Let's do a ritual on him!" shouted Greg.

I shook my head.

Walter reached out for me, "Let's sacrifice him."

Then they both cackled and I couldn't take it anymore.

It was a toad, a poor toad, but I needed to live and I needed friends; for once, I wanted to have friends. I tried to squeeze the creature, but the image of the yellow innards stringing out killed my strength. I almost dropped my toad. That would've been it, I was sure. If that toad hopped away those boys would sacrifice me.

The toad slid, slick in my palm and my arms revolted against the movement, sensing the consequences of dropping the thing. I didn't want to, but I had to. I threw the sliding toad as hard as I could against the plywood wall and it stamped a bloody print.

"Oh cool!" shouted Greg. His dire demeanour softened as he looked at the partial toad shape on the wood.

I wanted to cry. I didn't mean it. I'd go my entire life without killing another creature, anything. I'd go to church and say prayers every night, I'd ace every test, I'd wash my father's car and keep my room clean, anything! If I could just go back to the moment before I threw the toad. I would trade my life for that toad's. I didn't mean it!

"It's better if you squeeze em," remarked Walter. He continued to loom near me. "Can't add him to the museum, too smooshed."

"Yeah, but look at the print on the wall," said Greg. "It was a good sacrifice."

The twins added their dead things to the shelves and I noticed everything else on display. Everything deflated and dried. They were real killers.

There must've been fifty toads and frogs; some birds, mice, snakeskins and a bigger mass beyond my understanding on display behind the recognizable shapes.

I stepped closer despite the fear, like a jelly in my legs, my imagination jumping hoops to comprehend what I saw, "What's that?"

The twins looked at me and then followed to where my arm pointed, "Kittens," they said in unison. The shapes came to sense, the kittens were so tiny and it seemed as if they'd all belonged to one structure, a mound of skeletal remains of kittens.

"Did you kill them?" I asked.

The twins looked at each other, smirking, "Of course," said Walter. "We kill anything we want."

"Killed 'em good," added Greg. "You should've seen it. They was all mewing and screaming."

"Killed the mama too," said Walter. "Cool, huh?"

"Very cool," I heard myself say. I didn't think it was cool at all. It was horrid and awful. It made me want to hug my mother tight and beg my father to move us away once again.

The twins went through some of the artefacts, explained the pictures and told me stories of their greatness. They explained how things squirmed and writhed while they died, squealing and crying out in their animal tongues. I tried to follow everything they said, despite disgust commandeering my attention, and I knew it wasn't bullshit. Sometimes kids always lie to the new boy, but I'd seen the twins in the act and I knew, I knew!

"I guess I better go home," I said finally after Walter had finished telling me about the time he threw a spear the distance of three end-to-end football fields and got on the news for it because it nailed an eagle, dead.

"Yeah, okay, you can only come out here with us though, you're not a full member yet," said Greg.

"If you do," Walter said while making a throat slicing motion.

I never wanted to go back, but I wanted friends, so I shrugged and we all walked back to our bikes. We all rinsed our hands in the creek and then mounted. I led the way and didn't turn to wave goodbye when we came upon the property divide, the image of the exploding toad in my head. I couldn't look at them and let them see the tears in my eyes. I parked my bike in the garage on its kickstand and went inside.

I got to my room and slammed the door. It seemed with every second the death became more and more horrifying, more real. I imagined that the toad had family and friends waiting for him, his spot at the supper table empty.

My mother told me to wash my hands and my father asked about my new friends. So badly, I wanted to tell him the truth about the boys, but instead I said "Cool, cool."

That night I cried in bed as I listened to scratching in the walls. I was sure it was an army of toads seeking revenge and I would've let them take me. I deserved it, any *it* imaginable by the toad hordes. I had it coming.

***

My father spoke outside near my window. "Sure, bring them over and we'll let Sammy pick," he said.

It was morning. I'd forgotten about the toad and at the intriguing possibility of picking something. I dressed and ran out into the kitchen. I waited by the door to ask my father about what it was that I got to pick.

"Ears burning?" he said with a big grin on his face. "It's a Surprise."

An hour later, the doorbell rang and my father set down his screwdriver, he was busy putting together a TV stand. He nodded to the door and I knew right away that it was my surprise. I swung open the door, I saw the twins and then I saw the man and the woman. The man held a box and I heard small peeps within.

"You have to pick, Sammy," said my father.

The memory of the toad and of the feline skeletons roared back into my mind. I glared at him in disbelief.

My mother stepped from the kitchen and we all stood at the doorway while I looked at the kittens in the box. She put a hand on my shoulder.

I couldn't believe it. They wanted me to kill a kitten of my own. I imagined everything the twins did to the animals and then I imagined my own hands tearing apart the kittens, the peeping little kittens.

"Already got rid of two," said the twins' mother.

A lump of iron dropped into my throat and my legs wobbled. I felt like a battered pinball machine.

I'd trade my friends and family both, live out my life alone, I never speak another word again, I'd live a mute hermit's life just so I'd never need to choose. Hell would be fine, so long as I didn't have to kill any kittens.

I decided that I wouldn't, not even if they threatened me with sacrifice.

"I was thinking two maybe, what do you think?" my father asked. My mother gave her agreement face and the twins' parents thought it was a good idea.

"Lucky for these ones; the last batch didn't make it," said the twins' mother.

"Oh?" said my mother, petting a fluffy chin with an index finger.

"Terrible, the whole bunch died when the mama was fat with kittens. The kittens even survived in the belly for a few minutes after the mama died. It was quite a sight. The boys looked about ready to hide under their beds," said the twins' mother.

"Did not!" demanded Walter.

"Nuh-uh!" said Greg.

I heard it all, somewhere deep in my mind, but I didn't register. I was stuck trying to pick two victims of the four kittens in the box. I needed friends and I needed family.

“Uh, this one,” I said and pointed to a tiny kitten, black with huge blue eyes and white paws, “and this one,” I pointed at a cat of the exact opposite shades, same huge blue eyes. I couldn’t believe that I picked them. I’d sealed fates, executioner of cute.

“Good, good, look like good mousers to me,” said my father as he nudged me.

“Huh?” I groaned, my mouth had gone dry, I wasn’t ready to murder anything else, I wanted to change my choices. I’d promise anything so that I wouldn’t have to pick.

“Mousers, didn’t you hear all the mice in the walls, those kittens will take care of the mice soon enough,” said my father.

“Sure they will,” my mother agreed.

I was confused about everything. The twins and their parents left with two kittens in a box and my parents didn’t say a word about killing the cats. That night I finally asked. It seemed to worry my mother more than my father; he reassured her that boys get into such things sometimes. He explained the kittens and the twins’ need to impress.

Finally, I understood that the kittens weren’t for sacrifice. I hugged myself and smiled.

I spent the rest of the evening with a blooming happiness, I had friends that killed toads, but Dad said I didn’t have to and they’d probably still be my friends. My new friends didn’t murder cats as they said they had and nobody wanted me to sacrifice the kittens either. Dad said they probably found the rest of the animals already dead.

It was wonderful, my dread evaporating and raining down curious hope. I wouldn’t have to feel the life fleeting between my hands, didn’t have to sacrifice any lives for friendship.

I went to bed with a smile.

I smiled until I stopped.

I grew furious, those twins were liars and frauds and they turned me into a murderer.

***

In bed, late, unable to sleep, hearing the scratching in the walls, I think about my new friends, liars, both of them.

I've decided I'm done being a sacrifice, I'm done being at the bottom.

Their words stick with me and I wonder if it would be how the twins imagined it, a kitten sacrifice. The screams and cries, the blood and organs spilling like overfilled water balloons.

I wonder if it's like that when everything dies; toads, crayfish, snakes, mice, kittens and twin liars.

There's only one way to find out.

The Butcher's Apprentice

By David Basnett

It's fair to say that Nathan made an impression on his very first day at school.

We were all standing around choosing who was *it* for tag, and chanting *eenie meenie miney mo*, when Nathan pushed his way into the circle, his hair sticking up like a burst couch and two green rivers of snot running from his nostrils to his top lip, where he licked it away absently. He stood there in the middle looking at us with wild eyes and an untucked shirt and pointed to each of us in turn.

"My little monkey ran across the country," he chanted in a husky voice. "Fell down a dark hole and split his little arsehole. What. Colour. Was. His. Blood?"

Some of us had heard that swear word before, some hadn't, but none of us had ever used it. After a long pause, he realised that no one was going to offer up a colour so he continued himself. "Blue, B-L-U-E," he said with his finger pointing to me. "You're it. What's your name?"

"Aidan," I said.

"You're it," he repeated and everyone scattered across the yard.

And that was Nathan.

Never short of confidence and always stuck out like a dick in a bikini. There were other incidents. At the time, we dismissed them as just Nathan being Nathan, but someone - a grown-up - should have seen the warning signs. He lived close to me, on Attlee Terrace, which was part of the old pit housing, and was home to the less fortunate in the town. I guess these days we'd be classed as *deprived*. I often saw Nathan wandering the streets looking in windows and rummaging through rubbish bins.

It happened on the 16th May, 1998. I remember the date because it was the first time Newcastle United had made the FA Cup Final since 1974 when they were beaten 3-0 by Liverpool. The town, hell the whole *region*, was buzzing. Shops had black and white flags displayed proudly in their windows. The local radio stations had been building it up non-stop for weeks. Everywhere you looked there were people dressed in black and white stripes. It was the biggest day in the sporting calendar for a generation and it was the greatest, most exciting day that any of us kids had ever experienced.

And then there was Nathan.

He had taken to turning up at our back door and knocking on me to come out to play. I hated it, but my mother encouraged me to try to befriend him as it was obvious that he had no one else to play with. It was an hour before the match was due to kick off and when Nathan came knocking at the door, my father shooed me out on the proviso that I be back in time for kick-off. He didn't often want me under his feet, but today was special. A day when fathers and sons sat together and watched a little bit of history unfold.

I followed Nathan to the end of the street where a little stream ran east to west and separated the town from the fields and Jubilee Woods to the north. The sole of his right shoe was loose and it flapped as he walked but it didn't seem to bother him.

"You know how they kill pigs?" he said as he stared at the stream.

"What?" I replied, confused.

"They hang 'em up and slit their throats while they're still alive."

I stood silently, trying to banish the picture that my young mind was creating.

"Imagine that." He finally turned to me and I could see a light in his eyes. "Row upon row of squealing, dying pigs spilling their warm blood into gutters."

"Why?"

"Pigs is where bacon and sausages come from," he said. "Pork chops too. Think about that next time you're eating ya Sunday dinner. It don't bother me though."

It was the first time someone had explained to me where meat comes from. A conflict of emotions stirred in my body.

"Aren't ya going to say somefink?"

I shrugged then shook my head.

"Aren't going to cry, are ya?" He narrowed his eyes and balled his hands into fists.

"No," I said quickly. I knew enough from school to know that Nathan had a hair-trigger on his temper and could quickly snap into violence. "I'm not a crier."

"Good," he said, and laughed. "Cos I've got somefink to show ya."

The way he said it made my heart sink and I followed him with a growing sense of dread.

He led me deeper and deeper into Jubilee Woods, away from the well-trodden paths and into parts that may well have remained unseen to any other human footsteps since the trees were planted. The fir trees were thicker here, and seemed dead from the ground up, until they got way overhead where the brittle bare grey branches gave way to green needles and blocked much of the warm sunlight. The air was oppressive and still and seemed to suck the breath from my lungs. I could feel my heart thumping in my chest and I was certain Nathan was going to beat me for being a scaredy-cat.

"I need to be back soon," I said in a voice barely louder than a whisper.

Nathan turned and placed his face into mine. A thick vein throbbed at his left temple and a long string of spittle hung from his bottom lip. Our foreheads touched and he used his head to push me away. "Shut up, you little prick."

He led me further into the gloom.

"Do you believe in heaven?" said Nathan, suddenly.

"I–"

"I don't," he continued. "I think we can do whatever the hell we like in this life and there won't be any kind of reckoning after." He smiled at me. "Doesn't that change things? No consequences. We can do anything that takes our fancy. Things that people look down on... say is wrong or… evil." He stopped walking and stared at me. "As long as we don't get caught."

I thought about running, but he would be waiting for me at school and I knew his payback would be brutal, far worse than anything he had done there so far. Even worse than the time that he had put Johnny's fingers in the woodwork vice and tightened it until his fingers snapped and the screams had brought most of the teachers in the school running. He had been suspended for that one, but Johnny had said it had been his idea to see how much it hurt and had asked Nathan to do it. Nathan was back in school before Johnny came back from the sick.

"Do you ever have weird dreams?" said Nathan.

"Now and then," I said, trying to get him on my side.

"Sometimes, I dream I'm a painter or a sailor. One time I dreamt I was a Roman centurion fighting the barbarians at Hadrian's Wall. There was blood everywhere, men dying on the floor with their intestines spilled, steaming on the wet mud."

I nodded, thinking that Nathan sounded nothing like the other eight-year-olds in our class.

"Another time, I was a soldier carrying a tall red flag that had an eagle symbol with spread wings. I was marching along in a huge crowd and pride was nearly making my heart burst from my chest. Do you want to know what the weird thing was?"

I shrugged, not really wanting to know.

"My mother woke me up and said I was shouting in my sleep. But, here's the strange bit, I was shouting out in another language. They said it was German – and I don't speak a goddamn word of it."

"That *is* weird," I said.

"In most of the dreams I'm hurting people. Strangling, cutting, poisoning, shooting, gassing. In one, I cut out someone's eyes."

"We all have nightmares," I said, thinking that I'd never had a nightmare like the ones he was describing.

"Nightmares?" Nathan looked at me. "That's the thing. I never said anything about nightmares... I enjoy them."

I got goose bumps then, and a sick feeling grew in the depths of my stomach.

"Now, be careful around here," said Nathan. "Just go where I go."

"Why's that?"

Nathan smirked. "This is my place. I've got traps all over."

"Traps? What for?"

"To catch animals, of course. And to keep people out if they're stupid enough to come here." He pointed to the left. "I dug a pit there and covered it over. Soon as somefink stands on it..." he slid a finger across his throat that echoed of his earlier revelation about the pigs. "They're mine."

"How many pits?"

He smirked. "Loads. Nicked me dad's spade and took me all last summer to dig 'em all."

I knew then that he had me. I couldn't take a step home without his say so. My eyes darted back and forth seeking out the traps he had made. I could see a couple of places where the ground looked suspicious, but I was sure there were more.

"I don't like people," said Nathan, suddenly. "Is that normal?"

"Who don't you like?"

"My parents, the social worker, the police, kids at the school… everyone really. I don't like a single person." He stopped and looked at me. His tongue darted through his crimson lips and licked the snot from his top lip. "I don't like *you*, Aidan."

"Why did you bring me here?" I asked, determined not to show any fear.

"It's a test."

"Okay. How do I pass?"

"That's not how you play games," he said, chiding me. "There's no pleasure in cheating tests is there? I need to know if you're like me."

In the silence that followed, I heard it.

It was quiet at first. A whimpering then a rhythmical guttural call.

"A monkey?"

Nathan laughed cruelly. "A monkey? Where would I catch a monkey around here?" He led me to an uncovered pit and peered inside, beckoning me to do the same.

I thought I had been scared in the past, but I quickly realised that it was nothing compared to this. There was nothing I wanted less than to look into that pit. I would rather have jumped from an aeroplane or walked through a graveyard at midnight on Halloween. It looked innocuous enough... just a little hole dug in the ground by a kid. I could see some of the branches he had used to cover it, the ones that hadn't fallen into the pit when... whatever it was had fallen in. My heart felt like it had stopped and my eyes filled with tears as Nathan stood there grinning and urging me on.

"No," I said and shook my head.

Nathan looked up from the pit and blew out a big breath that rattled his pursed lips. "It's just a fox. A scrawny little thing. Just an animal. You eat animals don't ya? Can't be sad when they die then, can ya? What's the difference between me and a butcher killing 'em?"

There was a big difference. A *huge* difference, but I couldn't find the right words to explain that to Nathan. "You're not a butcher," I said.

Nathan bent down and thrust his hand into the pit. The cries from the fox increased and he stood with it grasped by the neck. It was deep red and snapped desperately at him with its sharp teeth as it wriggled and contorted in an effort to escape.

"Let it go," I said. My concerns for my own safety were momentarily forgotten.

"It's vermin," he replied. "Farmers shoot 'em."

He took a knife from his pocket and thrust it into the fox's chest to the gentle sound of small bones cracking. It screamed a long, lingering note that was all too human. He readjusted his slippery, bloody hands on the handle then pulled the knife sharply down. The fox opened up as easily as if Nathan had been unzipping a jacket and steaming intestines unravelled to the ground. The screaming and wriggling continued but lessened gradually until they both stopped at the same time.

"Come on! Have a look!" said Nathan. He was giddy with excitement, as if it were Christmas Day and there was a stack of presents waiting for him under the tree.

I kept my eyes averted and heaved my breakfast cereal onto the ground. My mouth filled with the mixed taste of acid and chocolate.

"You wanted to know if I'm like you, Nathan? That's what you asked me when you brought me here. Well, I'm not like you. I don't think *anybody* is like you. You shouldn't do things like this. I want to go home now. Take me back."

"Aidan..." He looked at me as if I had disappointed him. "I'll take you back. I promise ya. But you got to do something for me first."

"Depends."

"Come with me," he walked away.

I waited a moment and composed myself. Told myself that I could still get out of this alive and then, reluctantly, I followed him.

I almost turned back when the stench hit me. My legs buckled and I dry-retched.

"Isn't that bad, you baby," said Nathan. "Smell ain't much of nothing."

Animal skins hung from where they were pinned to tree trunks. Mostly rabbits, but some badgers, foxes, mice, rats, and a deer. The soil underfoot was darkened with blood and I was afraid to walk on it. The bones were gleaming white and laid out side-by-side. They all seemed to be in the correct location, down to the tiny bones of the mice feet. Nathan had been methodical, if nothing else.

Several plastic supermarket carrier bags hung from the branches of one tree. They bulged and were so heavy they hardly swung in the breeze. Nathan pointed to each one in turn, "Hearts, brains, livers, eyes…"

I switched off at that point, too shocked to take any more in.

"I keep 'em in the bags to stop 'em getting eaten. Pongs a bit when they're opened though," he said with a grin.

The entrails… Jesus. I quickly shifted my gaze back down. They were strung through the branches of the fir trees in big loops like tinsel on a Christmas tree. They were discoloured and rotten and several strands had snapped and hung down to the ground where digestive juices, liquefied food and faeces had leaked out and scorched the ground.

"Vell, vell, vell," said Nathan. His voice was low and gravelly – it was still his voice, but like someone was talking through him. His stance had also altered. He was stooped and his jaw hung looser than before. "Zey tried to catch me. Didn't zey? But old Hans hast tricks. Oh ja, scho many tricks. Vee schtripped zem naked like schvine. Cockroaches all of zem. Vat a schame vee vere schtopped before vee cut out zee cancer. Now zey grow in many, many numbers wit zere graspink little fingers."

I was too scared to cry. The transformation that had come over him seemed to have stopped the beat of my heart.

"That was the German," said Nathan, straightening up and as his normal, husky voice returned. "Sometimes I can tune out, make myself half-asleep and one of them can come along." His eyes narrowed. "Say hello to him then, you rude little boy!"

"H-hello."

Nathan nodded. "He's one of the more fun ones. I think they aren't dreams, Aidan. They're dead people I used to be, before I was me. I can remember how they all died."

I nodded and kept my silence.

"How would you like me to string you up and slit your stinking little throat?"

He waited for a reply but I was too scared to answer.

Nathan walked over and stood beside me. The knife went to my face and the sharp edge gently pressed into my cheek. "Lick the blade," he said, and put it to my lips.

It was still dripping with fox innards. I closed my eyes and licked. My tongue touched cold metal and cooled blood. A metallic taste filled my mouth and I could not suppress the shudder that overcame my body. "There," I said, opening my eyes. "I've passed your test."

"Okay," Nathan lifted an eyebrow to show grudging respect. "But that wasn't the test."

He led me back a little ways and stopped by another pit. There was no screaming or squealing from it like the fox pit, but I could hear heavy breathing.

"You do it this time," he said.

"Okay," I said in a small voice, trying not to think of whatever was trapped in there. "I'll do it."

He patted me on the back with a bloody hand. "I knew it! I knew you would understand!" He turned to the pit and thrust his hand down to collect the unfortunate animal.

Gathering up all of my courage for what was to come, I moved forward and pushed Nathan as hard as I could. He gave a cry of shock and anger as he disappeared head-first into the pit. I heard him land with a thump and a bellow of pain.

"Oh you've done it now," he shouted up to me. "Get me out of here and I might just take an eye or a finger from ya."

I was already moving and his shouts faded. Having no idea how deep the pit was, I couldn't be sure how long it would take him to get out… if he ever could.

I took one of the fir branches he had used to cover his pits and used it to feel my way forwards like a blind man with a white cane. *Too slow.* I could almost feel his breath lifting the hairs on the back of my neck. The trees of the wood stretched to the sky and crowded in on me at the same time. Warm tears dripped from the end of my nose. If he got out of the pit, his retribution would be merciless, and if he didn't? I never wanted to see him again, but I didn't want him to die either.

The woods started to look familiar and I recognised the point where he had said to watch out for the first pit. I dropped the stick and ran. I ran like my dick was on fire and there was a bucket of water at the end of the path.

My whole body was burning with the build-up of lactic acid and I had a crippling stitch, but I could not stop. I was over the stream before I thought to jump and I skidded onto Attlee Terrace, narrowly avoiding a reversing car. The honk of the horn followed me into my back yard, but I paid it no heed.

My father's shouts to me were ignored as I ran up the stairs and into my bedroom. The afternoon was spent, not watching Newcastle getting beat by Arsenal, but in a catatonic state, lying on my bed.

My mother eventually coaxed me downstairs at teatime and I sat silently, eating sausage and mash that turned to ash in my mouth.

"Cheer up son," said my father. He winked at me. "Newcastle will win next year, I'm sure."

I nodded, unable to process the feelings in my head, let alone explain them to a grown-up. My food was moved around the plate but very little made its way into my mouth and down to my rolling stomach.

My parents finished their tea and I sat with my cold plate. "Not hungry, eh?" My father tousled my hair as he cleared the dishes. "Bath time then, lad."

A sudden *rat-a-tat-tat* at the back door caused my heart to leap into my mouth.

"Who the hell could that be?" said my father.

"Sorry, John," called my mother from the kitchen. "Nathan's mam rang during the football and asked if he could have a sleepover. Seems he and Aidan have been getting on well and it was Nathan's suggestion."

My fork fell to the plate with a clatter and I stared at the window where Nathan stood looking in with a smile on his face.

"Well, go let the lad in," said my father and motioned to the door with his hands full of plates.

"No."

"For me, son," said my father. "I know he's a bit weird, but just put up with him for tonight and I'll have a word with your mam tomorrow. Can you do that for me?"

Unbidden, my head jerked into a nod and I dragged my feet to the door.

He was immediately in my personal space when I opened the door and I took a step backwards.

"Evening, Aidan," he said, and smiled at me. He had a cut above his right eyebrow that was still oozing a little blood and his cheek was scratched and bruised. His fingernails were broken and encrusted with dirt.

"Come on in, Nathan love," called my mother. She paused when she saw him. "You been in the wars today?"

"Tripped," said Nathan, and licked the snot from his lip.

“Do you need anything for it?”

“Nah,” he said, then smiled. “I’m just a bit tired. Would it be okay for me to go up to bed?”

“Well if you’re sure...” my mother gave him an appraising look. “Have you eaten?”

“Pork sausages,” he said, looking at me.

***

I woke in a panic, breathless and confused. My pillow was damp with sweat and my hair was plastered to my face and neck. I had meant to stay awake and could remember seeing in 2 am. The house was quiet… I couldn’t even hear my father’s snoring through the thin partition walls. My frenzied eyes fell on the sleeping bag lying by the side of the bed that I had been watching oh so fastidiously. It was empty. Where was he?

“Ve vanted to be friendsch.”

I’m sure the top of my head nearly hit the ceiling. My trembling hands pulled the sheets higher as I looked for the source of the voice. “Go back to sleep Nathan,” I said. “Tomorrow you’re leaving and I don’t want you coming back. You’re not right in the head.”

“Vee vanted to teachen you, ja? You took our gift and you schitten it out.”

There was a shadow by the bookcase, not standing, not sitting, but slumped.

“Now zer must be conze… contze. How you zay konsequenzen?”

The shadow stood and took a step towards me.

“Death ist not a schary zing. Embrasch it. Vee are reborn.”

Nathan took another step forward. Slack jawed and stooped, he grasped a sharp kitchen knife in his left hand.

"Killink ist inschide all of us. Mankind hast become more und more miserable the longer vee have suppresched zis inschtinct."

The knife rose.

"Zer is noschink more beautiful zan vatchink zee light leave schomeone's eyes as you twischt zee knife in zer gutsch."

He made it to the bed faster than I thought possible and strong hands pinned me down. The knife point went to my left eye and I felt it slide easily into my lower lid and come to a rest below my eyeball.

"I don't normally schtart with eyes," he whispered, his hot and stinking breath choking me. "I normally schpill zee gutsch. But I liked you and vill do you zee gut deed ov blindink you firscht."

"Mam! Dad!" I shouted, finally finding my voice.

A wet and clammy hand pressed over my lips.

"Juscht lie back und relax. You may enjoy zis."

He was bathed in the sudden light of a car passing down the street and for the first time, I noticed the blood. My god the blood! His face and clothes were covered and it dripped in a thick strand from the end of his nose.

"Oh yesch," he said softly. "Your parentsch ver real beautysch. Vee had such fun."

The face changed and I could tell it was Nathan again.

"Please, Nathan," I whispered as I felt tears and bile both rise at the same time. *My parents.* "Don't let Hans do this."

"Oh, but I'm learning so much from him… from Hans. He was famous," he whispered into my ear. "They called him the Butcher of Bielefeld." He pressed hard with the knife and I felt red hot pain as the point scraped to the back of my eye socket. He paused for a moment then twisted the knife. "I guess that makes me the Butcher's Apprentice."

The Seventy-Five Percent

By Brian Barr

Joseph Maxwell looked out of his Pontiac windows, forward, left, and right with wary nervousness, sipping his coffee as Baltimore's gutter trash wandered aimlessly down streets and alleys. B-More, the kids called it, a cesspool of sex and violence; a backwards calamity of destruction.

A hellish metropolis. Maxwell often wondered why he settled here after his retirement from the U.S. army, why he didn't pick a nicer location like Honolulu or Phoenix. Then, he remembered how much he hated the expenses of living in Hawaii when he was stationed there, and how the dry heat of Arizona made his dark skin suffer with its eczema episodes. The amounts of lotion he had to apply in modest temperatures just to keep his skin moisturized was torture enough.

Maryland was a choice he settled on for what seemed like a decent cost of living at the time, the suburban life comfortable there, but not *too* hokey and far removed from reality. Both Baltimore and D.C. were not too far from Maxwell's chosen home of Glen Burnie.

He came to Baltimore this evening to get his son back. The young man, Devon, had been lost to a life of street violence that he didn't have to live. Joseph often wondered where he went wrong. Did he not give his son a great role-model to look up to, a black male with a Masters in Communications, retired from the U.S. military, married, hardworking and modestly successful? His son grew up a military brat, living in apartments and houses on military posts. There were no rough starts for the child, and at a young age, Devon lived with the delusion that his family was rich. He was spoiled, and could literally get any toy he wanted, refuse food he didn't want to eat, simply because its taste didn't suit his tongue. "Military brat" was a more than suitable title to tag along Devon's name, a child that never had to hunger for anything, whom Joseph worked on supporting for fifteen years, along with his wife, Sandra.

Then, Devon ran away, months ago. He was nearly sixteen now, and he chose to come down to the roughest of Baltimore's streets, charmed by a bunch of fake thugs at his school. Joseph hadn't taken the signs seriously, his son imitating rap videos, wearing rags, claiming sets from famous gangs, and speaking crazy slang with his friends. One week, Devon was wearing blue, the next red. Joseph had always forced Devon to take the shit off, to dress like a man, but he couldn't stop the youth from wearing what he wanted at school. Twenty-four hour surveillance just wasn't given to a parent, and it certainly wasn't there when Devon decided to join a *real* gang.

The Mad Murderland was an exclusive Maryland gang, stretching out from the correctional facilities and prisons, active in Baltimore and surrounding counties; Prince George, Anne Arundel, and several others. Annapolis had chapters, Odenton and even Fort Meade, the last base Joseph had worked before re-entering civilian life. Partially a hot topic in the news and a dark secret along the streets, the gang was talked about, yet slightly ignored, not taken as seriously as it should have been.

Now, Joseph's son was lost to it.

No, Joseph thought, *I can still find him, still bring him back. He's not lost. Not just yet.*

On top of his son's claimed gang lifestyle and resettlement in Baltimore after running away from home, the streets were just calming down after a series of social protests. A young man, reputed to be a drug dealer, had died mysteriously while in police custody. The death tore a city apart, unleashing feelings of racial and class disparities, and protesters were calling police conduct into question, challenging brutality issued by law enforcement. The messages of peaceful protesters were drowned out by rioters in frenzies, angered members of impoverished slum communities who didn't hesitate to burn cars and devastate businesses, whether the property was in their own neighbourhood or not.

The riots may have only been a small part of the bigger picture, in terms of how many protesters turned out to address the issue peacefully, but the media didn't give a fuck. Riots got ratings, fear made headlines, and the news outlets made such topics their focus. Joseph Maxwell knew all too well, being a part of the media.

Pimps and whores strolled proudly in the middle of the day, not even caring to hide in night's shadows. These were their streets, their land, where they made their money.

Joseph Maxwell was convinced that his son may have died during the riots. He had heard of many of the city's gangs forming a truce that day, choosing not to engage in the violence and stopping people from rioting instead. Still, there were a number of gangs that were rumoured to not be a part of that truce. Mad Murderland was one of them, and they had been reported as a gang that was most active in *encouraging* riots. The gang was a newer one, rebellious to older gangsters well-seasoned and educated in the street life. The younger gangs often tried to outdo what had been done, throwing any sense of honour or protocol, even to fellow street hoodlums, out of the window. Perhaps those riots were a way for the MM gang to stand out and invoke terror amongst their own community, causing more problems than the truce forming gang members had hoped to solve.

Lost to MM, Devon would only be trapped in the negatives portrayed by the Baltimore riots, and it was probably already too late. If that video footage Joseph had seen in the newsroom truly *was* his son,

"Hey!" Joseph shouted at the bum leaning over his car with a bottle of Windex and a scrubber. Red lights could always mean a come up for a crack fiend in Baltimore. Parking his car temporarily, Joseph stood up to shoo the bum away, but the poor man ignored him, continuing to scrub the Pontiac's front window. Only when Joseph pulled out a wad of ones did the bum gracefully take the money and move back into a neighbouring alley. Joseph was able to get back into his car before the light turned green.

Record time, Joseph thought, mockingly to himself.

Back on the road to nowhere, Joseph was reminded of the tale of Orpheus, traveling into the underworld in order to save his love, Eurydice, from the clutches of Hades. Love was a hell of a thing, transcending all other emotions. The retired soldier was convinced a parent would risk even more for their children than a man or woman would for a romantic partner. The bond between parent and child was probably stronger than anything imaginable in the universe.

The last Joseph was aware; his son was in the Lower Park Heights area. The boy would call him randomly, settling with his gangster pals in apartment buildings ranging from Druid Hill to Towson, right outside of Baltimore, always on the move, never settling. Joseph likened his son to a ghost over the recent months, never seen, sometimes heard over a phone line or contacting him through email. School was officially out of the question, and he refused to consider pursuing a GED.

I've lost him, Joseph thought as he drove up those streets, restless, but failing.

Perhaps he had given him *too* much freedom. Joseph had tried being strict, easing up on the discipline, communicating. Whatever changed his son, made him embrace the unnecessary life of a criminal, he didn't understand. He had always reasoned it a fad, a way his son could escape the regular and bland existence given to him by army base neighbourhoods and Maryland suburbs, but maybe there was a deeper, underlying problem. Maybe something more pathological drew Devon to change, to play a part in a rough society that he had every odd to overcome, to even help in a positive way.

Devon's mother hadn't helped much. Perhaps Sandra had coddled the boy *too* much when he was younger, given him everything he wanted. But it wasn't all her fault, at least not exclusively. Joseph knew he had spoiled Devon too, given him too much freedom. Maybe that was why, when he finally got serious with him as an adolescent, the child already felt free enough to go wild.

***

"Look at those bastards," Joseph said, as he and Matt watched the footage once again.

Matt and Joseph had seen and reported on many a story similar to the video they were reviewing now, inner-city youths engaging in fist brawls. Another Baltimore playground, security cameras watching the kids as if they were in a maximum security prison. Young men getting stomped and punched by rival children, cursing, spitting, blood flying and pouring onto the concrete.

Matt shook his head pitifully. "A damn mess. If only they put that amount of energy into their classwork."

"That's the kid that died, right?" Joseph asked as he pointed at one of the kids struggling to get off the ground. His answer came in seconds, after the child's body became immobile. "Jesus. Only fourteen-years-old. Devon's age."

"Can't imagine if your kid was involved in shit like this."

"Hell no! I'd kick his ass! Me, and then his mother." Taking another sip of coffee, Joseph could hardly control his anger. "If these bad-ass kids had a better unit at home, none of this shit would happen. I'm always willing to bet they just got their mothers at home."

Matt rolled his eyes. "Here we go again."

"What? I'm just looking at the situation *truthfully,* Matt. How many of these little bad-asses come home to these single black mothers, letting them do whatever they want, running the streets late at night? They don't have a father to answer to. And these gangs. It's like a bunch of emasculated men trying to out-man each other, thinking that masculinity is going on the block, carrying a gun, or engaging in schoolyard fights that turn to murder and death. It all originates with these single mothers, just letting these rug rats do whatever they choose. Growing up in these shitty neighbourhoods, and even with the alternatives, you'd think they'd go to school and try to make something out of their miserable settings. I grew up around this mess. I didn't turn into a fucking monster."

"All because you had two parents?"

"And a mother that understood the importance of

a man in the home. I always say, look behind a deviant black male and you'll find an insufficient black mother."

"That's not really fair, Joe."

"It isn't? Well, what do you think *is* a fair assessment?"

"I doubt it's not like most of these mothers try, with the odds stacked against them and their kids. At least the mothers are around. Look at the fathers that just have sex with those women, and then leave."

Joseph laughed, placing his coffee mug on the desk before him. "Please. As if the bad judgment of these women didn't choose those men?"

And these men didn't choose to live up to their responsibilities. They produced these kids, then they fucking walk out on them. Worse enough, when these kids are born into poverty and the mothers have no help. You know that nearly three out of four black kids are born out of wedlock, with absent fathers in the home? That's almost seventy-five percent of black children, Joe."

"Exaggerate much? I've heard it's more like seventy-*two* percent."

"No fathers at home. And blacks are like, what, twelve or thirteen percent of the population in the states? If that isn't a fucked up situation, I don't know what is. I just don't think it's as easy as saying the mothers exercised bad judgment in the men they chose. Maybe they did. But these guys just dip when they should be taking care of their kids. We're only lucky that laws have changed enough for women to track these bastards down, make them do DNA tests and get child support. I can't stand deadbeat dads."

Joseph nodded. "I guess I can understand your logic. You grew up without your dad. So you probably see your father's flaw in the situation more than your mother's."

Matt's chuckle carried a hint of aggravation. "Absent fathers may not be as big of a problem in the white community. Probably about twenty percent or more of us grew up without our dads."

"What are you? A walking statistics board?"

"Just a topic I'm passionate about. I know firsthand what it's like to have a father walk out on you, and how much it fucks you up. You know I didn't even get a message from my father until I was sixteen? He wanted to come back into my life, wanted to apologize for not raising me. Fuck him. He was a fucking heroin junkie. And he died three years later. They found him in Bowie with a needle in his arm." Matt walked up to the monitor and turned it off before pulling out the tape. "I doubt the moral decay of America, or the world for that matter, can merely be pinned on absent fathers *or* negligent, present mothers. They're all just factors in a bigger problem of human delinquency. Pointing the finger in either direction is lazy, anyway. But to look at one issue or group of people and ignore the faults of another is just hypocrisy."

Joseph shrugged. "I've been known to generalize."

"At least your Devon has both parents at home to keep him on the straight and narrow."

"We do our best. He just started high school, you know? Freshman. He stayed on honour roll throughout middle school. Some of his friends, I worry about, but he's a good kid. I'm telling you, raising a kid is a team effort. If Sandra, or me, were out of the picture –"

"He'd end up like me?"

Laughing, Joseph slapped Matt on the back as they walked out of the review room. "Of course, not *every* kid without a dad ends up ruined by the experience. You worked hard, you made something out of yourself.

We're both hardworking reporters. Not everyone has that willpower. I'm just saying it *helps* to have both parents in the home."

"Is Devon the only child?"

"Yep. Sometimes, I wish we had given him brothers and sisters. They're good for the social aspects, help keep a kid humble, and lord knows we spoil the little brat. But we're proud of him, you know?"

"I can always tell. Well, only a few minutes until show time. Better make sure Becca's ready."

"She's a pro. I bet she's gotten her segments memorized."

"Nobody's *that* good. We'd all die if we didn't have a teleprompter. See you on the set, Joe."

"I'll be there."

Walking past a few crew members setting up their cameras, Joseph stepped to the side and pulled out his cell phone. He took a moment to text his son, musing about a less complicated time when a kid was lucky to have an Atari. At least cell phones were a good way of keeping in contact with family members, making them more of a convenience than an unnecessary vanity item for teenagers.

About to go on the air, he typed quickly. *Do your homework and keep your mom occupied.*

His texts were as laconic and straight-forward as his face to face interactions with Devon. He never wanted to impose himself too much into the youth's life, or get too involved. *Get too wordy like his mother, and you'll push him away,* Joseph thought.

The news director was calling from the side-lines of the set. Joseph straightened his tie and walked towards his boss's voice, ready for action.

***

Joseph didn't remember getting out of the car.

He remembered seeing Devon's face, but he looked so ruined, so dirty, his clothes wrinkled and spotted with stains. Only a few months in, and street life hadn't been kind to him. Joseph was convinced the boy *had* to be his son, standing on that corner, looking nervously back and forth before catching his father's eyes, freezing in fear, and running away.

Now, Joseph pursued him, feeling like a lion pursuing gazelle in some concrete jungle. He could see Devon's back, his hair a bit longer, his frame significantly slimmer and not the healthiest. The rain was coming down, the streets dirty around them, characters unsavoury from sidewalks and alleyways.

Joseph turned where Devon had, only a few feet away. The father greeted a dead end. The alley led nowhere but towards a trash can and a brick wall covered with graffiti, just like the surrounding buildings. His mind throbbing, heart racing, Joseph tried to reason with such a strange circumstance. The wall was too tall to climb in such a *short* time, if at all. Shards of glass and syringes lined the asphalt alongside paper debris and soda cans.

That was him, Joseph thought. *I know I saw him.* Like a ghost, some apparition, he had disappeared into the ether, almost as if he didn't exist. *When will I see him again?*

Turning around, tired, the father walked out of the alley, letting the rain pour on him. He inched back, slowly, to his car as the storm built around him. Thunder crashed in the sky, lightning descending behind buildings. Finally, after several feet, he could finally see his vehicle again, despite the murky evening rain making it difficult.

He could also see that his tyres were gone.

In shock, Joseph ran to the car. Yes, tyres gone, door handles removed, hubcaps stolen, headlights smashed. He hadn't been gone *that* long, had he? Only minutes, if that. Minutes long enough to be robbed.

"Damn it!" Joseph shouted as he kicked the car, fuming. Where the fuck was he? He wanted to say Sandtown, but it could have been Greenmount, Edmonson, 28th. He had driven down those streets for so long, searching until he was lost, and now rain and buildings were all he saw. He looked for a street marker, but his attention seemed tragically magnetized to the car, to the unending shock and anger that gripped him. He slammed his fists against the roof, as if denied access, and cried, tears melting with cruel precipitation.

"Daddy?"

Joseph turned around to see a young black youth, male, in a soaked white t-shirt and jeans. He couldn't have been older than eight, his eyes brown and lost, shining in sadness. *But that face. He looks like -*

Caught in silence for a moment, Joseph broke his hesitation, stammering as his head shook in the rain. "No, little man. I'm... I'm not your father."

"Daddy?"

Joseph turned again. This time, he faced a young girl, possibly twelve or thirteen. Her hair was braided. That nose, those eyes, so familiar.

"No, little girl." The ex-soldier shook his head, pressing his hands against the car. *Some kind of set-up. Might be some dealer's kids. Somebody's waiting to rob me blind.* "I'm not your –"

A sudden pain seized Joseph's head. The vision of the real world evaded him, and in his memories, he was brought back to hot summer nights in Arizona, the 80's, stationed in the barracks. He remembered beautiful military women in CEO balls, and roofies…

God no.

"Daddy?" said another child, crawling out from a trash can, and another, exiting the window of an abandoned building, and another.

"Stay back!" Joseph shouted. "I'm looking for Devon. Devon! *Devon, where are you?*"

The man began to run. The real world kept evading him, though he could feel himself *existing* in those Baltimore streets, his pursuit unending. He saw Devon in front of him again, running down another avenue, through another alley, and then, Arizona came back. Hawaii came back. Ft. Bragg. Texas. Sexy women. Beautiful ladies in and out of uniform, in gowns, in lingerie and naked.

"That's not my kid," he told another in a Schofield Barracks hotel, the tropics of Oahu bringing in a mellow heat. "You women just say that to tie a man down, to keep them locked down. You just want to steal my freedom from me."

"She's somebody else's," he told another woman in Texas. *Stupid slut, always trying to lock a man down.*

"Not mine," he told a staff-sergeant in Fort Bragg.

Women were clawing at him, digging their well-polished nails into his black skin. Their faces turned from seductive angels to horrid hags. Ebony women, pale, freckled ladies, Puerto-Rican, pacific-islanders.

We just fucked, bitch! That kid isn't mine. Those kids aren't mine!

One minute he was swimming in his own blood, skin ripped by clawing nails, hands and feet tugged by little hands attached to crying children, screaming harpy mothers. and the next, he was running down those dirty

Baltimore alleys. He could hear Devon playing with pistols, laughing with friends, enjoying the hell of a life he wasn't supposed to live.

I didn't raise you for this, Devon! Sandra was the woman I chose. You were my son, my only son. I didn't make you to fail. Come back to me-

The fires of an endless street inferno seemed to engulf Joseph, and Devon's laughter turned more demonic, more absent of human compassion.

***

"That can't be him."

Joseph and Matt had watched the footage five times by now. It would never go on the air, like many of the riot scenes, but that kid *did* look like Devon, and it *did* look like his head and face were stomped in by a bunch of other rag wearing kids. Then, the cops swarmed in, breaking them up. Cars were afire, the streets in smoke.

Matt's lips were frozen. He refused to speak, knowing comfort was impossible. Joseph could feel the sorrow and empathy somehow, even in the pain that engulfed him.

"I'm sorry," Matt said five minutes after they left the review room.

"That wasn't him. It couldn't have been him." He had been waiting. How long had it been since Devon called him, to let him know he was okay? A week? Two? The boy was always guaranteed to call randomly, to let him know he was still alive, despite the fact that he *knew* his father completely disapproved of his new lifestyle. He was fine. All of this was a phase, some game the kid was playing to belong. He would grow. He would realize his friends were ruffians and move on.

Dead.

"No. I have to get him, Matt. I have to. I can't just let him be out there. Or at least find him."

"But, Joe. They called you down to identify his *body*. And you saw the tape before they called. Aren't you just going to go to the station and –"

"I've got to find him." Joseph turned towards the lobby, his pace quickening.

"Don't worry about the broadcast, Joe. Just get to the station. We've got it."

Matt's voice died behind him. The newsroom died, the lobby, the station. Joe's Pontiac hit the street. He didn't bother to contact Sandra or look back, eyes forward and straight ahead, looking onwards until he could see his son.

His son. His *only* son, the boy that he had raised after marriage. Devon, the end of wild nights and endless affairs. The death of a debauched, lonely life. Unity was found in Sandra, and the symbol of their union was born in Devon, their shining star. He was their hope, their future doctor, future policeman, future lawyer, possibilities abound.

He wasn't dead.

The entire ride to that godless city, Joseph could remind himself of that simple fact. Devon wasn't dead. And now, chasing him from alleyway to corner, through parks and avenues, Joseph knew he wasn't too far away. They would be united, and he could take him home, set him back straight. His family could be together again.

***

They kept calling. Kept calling him *Daddy*. Kept asking why he had left, why he was never there.

Did he hear their prayers, receive their cards? A few of them were still living, in agony. Three had committed suicide. One was struggling through college now, another addicted to pain pills, robbing people, others in their own tragic, desperate attempts to survive a dark, shadowy world.

Mothers made lies, others told the harsh truth. Daddy was never coming. Daddy didn't care. Daddy denied them.

Alive or dead, those shadows, phantoms, felt so *real.* Along the streets, they pulled on him, ripped at him, tore through him. He couldn't distinguish reality anymore, as if he was caught in some psychic residue or dealing with the avenging angels of all the mothers and children he had wronged ignorantly. Somehow, that didn't matter. They wanted him dead.

Or they wanted to love him.

They wanted him to love them.

They were all crushing him, whether with hugs or with grappling claws and arms, he couldn't tell, whether in adoration or hatred, all seemed mixed. Mothers, sons, and daughters smothered him, holding his limbs, his torso. They pressed against his face, clawed at his ears. Blood poured down, fingers ripped. Kisses were delivered with rough, tearing bites.

Daddy. Joseph. Bastard. Deadbeat. Many a nail was delivered to him, from mature and prepubescent voices, the crying of babes sailing around him. He had forgotten names, remembering some, identifying a few of the women's faces, seeing his reflection in the visages of many a child. How many nights, how many lives? He couldn't tell, and they were all *killing* him with as much life as he had given them.

Devon was beyond those walls of tearing hands and scratching nails, those cries and sobs for a father. Devon had a father, and he didn't want him anymore, didn't care. Devon was laughing, the netherworld his new home, shooting guns with the ghosts of city children. The world was lost to him.

“Got to get you back,” Joseph whispered. “Gotta find you again, my son.”

His voice was drowned out by the bodies surrounding him. Children of different shades and flesh hues, fingers beginning to gouge his eyes, hands prying at his tongue, pulling. Joseph could only scream so long before he was sucked down into the blackness of that strange underworld holding him, denying him access to Devon. Above him, he could hear Devon continuing to laugh, in another level of hell so high it carried the illusion of traveling from heaven.

The children screamed. Daddy screamed. Existence disintegrated.

***

Joseph Maxwell’s death in a fiery car accident in downtown Baltimore was reported a day after his son had been found dead in a Baltimore riot. His colleagues would remember him as a skilled reporter and news anchor in the field, remaining objective in his work, despite his harsh criticisms held behind the camera. Former soldiers that worked alongside him would always remember him as the fun loving socialite that was always serious when it came down to business.

Above all, Joseph Maxwell would be remembered as a hard working family man. A few close to him knew the struggles he had with his son in the end, but no one held that against him. Kids got rebellious sometimes, but that wasn’t his fault, nor Sandra’s. At the funeral, people offered their condolences, offered to help out in any way they could with expenses or emotional support.

The mother was alone now, and no mother wanted to outlive her own children. Devon was her one and only, Joseph the man she had chosen to walk alongside in life.

They were a family, one solid unit, reduced to one lonely member. Sandra would try to forget the last troublesome year with her son, holding on to those bright memories of a fun loving kid taken care of by dutiful parents. She held Devon higher than the stars, along with a dad that had always been around in a world where many negligent fathers refused to take care of, or even acknowledge, their children.

Pregnant With Freedom

By Christopher Ropes

Before:

I guess my mistake, the biggest one, was in presuming that I would not be able to love a child if my wife died giving birth to it. Love may not conquer all, and blood may not always be thicker than water, but love conquers much and, when blood is thicker than water, it breaks the walls of flesh that keep us thinking we are islands, and makes of us one body and even one spirit.

The Beginning:

Melissa was so happy to give me the news. The test was blue, her eyes were blue, and her smile was golden. I was going to be a proud papa. It was all I could have asked for, barring that one caveat I mentioned above. But that wouldn't happen, not in the day and age of modern medical science, right?

Of course not.

I held her hand, feeling her quick squeezes on my fingers, as the doctor explained to us all that we could expect from the pregnancy, and how he would be there to help us through anything, anything at all. The first appointment – it was a reassuring pep talk, exactly as it was designed to be, giving us confidence that nothing untoward could possibly happen with Dr. Matthew Schneider on our team. Middle-aged, but still brimming with a certain youthful idealism, at least to our eyes, Dr. Schneider was the perfect cheerleader.

Melissa and I walked from his office, took a quick drive in our Toyota to the nearest Starbucks, and talked like we hadn't since before we were married. A heart-to-heart where we laid bare all our hopes and fears and dreams over a hot latte.

When I took her home, we made love, in the truest sense of the words. It was tender and it was magical and it was our eyes staring into the depths of each other's souls as our bodies conjoined. We were one, perfect being, and our marriage was never better. This is the memory I return to most often.

Well, of the happy memories, anyway.

First Month:

Morning sickness and mood swings, shopping for uni-sex baby items we would need, me quitting smoking, but mostly life going on as normal. I went to work at the school, teaching English, Melissa went to New Bouquet Scent Florist where she was a manager, and life was normal. Life is always normal, right? Because, if something is happening to us, in an infinite cosmos, that thing happening must have a degree of normalcy, I would imagine. Or maybe I'm making this shit up, I failed physics.

I'd had a pretty tough day and we were planning on having cheeseburgers for dinner. Coupled with a few brews, I was down for some of that action, no doubt. Traffic wasn't too bad, and I got home a little early. I walked in, threw my jacket over the hat rack, yanked off my tie and tossed that over my jacket, and strolled to the kitchen.

There she was, with the ground beef. She was rolling it around in her hands, squeezing it so cascades of red cow muscle squished through her fingers and plopped to the floor. What remained, she put on the counter and began punching it and making a strange sound, almost like a hyena's yipping laugh. I cleared my throat and she turned to me and instead of any of the expressions I expected to see, perhaps madness or savage glee, I saw she was terrified, and yet defeated. I almost asked what was wrong, but instead, I dropped my briefcase right there on the floor, ran to her, and took her in my arms. She pushed me away, grabbed a handful of the beef and stuffed it into her mouth. Then she meandered off, out of the kitchen to our bedroom upstairs, her walk a staggered and sulky slog, almost as if she were wading hip-deep in swamp mud. That's when I knew something was amiss and that's when I missed maybe my only chance to do anything.

Now, I'm not sure if I regret that or if I'm glad.

(Interlude: I look at her and she looks at me as I write. I love this girl… my girl.)

Second Month:

"You could get very sick, maybe die. I recommend at least considering the termination of the pregnancy."

"No," Melissa said, a firmness in her voice that I hadn't heard since she said, "I do," at the altar three years before.

"Mrs. Hartley, please, consider your options. I don't want to end any pregnancy, but you are my patient, first and foremost. I must do what is right for you."

"With all due consideration, Doctor, fuck yourself." She was so beautiful in her anger and determination and bizarre habits. The meat hadn't been the end of it. Just the beginning, in truth. Needless to say, we never saw Dr. Schneider again. He didn't guide us bravely and kindly through the pregnancy storm. Instead, he vanished into a past that, now, is blurry and somehow anonymous, as if it were the history of a stranger that I was spying on.

We never saw any other doctor either for the remainder of what lay ahead. Her health still seemed strong at this point, though Dr. Schneider made it clear that it most likely would not remain so. Melissa knew, somehow, that any other doctor would say the same thing she'd already rejected, so we avoided it entirely. It was understood that I either had no opinion on the subject or was wise enough to not share it. That much went unspoken.

Much went unspoken, looking back on it. I never commented on the many times we would be watching television and her eyes would drift to her own belly, and she would mouth words to whomever was growing in there (*my* beautiful girl,) and she would not remember I was there or the TV was on in the background. When she came to again, it was always with a jolt of surprise and it obviously took a moment for her to regain recognition of where she was and who I was. My heart was troubled often.

Worse were the times I would return home from work, and she would be home, having taken an indefinite leave from her florist job, and she would be on the loveseat, clutching her own clothing and rocking herself back and forth making whimpering sounds. Naturally, I never mentioned this either. Aside from locking herself up inside her own head, Melissa had decreed that I would be locked in my own head as well. Without her to talk to about what I mistakenly thought we were both going through, I had no one on my side. I just had my thoughts and my fears and my hopes. I took to prayer, a practice I had abandoned many years before, after deciding the Roman Catholic Church was some kind of holy pyramid scheme.

"Dear God, whatever or whomever you may be, save us . . . save us from you. Amen.

Third Month:

What's love but a second-hand intrusion of the madness of one animal putting another animal's being before its own? She lost that for me, but certainly gained it for the baby. It shames me to say it now, but I did not share her devotion to the creature growing within her. The third month is when I began to notice her weight loss and the paleness sucking even a feint at vitality from her. Every time her acting attempted to approximate liveliness, it was more grotesque than the chest-bursting scene from the first *Alien* film and less natural. I can't say I was managing the role of loving husband with verve and panache either. The sight of her looking so unhealthy and shutting me out emotionally eventually made me give up on reaching out to her much. In truth, the sight and even sound of her began to make me feel sick.

I would help around the house when I could, mainly because I was not a sociopath and knew it was the right thing to do. I was a capable cook, though her appreciation for my efforts resulted in little more than her being a smidge more pleasant to me for an hour or so after mealtime. But couples don't split up when a baby is on the way. That's what I told my very few friends and family members who had any clue about the difficulties.

Melissa probably told no one anything. She barely spoke to anyone at all. I met her sister while grocery shopping one time and was accused of being abusive.

"Planning on letting Mel out of prison to talk to me once in a while? Maybe join me for lunch?"

"Um, what are you talking about, Sarah? Nice to see you, by the way."

"You think no one has noticed that you haven't let her have a life outside the house since she got pregnant?" Her hostility was bizarre to me, since she'd always been pleasant before, and because I had no idea that Melissa hadn't been speaking to anyone.

"I haven't been forbidding her from doing anything. I swear. I will put the phone in her hand myself when I get home from shopping. I don't want to keep her from her family or her friends. I'm actually worried about her not being in touch with people."

Her eyes showed a hint of remorse, perhaps, or just worry for her sister. "Is she… the baby…"

"As far as I know, they're both okay, but…" Things were getting awkward. I took the dive with information that I knew wouldn't make Sarah happy, because it made me extremely concerned. "I have to tell you, Sarah, she hasn't been keeping any doctor's appointments. She's been doing nothing, seriously, nothing at all, to take care of herself or the baby. She's…" I trailed off again. How I to tell someone their beloved sister was possibly going insane?

The clues in my gaze, my troubled and deadened stare into the distance at nothing in particular, gave me away. "Something is wrong with her? Something," she reached for some kind of euphemism for *nuts*. "Something not physical? Mental? Emotional? You know." Her eyes pleaded with mine for there to be nothing wrong with Melissa's mind and I couldn't give her that reassurance. I couldn't give anyone, least of all myself, any reassurances about anything.

We talked and agreed to meet each other the next weekend for lunch and to discuss matters. Fast forward to…

Fourth Month:

The affair begins. So does guilt over the affair. Fast forward to…

Fifth Month:

The affair continues. The guilt over the affair doesn't. Fast forward to…

Sixth Month:

She knew and she didn't care. As a matter of fact, she preferred it that way.

"Fuck her all you want, I don't really want your nasty cock near me or the baby." She really said it that way, really made me sound like some kind of foetus molester. I had just about had enough, but the "just about" trumped all with me; my non-confrontational, downright pussy-ish ways. I was starting to make myself sick. Why wasn't I forcing her to see a doctor, or confronting her about the oddness and nastiness that had pushed me into the arms of her sister? Into the literal and figurative warmth I wasn't getting at home? Psychoanalyze it however you will, start with my relationship to my own mother if you must, but the bottom line was that I was a wimp. And I was just simply starting to not care. This woman housing this parasite I'd helped create was not someone I wanted to spend five minutes with, let alone the rest of my life. I harboured a vague hope that things would be better after the birth, or after Melissa dropped dead in the attempt to give birth. It simply didn't matter anymore.

She was certainly getting pale. And thin. Oh well.

Seventh month:

I stopped contacting Sarah, started missing days of work. The entire situation was starting to prey on my spirit as it seemed to be preying on Melissa's sanity and body. Late at night, I heard the ruinous sound of her dry heaves, the ones that left drops of blood on the toilet seat she never cleaned up, on nights she'd eaten nothing at all. *Just die already, bitch. Just die.*

Of course I'm ashamed, but it's easier to be ashamed *now* than it was to live with her like that *then.* Much, much easier. I knew things were drawing to a close, would be over one way or another soon, and that some kind of freedom was beckoning, freedom from her or the child or from all of it, *forever.* I wasn't praying anymore, but I was meditating on freedom, ruminating on the many ways that death could be construed as the ultimate liberty. Her pregnancy had turned me into the bleakest of existentialists.

Eighth month:

Melissa, sitting nude on the kitchen floor, surrounded by raw steak, torn to shreds. Rubbing it on her body, leaving bloody juice trails on her sickened white skin.

My long walks, pondering whether I should just kill her, go to prison, live out the rest of my life as a con-monk, praising death and my own ruination, and sleeping endlessly in my requested solitary confinement cell. Strange dreams for a strange man in a strange world.

The one anonymous call I made to a doctor, speaking only to a nurse, who informed me I had to drag her into the emergency room, bodily if necessary. Bad things were happening with this pregnancy. I couldn't be bothered.

She stopped getting out of bed entirely one day, in the third week of the eighth month. I would stand there as she thrashed about in bed, weak but determined to expel the creature within her. I hated her more watching those struggles than I ever had before. Vile woman, vile process of procreation, vile emotions that tricked us into loving anyone, including ourselves. Oh, how wrong I was.

Ninth month:

There was a Twins game on, and we were leading the Yankees 7-4 in the 9th inning. I heard thuds from upstairs and then repeated thumps coming down the steps. She crawled on her belly into the living room, leaving a blood trail behind her, from between her legs. One clawed hand reached out for me. My eyes settled on her, the entirety of my deadened heart's lack of feelings for her resting on her in that gaze. Whatever love or anything else I had ever felt for her had become an emotional abyss beyond any hatred I had ever felt for anyone. A void that couldn't even be called apathy. She lacked any kind of substantial being to me in that moment, and I knew she was nearing the end.

It began subtly, her face becoming more drawn, and her mouth opened to scream, but no sound came forth but a strained *eeeee* sound. Then I saw her eyes were not at the same level, and the disparity was getting worse and worse, and the flesh and bones were collapsing inward, as her belly began to swell. Blood seeped from her very pores, dripping down her face in thick, clotty masses. Her mouth worked in a strange rhythm and chewed at her protruding tongue, and she spat gnawed bits of it from between her lips. I was entranced.

Her head, her once so beautiful face, fell apart, skull and brain tissue plopping thick and fluid onto the beige carpeting. Her distended belly grew even more, and her legs drew up, up, until they were being slurped into her vagina, up into her womb. Her arms folded across her withered breasts, and her chest caved in, sucking the brittle arms in with it, a wet *glorp* a testament to the utter wreckage of her body. And slopping about in the bloody, fleshy remains, my girl.

She appeared to be about five or six already. I saw what must have been her umbilical cord and her placenta get slorped up into her mouth like cannibal spaghetti. Her small hands wiped gore from her face and eyes and she smiled such a bright and loving smile at me. I ran to her and took her in my arms. "Abigail," I said, just knowing that was her name. "I love you, my little girl. I love you."

We've been on the run ever since, me and the darling creature who destroyed my wife. She's aged another ten years since then, grown into a beautiful teenager. As her father, it is my duty to control the bizarre lust she inspires in me, to quash the sickening feelings I get when I look at her, and I do this successfully, though not without exacting some penance on myself. I've taken to inserting jagged stones and small pieces of broken glass in my shoes, to punish me as I walk. I deserve punishment after all, don't I?

She has taken a few lives since her mother's, usually police or snoopy motel management. There is a manhunt on for us, and it will never end until we are both caught or… I don't know what the "or" is, but Abigail assures me there is another option.

She encouraged me to write this, so I've jotted down the most important parts, while she watched. Now that I'm nearing the end, she is grinning at me, a happy grin, and a most pointed grin. I've seen the look in her eyes and, once again, I wonder what I helped bring into this world. A human girl or something more? She seems to feed more on the demise than the flesh or blood of her victims, an existential vampire. And I know she won't brutalize me like she brutalized those others. She has another plan for me.

The trip to the store she insisted she go on alone. Why did I let her? I trust her, that's why. More than I trust myself. She shows me the package of rat poison. I can only nod and wrap this up. I will feed her in my own way, my penitential way, my way that refuses my own life in favour of absolute freedom. She will feast, daddy will be gone, and the world will be her buffet table. I pity you, mere humans, for you shall see the splendour of my beautiful daughter's smile, and she is coming for you. I expect the pain I will soon experience to be most cleansing.

The spasms of my ending start to wrack my ragged body and it is a beautiful rebirth. *My girl.*

Detention

By Stuart Keane

Thanks for reading my debut anthology for Dark Chapter Press. Before I get into the afterword, I wish to thank Rob McEwan for giving me this wonderful, phenomenal opportunity. Back in 2015, when Rob first approached me about possibly working for DCP, I was humbled and astonished. We'd worked together in the past on several projects, and grew close through our shared admiration for the very genre we love, but for him to reach out and offer me a chance to work for *his* company, a fast-moving British horror press who are quickly going places, one he started all on his lonesome in his little office in Alnwick, I was stunned.

Needless to say, I quickly accepted. Opportunities like this don't come along every day.

At the time, DCP was still in its infancy. When I signed on, the company comprised of Rob alone. I totally wasn't worthy to be the second person involved. However, Rob has a keen eye for detail, and a wonderful ability for spotting amazing talent. He also has a passion for the horror genre that I rarely see in many of my peers, one that drives him to produce the best possible quality for his press, a publisher who adheres meticulous detail and dedication to its portfolio. A man who stands by his morals, doesn't bend in the face of adversary, and is true to his word.

Did I want to be part of this company? Hell yes.

The first thing I noticed about DCP was the quality of the output. True, DCP aren't what you would call prolific, in the loosest sense of the word, but they ensure the work they publish is of the highest quality. You only need to read Kill for a Copy and Eight Deadly

Kisses, or participate in their monthly Flash Fiction competition to see where I'm coming from. Quality over quantity? I'll take it any day of the week. If I'm honest, I prefer reading an anthology that took months to prepare, collate, edit, format, and polish. It seems much more rewarding, and you know the product is of a superior quality. I don't care if I only get one a year, the wait is worth it.

Which is where Kids comes in.

Some of you don't know this, but Kids was my DCP audition, my key to the hallowed halls of Dark Chapter Press. Rob wanted to severely test me, bring the best out in me, and the only way to do this was simple – he proposed I head an anthology. I choose the theme, I collect the authors, and I decide on the stories. I put the collection together, and we go from there. So, that's what I did, following an exhaustive, popular submission call (which resulted in producing two excellent books, rather than one), two eye-opening rounds of edits, and a detailed editing process. It took time, yes, but the finished product is nothing short of exemplary. For the authors who have been following this anthology from mere thought to printed page, you know what I'm talking about. For readers who just picked up this anthology for the first time – do you agree?

So, thank you for reading the first volume of Kids. Volume 2 is on the way, but until then, revel in the beautiful horror of it all; eighteen stories that feature the children of your worst nightmares, all written by some of the brightest talent in the horror genre today. For me, Kids are the epitome of horror, an innocent being that twists your feelings and emotions, and leads you astray until it's too late. By then, they have you, you're its victim, and there isn't much you can do about it.

Kind of like this book. Well, kind of. At least you'll live to see another day after reading Kids, if the nightmares don't consume you.

Stuart Keane
February 2016

Contributor Biographies

Authors

James Walley

Arriving in the rainy isle of Great Britain in the late '70s, James Walley quickly became an enthusiast of all things askew. Having grown up in a quaint little one horse town that was one horse short, on a steady diet of movies, '50s sci fi and fantasy fiction, creating creepy nonsense seemed like the only logical step to make.

Sure, he can sometimes be found behind the desk of a nine to five job, but has kept himself sane by singing in a rock band, memorizing every John Carpenter movie ever made, and learning the ancient art of voodoo.

His debut novel, *The Forty First Wink*, was published in 2014, and with a clutch of short stories also in the offing, the sequel is prepping for launch."

Facebook: https://www.facebook.com/TheFortyFirstWink/
Twitter: @JamesWalley74
Author Page: http://www.ragnarokpub.com/#!the-forty-first-wink/c1c1q

Feind Gottes

Feind Gottes is a horror writer with his first published work, **Hell Awaits**, appearing in **Kill For A Copy** from **Dark Chapter Press**. His zombie flash fiction tale, **Tamed Brute**, can be found in **Flashes of Darkness: Halloween Special 2015** and his tale, **Known But Not**

Named, recently won **Dark Chapter Press' DreAdvent Calendar** contest. Feind recently finished his first novel and will have another short story published in the anthology, **KIDS**, to be edited by **Stuart Keene** for **Dark Chapter Press** due out in March 2016.

Feind is also the editor for *ThyDemonsBeScribblin.com*, his website dedicated to all things horror & heavy metal. Feind is also a contributing writer for *Occult Rock* and formerly for *Doommantia*. Feind currently resides in Tucson, AZ working non-stop to promote and support independent music, movies and writers like himself.

Website
Facebook
Twitter

Josh Pritchett

Josh Pritchett was born in Charlottesville, Virginia in 1970, the home of the University of Virginia where Edgar Allan Poe first went to college. When he was twelve, he read Stephen King's "Night Shift" and found his life's calling. Sadly feeding people to rats is not a growth industry, so he became a writer instead. He has previously been published in the anthologies Brave New Girls, Bones III, and Bizarre Tales from Three Notch'd Road. You can follow Josh on Facebook at Josh Pritchett Jr.

Sharon L. Higa

Sharon L. Higa is an East Tennessean who lives smack in the middle of 'hauntsville' – much to her delight. She revels in penning tales of Horror, supernatural thrillers, fantasy/action and pretty much anything else that is creepy, crawly and downright spine chilling. She has three novels, one novella and several short stories printed in a wide variety of anthologies.

To check out her offerings to the world at large, you can go to her website: www.leapingunicornliterary.com

Check out her facebook page under Sharon L Higa or catch up with her on twitter. She posts as: elf126

Sharon also has a wordpressblog under blueunicorn1, where she spreads the word about her up and coming projects as well as those of her fellow authors.

Douglas F. Dluzen

During the day Douglas is a geneticist and studies the genetic mechanisms of aging and age-related diseases.

At night he continues to write his science fiction, fantasy, and horror stories. He is currently editing his first novel and working on a science fiction trilogy.

He is also deeply interested in the meeting of everyday science and the supernatural and that's where he draws much of his horror-writing inspiration. Douglas enjoys traveling, hiking, and air drumming.

Twitter: @ripplesintime24
Website: http://douglasripplesintime.blogspot.com/

Erica Chin

Erica Chin was born and raised in Malaysia, a country with a diversity of ethnics, cultures and cuisines. She enjoys learning about and writing in Mandarin and English. She revels in plotting stories that unnerve people. She currently lives in Kuala Lumpur, Malaysia. Find Erica Chin on Facebook at www.facebook.com/ericachinstories

Andrew Lennon

Andrew Lennon is the author of A Life to Waste, Keith and Twisted Shorts.

He has featured in numerous anthologies and is successfully becoming a recognised name in horror and thriller writing. Andrew is a happily married man living in the North West of England with his wife Hazel & their children.

He enjoys spending his time with his family and watching or reading new horror.

Website: http://www.andrewlennon.co.uk

Pete Clark

Pete Clark has had a number of stories published on webzines, and in the anthologies 'Detritus' (Omnium Gatherum), 'Short Sips' and 'Here There Be Dragons' (Wicked East Press), 'Fresh Blood' (MayDecember Publications), 'Thirteen Volume 3' (13 Horror), 'Time of Death' (Living Dead Press) and 'Darkness ad Infinitum (Villipede). He was awarded an Honourable Mention in the L. Ron Hubbard Writers of the Future contest (2nd Quarter 2011). He includes Stephen King, Clive Barker and China Miéville among his many influences. Writing numerous short stories and his first novel, he lives in North West England with his wife, two children and a growing collection of guitars.

Mark Parker

Mark Parker is the founder, publisher, and managing editor of Scarlet Galleon Publications. His editorial credits include *Dead Harvest: A Collection of Dark Tales (2014); Dark Hallows: 10 Halloween Haunts (2015);* and the much anticipated *Fearful Fathoms: Collected Tales of Aquatic Terror (2016).* Parker is the author of *The Scarlet Galleon, Biology of Blood, Way of the Witch, Banshee's Cry, Lucky You, The Troll Diner, Killing Christmas,* and *Born Bad* to be featured in the forthcoming anthology *KIDS: Vol. I* coming soon from Dark Chapter Press. Bestselling author of the *Witching Savannah* series writes of Parker's *Way of the Witch:* "Parker has a strong voice and is able to convey a sustained sense of time and place. Similar in feel to Richard Laymon's *Traveling Vampire Show.*" You can learn more about the author/publisher by visiting his website www.scarletgalleonpublications.com

Michael Bray

Michael Bray is a horror / thriller author of more than ten novels. Influenced from an early age by the suspense horror of authors such as Stephen King, Richard Laymon & Brian Lumley, along with TV shows like Tales From The Crypt & The Twilight Zone, he started to work on his own fiction, and spent many years developing his style.

With books sold in over forty countries and rights optioned for movie and television adaptations of his work, he recently signed with Media Bitch literary agency where he intends to take the next step in his writing career. He currently resides in Leeds, England, with his

wife Vikki and daughter Abi.
Where to find Michael Bray online

Official website: www.michaelbrayauthor.com
Facebook: www.facebook.com/michaelbrayauthor
Twitter: www.twitter.com/michaelbrayauth
Instagram: www.instagram.com/michaelbrayauthor
Google +: www.plus.goggle.com/michaelbrayauthor

Matt Hickman

Matt is an avid fan of horror fiction. He spends a majority of his free time reading books from both established and independent authors. With a diverse knowledge of the genre, he has now tried his hand at writing horror. With the support of his peers, some of which are established writers themselves, he now approaches a new career, one that will see him take horror by storm.

His debut, a collaboration with Andrew Lennon; Hexad is available on digital download from Amazon, to be followed by inclusion into an anthology from Dark Chapter Press – Kids.

Alice J. Black

Alice lives and works in the North East of England where she lives with her partner and slightly ferocious cats! She writes all manner of fiction with a tendency to lean towards the dark side. Dreams and sleep-talking are currently a big source of inspiration and her debut novel, *The Doors*, is a young adult novel which originally came from a dream several years ago and grew from there.

Chantal Noordeloos

Chantal Noordeloos (born in the Hague, and not found in a cabbage as some people may suggest) lives in the Netherlands, where she spends her time with her wacky, supportive husband, and outrageously cunning daughter, who is growing up to be a supervillain. When she is not busy exploring interesting new realities, or arguing with characters (aka writing), she likes to dabble in drawing.

In 1999 she graduated from the Norwich School of Art and Design, where she focused mostly on creative writing.

There are many genres that Chantal likes to explore in her writing. Currently Sci-fi Steampunk is one of her favourites, but her 'go to' genre will always be horror. "It helps being scared of everything; that gives me plenty of inspiration," she says.

Chantal likes to write for all ages, and storytelling is the element of writing that she enjoys most. "Writing should be an escape from everyday life, and I like to provide people with new places to escape to, and new people to meet."

Chantal started her career writing short stories for various anthologies, and in 2012 she won an award for 'Best Original Story' for her short 'the Deal'. Coyote is her first big project.

Gary Pearson

Gary Pearson is an indie author that has published two Novella's within the thriller genre, and is currently working on further pieces and submissions for anthologies.

He became interested in writing at a young age

when watching his local football team, he was inspired by the sports writers of the day and began writing his own articles detailing the events of the games for his local newspaper. Gary has also started a novel, which began when he partook in NaNoWriMo 2014, a writing challenge which requires contestants to write 50,000 words in the 30 days of November. He completed this challenge and emerged as a winner, this spurred him on to complete the Novel which will be a significant milestone once published.

Find out more about Gary by going to one of the following:
Website: http://www.garyipearson.com
Facebook: https://www.facebook.com/pages/Gary-Pearson/733279940055214?ref=aymt_homepage_panel
Twitter: https://twitter.com/GaryP04

S.L. Dixon

Former homeless hitchhiker and high school dropout, S.L. Dixon grew up in Ontario, Canada and his short stories have appeared in magazines, digests, literary journals and anthologies from around the world. Currently, he's married, has a cat and resides in a small coastal community in British Columbia, Canada.
@SLDixon1
www.sldixon.ca

David Basnett

Hailing from north of Hadrian's Wall, the true life inspiration for Game of Thrones' The Wall, that was built to keep the Roman empire intact, David was raised amid the foothills of the Cheviots and in the shadow of the sprawling and inspiring Northumberland National Park. His fast paced yet still descriptive style of writing and knack of breathing life into tired genres has established him as a horror and young adult author to watch out for.

David is a regular contributor to Dark Chapter Press having won one of their flash fiction competitions and is part of the Kill for a Copy anthology.

A regular on social media to talk with fans of his books, you can keep in touch with David on:
twitter.com/dbasnett
facebook.com/officialdavidbasnett
davidbasnettauthor.wordpress.com/

Brian Barr

Brian Barr is an American author of novels, short stories, and comic books. Brian has been published in various short story anthologies and magazines, including Queer Sci Fi's *Discovery,* NonBinary Review, Nebula Rift, New Realm, Mantid, Dark Chapter Press's *Kill for a Copy*, and many J. Ellington Ashton Press publications. Brian collaborates with another writer, Chuck Amadori, on the supernatural dark fantasy noir comic book series Empress, along with Pencil Blue Studios' Marcelo Salaza for the art. His first novel, Carolina Daemonic: Confederate Shadows, was published by J. Ellington Ashton

Press in 2015. Carolina Daemonic will be a four-volume novel series, along with various short stories which have already been published and will be eventually be gathered in collections.

Facebook: www.facebook.com/brianbarrbooks
Facebook Group: www.facebook.com/brianbarr-booksdotcom
Dark Chapter Press Author Page: http://www.darkchapterpress.com/brian-barr/4590071515
Website: www.brianbarrbooks.com
Twitter: @brianbarrbooks

Christopher Ropes

Christopher Ropes is a horror and occult author and poet living in New Jersey. He lives with his two kids and his fiancee and their menagerie of pets. He's been published in the first two J. Ellington Ashton Press "Rejected for Content" anthologies, and has stories soon to be published in Xnoybis #3 and Despumation Journal #2. He also has a book of transgressive poetry, "The Operating Theater," available from Dynatox Ministries. Various occult journals have published his work as well. You can connect with him at: https://www.facebook.com/ChristopherRopes/

Stuart Keane

Stuart Keane is a horror/suspense author of several novels. Currently in his second year of writing, Stuart is developing a reputation for writing realistic, contemporary horror. With comparisons to Richard Laymon and Shaun Hutson amongst his critical acclaim – he cites both authors as his major inspiration in the genre – Stuart is dedicated to writing terrifying, thrilling stories for real horror fans.

He is currently a member of the Author's Guild, and an editor for emerging UK publisher, Dark Chapter Press. With books sold all over the world, and his first novel, All or Nothing, currently in development to be turned into a TV serial, 2016 will be a busy year for Stuart. He has several novels in the works, including Oedema, Outbreak, and the continuation of his Charlotte Chronicles trilogy, Awakening and Amy.

Stuart was born in Kent, and lived there for three decades. A major inspiration for his work, his home county has helped him produce numerous novels and short stories. He currently resides in Essex, is happily married, and is totally addicted to caffeine.

Feel free to get in touch at www.stuartkeane.com **or** www.facebook.com/stuart.keane.92
He can also be found on Twitter at @SKeane_Author.

www.stuartkeane.com
www.facebook.com/stuartkeanewriter
Twitter - @SKeane_Author.

Jack Rollins

Jack Rollins was born and raised among the twisting cobbled streets and lanes, ruined forts and rolling moors of a medieval market town in Northumberland, England. He claims to have been adopted by Leeds in West Yorkshire, and he spends as much time as possible immersed in the shadowy heart of that city.

Writing has always been Jack's addiction, whether warping the briefing for his English class homework, or making his own comic books as a child, he always had some dark tale to tell.

Fascinated by all things Victorian, Jack often writes within that era, but also creates contemporary nightmarish visions in horror and dark urban fantasy.

He currently lives in Northumberland, with his partner, two sons, and his daughter living a walking distance from his home, which is slowly but surely being overtaken by books...

Jack's published works are as follows:

The Séance: A Gothic Tale of Horror and Misfortune
The Cabinet of Dr Blessing
Dead Shore, **in** *Undead Legacy*
Anti-Terror, **in** *Carnage: Extreme Horror*
Home, Sweet Home **in** *Kill For A Copy*
Ghosts of Christmas Past **in** *The Dichotomy of Christmas*

Jack can be found online at:
Twitter: @jackrollins9280
Facebook: www.facebook.com/doctorblessing
Website: jackrollinshorror.wordpress.com